LYSSA'S JOURNEY

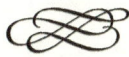

CIN MEDLEY

MED'S PUB
PUBLISHING

Lyssa's JOURNEY

CIN MEDLEY

Published by Med's Pub Publishing
Copyright © 2018 Cin Medley
All Rights Reserved
ISBN-13: 978-0-9989748-4-2
ISBN-10: 0998974846
Cover Artwork Used with permission from Bigstock ©
Cover Design by: Amanda Walker P.A. and Design Services
Edited by: Kendra's Editing and Book Services- Kendra Gaither
Formatting by Med's Pub Publishing

As always, I write the bits of naughty for Veronica. She made me do it. Love you.

My husband David, I love you for your encouragement, and your endless confidence that I am doing the right thing.

Kendra, I know you laugh at me more than you correct me, it's what you do. My beautiful sista by another mother…I love you, without you my stories would-be run-on sentences with comma's everywhere.

CHAPTER ONE

It was one in the afternoon when Lyssa returned from her lunch break. Her boss, Mr. Slate, was waiting for her when she walked through the door.

"Lyssa, can you come into my office, please?" he asked. She nodded and followed him into his office. "Have a seat."

Wondering what this could be about and if she'd done something wrong, she said, "Mr. Slate, is everything all right?" For the past six months, she had been working on a big case for the firm.

"Oh, yes, Lyssa, everything is fine. I want you to go out to Greenvale Ranch and talk to Mr. Greenvale. He can't make it into the office. He has received some mail concerning his case."

"Mr. Slate, Mr. Greenvale's daughter, Kennedy, is my friend. Should I be doing this interview? Isn't that a conflict of interest? I don't want to do anything to jeopardize his case. Mr. Greenvale has a very good chance of winning this."

He smiled at her. "Lyssa, it's not a conflict of interest. You are not the lawyer assigned to this case. You are just an assistant to Stanly, who has nothing to do with this case. It'll be fine; besides, we are hoping that since you know him, maybe you can help calm him down."

Lyssa smiled at him. "You do know his daughter is getting married in three months, and I'm part of the wedding party?"

"I wasn't aware of that, but it shouldn't matter. So, you go out there and see what's going on. There will be a company car waiting for you down in the garage. You do know how to drive?"

She laughed. "Yes, Mr. Slate, I know how to drive."

"Good, good, now get going. I know it's a bit of a drive out there, so just keep the car until tomorrow."

She nodded and left his office, then headed to hers to grab her files and briefcase.

It took a little over an hour before she pulled up to the gate. She had changed her shoes, into her tennis shoes, so she jumped out and opened the gate.

As she moved up the drive, she looked around. Nothing had changed in the past ten years. She hadn't been out here since they were in high school. She wondered if Mr. and Mrs. Greenvale remembered who she was.

Pulling up to the house, she grabbed her briefcase and got out. Her smile was automatic; the memories she shared with Kennedy here were everywhere she looked. She turned to look at the barn, remembering all the hours they spent in the loft, singing and dancing. She turned again, her back to the house, to see the stables. Closing her eyes, she could still remember Midnight. That horse hated her, hated her so much he threw her, nearly stomping her to death. Shaking her head, she smiled again. It's probably why Kennedy was getting married out here. Just to make her ride that damn horse.

The voice threw her. "Lyssa? Is that you?"

She spun around to see Kennedy's mom coming off the porch. "Mrs. Greenvale." She headed toward the woman, who wrapped her in her arms.

"Oh my goodness, how have you been, dear?"

She chuckled. "Very good. How have you been?"

"Oh, you know me, I love this life. Why don't you come in? I just made some sweet tea. Can I get you a glass?"

Kennedy's mom made the best sweet tea. "I'd love some."

As they walked up the sidewalk, they talked about the wedding and how excited they all were that it was going to be on the ranch. The girls had been friends most of their lives, so it was a given that she was going to be a part of the big day. Lyssa's family had a little farm, if that's what you wanted to call it, down the road. It was nothing compared to the huge ranch and estate the Greenvale's owned. But they never acted like they were better than anyone else. In fact, they were just the opposite.

Lyssa went in and was greeted by Mr. Greenvale, and they sat down in the living room to talk. "Mr. Greenvale, I don't know much about what is going on. My boss, Mr. Slate, sent me out here to talk to you about some letters you've been receiving?"

"Yes, let me get them for you. There are a few from some company; they want to buy the land to build some kind of hoity toity complex on it. They said something about owing back taxes, and that my time was up for paying them. Something along the lines of three million dollars. Imagine that." He chuckled. "I can pay that eight times over and still have money left in the bank. It just doesn't make any sense." He handed her a bunch of envelopes. "There are also letters from the county and state about owing back taxes."

"Mr. Greenvale, how long has this been going on?" she asked as she looked through the envelopes.

"Oh, a little over a year, I guess. I've been talking to Mr. Slate about this, and he keeps giving me the run around. He gave our case to that fool, Knox Fairfield. I don't know why I bother paying that man all the money I pay him when he hasn't done a thing about this."

She opened one of the letters, and as she read through it, she just sat there shaking her head. *What in the hell is this?* Lyssa knew for a fact that this ranch was one of the biggest and greatest producing ranches in the State. *How is this possible?*

"Mr. Greenvale," she said.

He chuckled. "I think you can call me Charles. I've known you for most of your life."

She smiled a warm smile. "Charles, I don't understand how this is possible. But I am going to find out. Something isn't right. I'm going

3

to be taking over this case. If my boss doesn't like it, I'll quit my damn job and do it on my own. You have my word; I will figure this out. Please, don't worry. This should be an exciting time. Kennedy is getting married in three months."

He patted her on the knee. "Don't go quitting your job over this."

She chuckled. "I don't do much there anyway. I was looking for a change of pace. I was actually thinking of moving on to another job, maybe in the city, but I'm not sure. Opening my own office here in town is an option as well."

"Like our Kennedy," Mrs. Greenvale said. You could hear the sadness in her voice. "You girls were always talking about how you couldn't wait to go to college and live in the big city."

"Well, Mrs. Greenvale, my heart has always belonged here. To be honest, I think the city would scare the crap out of me. Kennedy keeps hounding me to move up there with her, but now that she is getting married, I don't think it's going to happen. I'm a small-town girl, a farm girl at heart."

She smiled a forced smile. Lyssa knew she missed Kennedy. She took the letters and put them in her bag and finished her tea. "Well, I'm going to go and see what I can find out. When I know something, I'll come back and we can have a talk. But I'll get to the bottom of this."

"Thank you, dear." Mr. Greenvale smiled at her, walking her to the door.

Lyssa hugged them both and walked out. She stood on the porch and looked out at the ranch. Mr. and Mrs. Greenvale were like her second parents; she'd spent that much time here when she was young.

She stepped off the porch and walked to the car to put her bag in it, and then walked around to the back of the house, all the way to the fence. Leaning on the fence, she stood and took deep breaths. Remembering.

~

He had heard the car pull up as he walked through the barn, his silhouette barely visible against the doors. He watched the woman with pale blonde hair get out of the car. She looked right at him, but he knew she couldn't see him in the shadows since the sun was high in the sky.

As she moved from the side of the car, he felt his mouth go dry. "Who the fuck are you, sweetheart?"

The further she moved up the walk, the clearer the view he had of her. "Fuck," he whispered. Her skin-tight pencil skirt hugged her perfect curves. Buck felt himself get a bit hard. When she turned to see the missus walking up, he got the perfect side view of her. Her breasts weren't so big, but he shrugged his shoulders. "Well, you can't have an ass that tight and have a rack as well." He wasn't so sure how long her hair was, it was pinned in a tight bun on top of her head. He watched as the two women embraced as if they had known each other for years. *Is she a friend of Emily's?* He wondered.

Buck had been the ranch manager for the past eight years or so. He took the job when the old man had a minor heart attack. He left the corporate world in Chicago when his fiancé maxed out his credit cards, emptied their bank account, and then left him. He was done. He sold his company, his penthouse, his fancy cars, everything, and bought a pickup truck and headed west.

He had planned on buying his own ranch, but he spent a few months having a pity party for himself and fucking anything with legs. He must have gone through half the county. One night, he was so drunk, he crashed his truck into one of the fence posts at the end of the property on his way home from yet another one-night stand, and he'd passed out. Mr. Greenvale found him with a nasty gash on his forehead. They took him in and took care of him. He had never met people like them, so kind and giving, wanting nothing in return.

Buck had offered to pay for the fence, but they wouldn't have it. So, he fixed it instead. His truck still has the smashed in grill, which he decided to keep to remind himself that he was an asshole. About a week after he arrived here, the old man had his heart attack, so he stayed until he was fine. He'd been here ever since.

When they asked him his name, he told them it was Buck. He didn't want Callen McCabe anywhere near him. That part of him was dead, and looking at the blonde walking up the sidewalk, he knew the kind of woman she was. He could tell by the way she held her head and carried herself. She was after something bigger than herself. He knew from experience that women who dressed like that and walked like that were nothing but trouble.

Shaking his head and chuckling, he turned and walked away, forgetting his natural instinct to fuck her stupid. He wanted no part of that shit. Once was enough for him.

Buck was about done for the day, so he put his tools away and was walking out of the barn toward his truck. The woman's car was still parked in front of the house. As he rounded the back of his pickup, he saw her standing in the backyard leaning on the fence. He smiled, looking at her perfect heart-shaped ass, and found himself stopping to gaze at her. After another moment, she turned and headed straight for him. She was watching where she was walking, so she didn't look up to see him gawking at her. He opened the door and climbed into the truck. When he started it, she looked up, and his breath hitched in his chest when their eyes met. *Holy shit!* Her eyes were so blue and huge; she smiled a small smile at him, and he nodded as he put the truck in reverse.

"No fucking way," he mumbled to himself. He hit the gas, spinning his tires, and shooting gravel and dust into the air, right in her face. Buck chuckled to himself as he heard her yell.

Lyssa stood looking out at the field she and Kennedy used to ride through. She could even see the path to the creek just beyond the trees. This was a wonderful place to grow up, but it sure wasn't the right setting for two young girls to learn about the world.

Once they headed to college, they were faced with a whole new world. Boys surrounded them everywhere. Kennedy was stunning, and they would follow her around like puppies. It scared the shit out of Lyssa. These boys were nothing like the ones they went to school with. These boys were men—men who wanted more than a kiss in the field. They wanted much more. Lyssa wasn't buying into it like Kennedy did. God, so many men hurt her, telling her she was beautiful and special and then having sex with her and never calling her again.

Lyssa could still remember all those nights her friend cried because of one guy or another. But she wasn't going to fall for that shit. No way. Lyssa was still a virgin, a fact she was proud of. She was proud she hadn't been so stupid as to fall into the game of college boys. Hell, most men now in the city are the same way. She knew she wasn't a dog, that she was kind of cute. She may not be as beautiful as Kennedy, but she took care of herself. Looking down, she wished she had bigger boobs, but hey, it didn't matter to her. She was happy with her choice, with her decision to not be someone's stepping stone.

Checking her watch, she knew she needed to get back to the office, where either Mr. Slate was going to give her the case or she was quitting and taking it with her. No way was someone going to hurt the Greenvales, not as long as she had a law degree.

Turning, she headed back to her car, walking carefully through the yard, when an engine startled her. Looking up, she was about ten feet from a pickup truck. Sitting behind the wheel looking at her was probably the most gorgeous man she had ever laid eyes on.

What the fuck? His brown eyes seared right through her. She smiled, and he nodded at her. Then the truck was moving backward. He said something, but she couldn't make out what he said. She stood there watching as the truck turned to drive away. When he hit the gas, rocks flew up, along with dust, covering her and the rocks hitting her in the face, cutting her eyebrow. One hit her in the mouth, splitting her lip open.

She screamed as the rocks sliced at her face, her hands coming up stop the pain. Pulling them back, she could see the blood on them. "Oh my God," she said. Looking at the truck, she yelled, "Fucking Asshole!"

Walking to the car, she opened the passenger door and grabbed

7

her bottle of water. She pulled her blouse off and poured water on it. Standing in the driveway in her camisole, she wiped at the blood and cuts. When she finished, she got in the car and headed after the truck. It wasn't hard to tell which direction it was going; the dust was still hanging in the air on the gravel road.

Driving through town, she saw the truck sitting out in front of the only bar on the street. She was pissed so she pulled in behind it, got out of the car, and stormed into the bar. He was sitting on a stool talking to some leggy brunette with his back to her.

Walking over, she shoved him on the shoulder. "Excuse me, asshole," she shouted. He chuckled as he turned around, thinking it was some girl he fucked. He nearly choked on his beer when he saw she was half-dressed. "What the fuck is your problem?" she shouted at him.

"I don't have a problem," he snapped.

"Really? Is that what you think? Do you see my face, dickhead? You just did this to me, and you don't have a fucking problem? Well, sweetheart, you do now." It wasn't like her, but she was pissed, and she swung her fist, connecting with his mouth and splitting his lip. Then she swung again, connecting with his eye. All the guys were cat-calling her and cheering her on. "You want to be a dick? Well, I can be a dick, too."

Turning and storming out of the bar, she was shaking. She had never done anything like that in her whole life. "Oh my God," she whispered to herself. Her hand was on the door handle when she heard him.

"What the fuck is your problem? I told you, I'm not the staying type. A fuck is a fuck."

Lyssa froze, then she spun around, trying not to giggle when he stepped back. "Oh, you think this is about a fuck you gave me? Boy, you're pretty full of yourself, aren't you? Trust me, sweetheart, if I let you fuck me, you would have never left my bed. You spun your fucking tires and the rocks did this to my face, dickhead. Are you that fucking stupid that you don't remember fifteen minutes ago? Oh, wait," she looked past him at the brunette standing a few feet behind him with the rest of the bar, "let me guess. The only thing you can think about is your next fuck? Well, there you go." She nodded toward the brunette. "Don't let me keep you."

She turned and pulled the car door open, but he made the mistake of grabbing her arm. "Wait a fucking minute. You walk into a bar and punch me in the face, and you think this is over?"

Her reaction shocked the hell out of her. She spun around, connecting her fist with his jaw. "Don't fucking touch me. I know men like you, one-stop shop. The only thing you care about is shoving your dick into someone. So, go shove it."

She got in the car, locking the door. When she pulled out, she made sure to spin the wheels, leaving a cloud of dust behind her. Luckily for her, the hospital was only a few blocks down. Well, it wasn't really a hospital.

After the doc cleaned her up, she ended up with a few butterfly bandages on her eyebrow. The rest of the cuts were minor. When she left, she went back to the city, back home, swearing all the way there. "Who the fuck? What the hell? Fucking asshole."

Pulling into the parking space that was hers, she made her way to her apartment, slamming the door behind her. "God, what an asshole," she murmured on her way to the bedroom. Stripping out of her clothes, she got in the shower, being careful of her eye.

As she stood looking in the mirror, she could see the cuts and faint marks on her face and chest. "Fucking asshole," she whispered. After she got dressed, she made something to eat and sat down on the couch with the letters, a dish of paperclips, and a pen and paper. "Time to get to work."

CHAPTER TWO

Buck stood in the parking lot of the bar, shaking his head. The brunette walked up. "Oh my God, are you all right?"

He looked at her. "Sorry, sweetheart," he said and walked away, climbing into his truck.

Driving home, he happened to drive past the doc's office and saw her car was parked in front. He almost stopped. Shaking his head, he just drove home.

His house was small. It didn't have much furniture in it. He didn't care for fancy things anymore, not since *her*. There would never be another *her*. Once was enough for this lifetime.

Standing in front of the mirror looking at his face, a small smile crossed his lips. He hadn't smiled a real smile in a very long time. He didn't know who that woman was, but damn, she had a hell of a right hook. Peeling off his clothes, he jumped in the shower. As he washed the day's dirt from his body, her eyes popped into his head. *Who the hell was she?*

Being single-minded these days, he didn't put two and two together. He hadn't figured out that the woman on the ranch was the same woman who jacked him in the bar. When he got out, he headed to the kitchen, still naked. He grabbed a beer before sitting in his chair and thought about that little spitfire who'd left him bloody. Yeah, he could tame that shit; she probably needed a good fuck. With her long hair hanging in her face, she had the look of a crazy woman in those beautiful blue eyes. He couldn't for the life of him understand why she thought he had hurt her.

Shaking his head, he finished his beer and went to bed. Five in the morning would come early. He loved his job. It wasn't nine to five, and it had nothing to do with the corporate world. It was an honest living, and he really did respect and like the Greenvales. Their daughter, not so much. He met her a few times, prissy little thing. In it for the money, that's who she was. She was marrying some rich pompous ass from the big city. That was him eight years ago, the same pompous asshole, thinking, no, knowing he was untouchable. That was until *she* came along, fucking bitch.

He was a bit disappointed. He really wanted to fuck someone, but that spitfire blonde put a damper on that, and with this split lip, it looked like he'd be celibate for at least a week or so. Buck closed his eyes and crashed.

When morning came, Lyssa pulled herself out of bed. She had some investigating to do. By the time she arrived at work, Mr. Slate was already there. When she walked into his office, he looked up. "Jesus, what happened to you?"

She laughed. "Some asshole cowboy thought he was funny. It's fine."

"Well, I hope you gave as good as you got."

Looking down at her bruised hand, she laughed. "Sure did. But that's not what I want to talk to you about. You sent me out to the Greenvale Ranch, and I had a talk with Mr. Greenvale. Mr. Slate, I want this. I want the lead. I want to investigate this."

"Lyssa, you know I can't do that. This is Knox's case."

"Yeah, well, Knox is sitting on his hands. There is something here, and I want it."

He smiled. "I'm sorry, Lyssa."

"So am I. Mr. Slate, I quit."

"Now, Lyssa, don't be silly."

She laughed. "I quit and I'm taking Greenvale with me. His ranch is one of the biggest in this state, and there is no reason this should be happening to them. There is no way the taxes are in arrearage as these letters claim. There is something more going on here."

"Where did you get those?"

"From Mr. Greenvale. I'm taking this case. These people, I've known them for nearly my whole life. I won't let this happen, so either you give me the case or I'll quit and take it with me."

"Miss Dawn," was all he got out before she interrupted him.

"Mr. Slate, I quit. I'll have Mr. Greenvale contact you in regards to him relieving you of your services. This should have been dealt with after the second letter. I hold in my hand eighteen letters. Your inability to move forward with this is a breach of contract."

He sat there smiling at her. "What has gotten into you? You've always been a mousy little thing."

She stood and leaned across his desk. "Your biggest mistake was assuming you had a clue about me. I'm a mousy little thing because it suits me. Did you even read my transcripts when you hired me, or did you hire me because I look good? You haven't seen shit. I quit."

Turning, she walked out of his office, heading to hers to get her things. Knox walked up to her. "So, word around here is you went out to the Greenvales' yesterday. Why are you after my accounts? Can't land any for yourself?"

She looked at him. "You know what, Knox? You're a fucking egotistical piece of shit. You have fucked every girl in this office except for me, and do you know why that is?"

"Because you're some kind of prude. Trust me, sweetheart, you could use a good fuck."

She busted out laughing. "I suppose you and your little dick can give it to me?" Leaning in, she whispered, "Trust me, girls talk. I wouldn't waste my time giving my virginity to a guy with a little dick. No, I'm waiting for the big one. You know, the big ten-incher."

She grabbed her things and walked out, leaving him standing there with his mouth open. She held her head high as she moved through the office. Once in her car, she burst into tears. What the hell was she going to do now? After a few minutes, she pulled herself up and squared her shoulders. She wasn't this girl; she was tougher than this shit. Once she got home, she did what she does best. Research.

Hours passed, and she had discovered more than a few things, so she gathered her notes and tablet and headed to the city. She was going to figure this shit out. Too many companies were involved here. First stop was the State Treasurer to find out what was going on. Walking into the building was the easy part. She was shuffled from one office to the next, finally ending up in the billing department, where she turned on her innocent charms and talked some geeky guy into giving her copies of the last twenty years of the Greenvales' land taxes.

As she sat in her car, she called Mr. Greenvale. "Hi, Charles, this is Lyssa."

"Yes, dear, how are you?"

She chuckled. "Well, unemployed right now, but that's fine. Listen, I'm up here in the city. Do you have copies of the checks you sent to pay your taxes for the last ten years or so?"

"I'm sure Emily has them. If not, we can get copies from the bank. Why are you unemployed?"

She laughed. "Can you please get them? My boss wouldn't give me your case, so I quit and took it with me. I'm now your lawyer if you want me."

He chuckled. "I would love for you to be our lawyer."

Letting out the breath she was holding, she said, "Great, you are going to have to let Mr. Slate know that you are dropping him. Would it be all right if I come by this evening on my way back? I think we need to talk."

"Of course, we'll see you then."

Lyssa hung up, then pulled out her tablet and did a search for this company that was making a bid on the land for when the default expires in two months. She found the address and headed there.

When she pulled up, it was a vacant lot. Sure she had the wrong address, she called the number associated with the company.

"Alexander Corporation, how may I direct your call?" the woman answered.

"Hello, I seem to be lost. I am supposed to be delivering some paperwork to your company, and I am sitting in front of an empty lot. Could you please give me the correct address to your building?"

"I'm sorry, Miss, who are you?"

"My name is Alice Knox, I'm from the law firm of Slate and Slate."

"Oh, Miss Knox, our address is 1492 Warf Drive."

Lyssa tried not to giggle. "I'm sorry, but I am sitting at that address and there is no building here. Is there a secondary Warf Drive?"

"Are you at East Warf Drive?"

Lyssa looked at the street sign. "I am."

"We are at West Warf Drive."

"Oh my gosh, I feel like such an airhead. Thank you so much. I'll be there shortly."

"No problem, Miss Knox. We are on the eighty-fifth floor."

Lyssa hung up. For some reason, she felt a bit odd. Something just wasn't right. She finally found the building and parked. Making her way inside, she stopped to look at the building index. Finding the company she was looking for, she couldn't believe what she was seeing. The floor was shared with Kennedy's fiancée's company. Bell International.

She decided to go up and have a look around. When she got off the elevator, there was only one door, so she went in. On the wall was just the name of Hugh's company. A cute little brunette sat behind the desk.

"Can I help you?"

Lyssa just stood there looking at her. "Hi, I'm looking for Hugh Bell."

"Do you have an appointment?"

"No, I don't. You know what, never mind." Lyssa turned to walk out, and that's when she heard him.

"Lyssa?"

She turned her head, and sure enough, it was Hugh Bell, Kennedy's soon to be husband. She smiled. "Hugh."

"Is everything all right?" He was walking toward her.

"Oh, yeah, I was just looking for Kennedy. I was in the city and thought maybe we could have dinner. Your receptionist said you weren't available, so I was just leaving." She couldn't think of anything else to say.

He smiled at her, giving her a hug. "She had to go out of town for a few days, but she should be back tomorrow sometime."

Lyssa hugged him back. "It's not a problem. That would explain why she hasn't answered her phone. I guess I'll just head back. It was good seeing you. Hey, are you coming down to her parents' this weekend for the barbeque?"

He laughed. "Wouldn't miss it. I'm bringing my best man and a few of my groomsmen. Kennedy tells me you are single."

Lyssa felt her cheeks flush. "Don't you dare think of fixing me up. No, thank you."

He laughed. "Never, just putting it out there."

She laughed. "Listen, I should get going. I'll see you at the weekend."

Hugh hugged her again. "Yes, you will. Be safe out there."

"You too." She smiled and walked out. The elevator doors were still open, so she got in and got the hell out of there.

Once safely inside her car, she mumbled to herself, "What the fuck was that?" Shaking her head, she started the car and headed back to the Greenvale ranch. It took about two hours to get there. When she pulled up, she just sat there, her hands still shaking. Looking at the house, her mind spun in a million directions. *This is not good. Something is very wrong here.*

Finally, she got out, leaving everything in the car. Sitting down with Emily and Charles, she told them about what she found. Emily gave her the copies of the cashed checks.

"So, now we have the proof they were cashed," she said.

Emily stood as the phone rang. Lyssa watched as she walked out of the room. "What aren't you telling me?" Charles said to her.

"A great deal, I'm afraid. But I don't think Emily needs to know. Can you meet me in town tomorrow for lunch, so we can talk?" she whispered.

"I can have Buck drive me in. Say noon?"

"That's perfect. I'll see you there." She stood and made her way to the door. "Goodbye, Mrs. Greenvale," she yelled.

"Goodbye, sweetie," she yelled back.

Lyssa walked out of the house and down the walk to her car. As she opened the door, she happened to look up as a man walked out of the barn. When he looked at her, she realized who it was and smiled a small smile of victory. He had a split lip and a black eye. Nodding her head, she got into her car and drove away.

Buck heard the car, but by the time he looked up, the only thing he saw was long blonde hair walking in the front door, with a mighty fine ass attached to it. Smiling, he was a bit pissed off that his lip was split open. He needed to get laid, but not looking like this. He finished up what he was doing. It was quitting time, and he needed to release his aching cock.

As he was walking out to get into his truck, he saw the blonde bombshell walking out of the house. Her legs were thin and long in her blue jeans. Her hair hung down to her waist; man, he could wrap his hand in that as he rode her from behind.

Buck knew what he looked like, and he knew his cock was bigger than most. He could fuck anyone he wanted. Women did not deny him. In fact, they flocked around him for his attention. He was sure he wouldn't have a problem with her. The way she carried herself, he was sure she was a spitfire in the sack. She had a bit of sass about her.

It was when she looked up at him that he realized who it was. The tiny woman who handed him his ass yesterday. He was stunned to see her again, so much so that he just stopped in his tracks. It was when she smiled at him and then nodded that he felt fury rise up inside of him.

As she pulled away, he reached up to touch his mouth. Oh, she would pay for this, and his cock would make sure of it. Sassy little thing. He climbed into his truck and headed home.

As Lyssa pulled out of the driveway, she laughed. "What an asshole," she said to the car. But still, she giggled. He had a fat lip, split wide open, and he was sporting a nice black eye. "Serves his ass right, the jerk."

When she got home, her phone was ringing as she walked in. Grabbing it off the wall, she said, "Hello."

"Hey, stranger," Kennedy said. "Hugh said you stopped by his work today."

"Yeah, I was in the city for work, and I thought we could have dinner, but you didn't answer your phone. I was a few blocks away from his office, so I thought I'd stop and see what was up."

"I'm in New York until tomorrow. When are you coming back up?"

"Not sure, but the big barbeque is this weekend. We'll see each other then."

"I know, and I can't wait for you to meet Hugh's groomsmen. Oh my God, Lys, you are going to die. They are drool-worthy for sure."

She laughed. "Will you stop trying to hook me up? I'm not interested. But we are going to do some dancing, so you better not wear something prissy."

That sent Kennedy into bellowing laughter. "I promise, I won't. I'll wear jeans, and yes, it has been a long time since we tore up a dance floor."

"I know, right? So, what are you doing in New York?"

"I'm here, actually, for Hugh. One of his companies is moving shop, and he wanted me to help out."

Lyssa laughed. "So, now you're the helper?"

"Ha-ha, funny. No, I do PR. You know that. And, well, this Alexander Corporation is his baby. He and a few of his buddies started it, a side business. They are buying up land all over the country to build eco-friendly towns or something or another. Right now, it's just in the beginning phase."

"Sounds pretty impressive if you ask me."

"Sounds pretty boring to me, but hey, on the upside, I get to shop."

Lyssa giggled as she was writing down everything Kennedy was saying. She wasn't comfortable about taking this information from Kennedy. Knowing she was going to use it possibly against her soon to be husband made her feel even more uncomfortable. Hopefully, she would understand. After all, it is her parents' ranch Lyssa was trying to save.

"Okay, so listen, I need to head out. I will see you Friday at the ranch," Kennedy said.

"Oh, you better believe it. I miss you," Lyssa said.

"I miss you, too. Remember when times were simpler, and we lived down the road from each other?"

"God, do I long for those days. You stay safe."

"Safer than safe. I love you."

"I love you, too," Lyssa said as she hung up the phone.

God, she felt guilty, but Kennedy would understand. Hopefully. Kicking off her shoes, she got busy. Hours passed and the only clue she had was a guy named Brody Buckingham. Seems he was the C.E.O. of this Alexander Corporation.

She started her investigation into him and his connection to Hugh. A half-filled notepad of paper later, she had discovered more about Brody than she wanted to know. Spoiled rich kid, a college buddy of Hugh. Came from old money, old hotel money. His family owned the Alexander Hotel chain. Oldest son of Martin and Georgia Buckingham. This guy was bad news all the way around.

By the time she was finished, it was going on eight at night. Lyssa hadn't eaten all day, so she put her shoes on and headed out for a burger, then went to bed. Tomorrow would prove to be a very interesting day.

Man, Buck hated jacking off in the shower. He would much rather have a warm body underneath him. He wanted the blonde bombshell under him, or on top of him. He wasn't picky, as long as he was feeling the silky smoothness of a tight core wrapped around his cock.

It didn't take long for him to spill his load all over the shower wall, but thoughts of those blue eyes and that tight ass kept him hard. "Fuck," he moaned as he got out and dried off. He'd been hard since last night when she spun around and jacked him in the jaw. His hand reached up to touch his face.

He couldn't help but chuckle. That woman had some fire inside of her. He wondered who wronged her. "She probably has some serious daddy issues," he said to the room.

He plopped on the couch with his erection standing straight in the air. Looking at it, he laughed, taking a drink of his beer. He put his head back, closing his eyes, and there she was—that tight ass walking away from him, her long thin legs, those fucking tight ass jeans he wanted to peel from her body.

His hand wrapped around his cock, moving slowly up and down. Gripping tighter, he imagined how fantastic that little body would feel as she rode him. It was a matter of minutes and he was coming all over the place.

"Aww, fuck. Yeah, that's it," he groaned out as he imagined her tits bouncing in his face.

When he finished, he chuckled, shaking his head. He reached for a towel that was lying on the coffee table and wiped himself off.

Never had he felt like this. He really needed to get laid. Finishing his beer, he headed to bed. Maybe if he slept, she would get the fuck out of his head. This woman was going to be a problem for him. The sooner he fucked her, the sooner he could get on with his life.

When his alarm went off, he actually struggled to wake up. But, none the less, he had no choice. Well, he had millions of choices, but he liked his job. He liked that he felt as if he was doing something. He respected the Greenvales, and they needed him. So, he dressed and grabbed something at the diner, then headed out to work.

A few hours after he got there, old man Greenvale came out to the barn. "Buck, how's it going out here?"

He found it funny that he asked him that all the time. "It's good, sir. How are you feeling today?"

Charles chuckled. "Old. Hey, I was wondering if you could give me a ride into town this afternoon. I have a lunch date at noon at the diner."

Buck looked at him. "Isn't Emily going with you?"

He shook his head, leaning in to whisper, "No, not today. It's just me."

Buck found that statement to be a bit odd. "Are you having an affair?" he asked jokingly.

"Oh, heavens no. There isn't a woman who could pull me away from my Emily."

Buck chuckled. "I had... well, I thought I had that once."

"Is that why you're here? Because a woman hurt you?"

Buck smiled at him. The old man didn't miss a beat. "Yeah, she took me for all she could and then she left."

"Then she wasn't the one for you. She is out there somewhere, the one for you."

"Ah, Charles, I believe that ship has sailed for me."

"Nonsense, you're good looking and young. Your life has just begun. You'll find her one day."

"I'm not as young as you might think I am."

Charles laughed. "You're certainly younger than I am." After a short pause, he continued. "So, we should head out around eleven-thirty. I don't want to be late."

"Sounds good to me," Buck said as he looked at his watch. He had about an hour until he needed to go. He stood there watching Charles walk back to the house. Then he got back to work.

An hour later, he headed out of the barn, only to see Charles standing by his truck. Chuckling, he headed over to it.

On the drive into town, Charles said to him, "I would appreciate your discretion today. Emily doesn't need to know about this. I told her you and I were going to the hardware store. With Kennedy's wedding coming up and the barbeque this weekend, she has enough on her plate."

"Charles, is everything all right?"

"Not really, but I'm hoping I can get it all settled before Kennedy gets married."

Buck didn't want to push him, but he was feeling a bit uncomfortable, more so as they pulled into the parking lot at the diner and sitting in the window was the blonde bombshell. He watched a smile cross her mouth when she spotted the old man. Buck took a deep breath. She was fucking stunning up close. He didn't want to feel this way. He knew the kind of woman she was, and he wanted no part of her.

"Did you want me to come in with you?" he asked Charles.

The smile on his face indicated he didn't need him there. "No, Buck, I've got this."

He watched him climb out of the truck and walk into the diner, where the blonde bombshell stood and hugged him. Buck heard himself moan as she wrapped her arms around him. "What the fuck?"

What the fuck is wrong with me? She is just like the rest of them. Women who look like that are out for one thing and one thing only. Money, a leg up.

Shaking his head, he closed his eyes and put his head back, willing his fucking erection to go away.

CHAPTER THREE

Since yesterday, Lyssa had discovered more than she ever expected. Taking her notes with her, she headed to the diner to meet Mr. Greenvale. She was more than a bit nervous. What if she was wrong? What if the information she uncovered was wrong and Mr. Greenvale instantly hated Hugh? But what if she was right, and his soon to be son-in-law was about to steal his land and have him thrown out in the street?

Sitting at the table with her leg bouncing up and down, she figured she didn't need any more coffee, so she ordered a glass of unsweetened tea. She sat there staring at the clock, and exactly at noon, she turned her head to see that asshole's pickup truck pull into the diner parking lot.

"Great," she whispered to herself. But when she looked again, Mr. Greenvale was in the passenger seat. Her smile was automatic. She stood up as he walked in and greeted him with a hug. Ignoring the asshole should be easy with all the information she had to disclose to Mr. Greenvale.

"Good morning, dear," he said to her as he sat down.

She smiled at him. "You might not think so when I tell you what I've discovered. Mr. Greenvale, what do you know about Hugh?"

"Not much, really. He owns his own company, went to Harvard, came from money, and he makes my Kennedy happy. That's what this weekend is about, getting to know him, I suppose. All we ever wanted was for her to be happy, and if this young man makes her happy, then he's all right in our book. Why do you ask?"

"Well, in my research into this mess, I've discovered that there is a company out there that is pushing to purchase your land in two months when the bank forecloses, or if the state takes it for unpaid taxes."

"Is that right? Well, you have the paperwork, so can't you go to court and get an injunction or something like that?"

She smiled at him. Reaching across the table, she took his hand in hers, unaware that the asshole was watching them. "Mr. Greenvale," she began.

"Charles, call me Charles."

She smiled. "Charles, the path to this company led me to Hugh's company. I spoke to Kennedy last night. She is, in fact, in New York, setting up the offices for this company. It's called Alexander Corporation. Apparently, they are buying up land across the country to build eco-friendly towns, or housing, something like that. Although Hugh is a part of this company, the C.E.O. is a guy named Brody Buckingham. He is Hugh's best friend, the best man he chose for their wedding. I think they all agreed to come out for the weekend so they can check out the property. Kennedy has no idea what is happening, and I'm afraid that when she finds out, she is going to be devastated."

"Then this weekend should be very interesting." He chuckled, contradicting the slight frown marring his face. "It's been some time since I have had to deal with snakes, but they are all around us."

She turned her head to look at the asshole in the truck, his eyes boring into hers. Turning her head, she smiled. "I suppose they are. Mr. Greenvale, you can't say anything about this to anyone. Not until I can get more evidence. I can't get in front of a judge with just circumstantial evidence. I need solid proof, or you just might lose your land."

"Oh, I am not going to say a word. You have done more for me in two days than that idiot Slate has done in a year."

"It isn't Mr. Slate, it's Knox Fairfield, and now that you say that, I can't help but think he has something to do with this as well. Which would put him in a very real position of being disbarred. Trust me when I tell you, I would love to see it happen." *Almost as much as I loved punching that asshole in the face,* she thought.

He just nodded his head as the waitress came over to take their order. When she walked away, he looked at Lyssa. "I know your parents would be proud of you. I never told you this, but I was the one who bought your farm."

She sat there looking at him. "Why would you do that?"

"Because I thought that one day you would want it. That and I thought you could use the money to pay off your college loans. I know how much it cost to send Kennedy to that fancy school."

"Mr. Greenvale, you paid far too much for it. I will admit I was shocked when the lawyers came to me and told me how much was offered for the land. You didn't have to do that."

He smiled. "Yes, I did. I also had the place renovated, so if you want to move in there, you can. Let me give it to you as payment for your help."

She shook her head. "No, I won't let you do that. I still have the bulk of the money you paid for it. If anything, let me pay you what I have for it."

He chuckled, placing his hand on hers. "Don't be silly. That land is part of what they are trying to take away from me. So, you'll be fighting for your home as well."

She laughed. "Let me think about it, but for now, I think it's best I stay where I am, at least until this is finished."

The waitress came with their food, and they ate and just chatted about things. When they finished, she went to pick up the bill, when his hand came down on top of hers. "This is on me. You be careful," he said as he picked up the check and stood. "I don't want anything to happen to you. Kennedy would never forgive me."

They walked out together, and she hugged him at the door of the truck. "I'll talk to you soon. If not, I will see you this weekend." He opened the door. "Keep your ears open," she said softly.

"Watch your back, dear. There are plenty of snakes out there."

Lyssa locked eyes with Buck. "Yes, there are," she said, her eyes moving back to Mr. Greenvale's. "I'll see you soon." He climbed into the truck while Buck watched her every move as she walked to her car.

~

Who the fuck are you? He thought.

"Well, I suppose it's back to the ranch." Mr. Greenvale snapped him out of his stare.

Buck started the truck and pulled out. As they were headed back to the ranch, he asked, "Charles, is everything all right?"

"There seems to be a snake in my garden, Buck."

Buck chuckled. "If that isn't a loaded statement, I don't know what is. Care to elaborate?"

"Not yet. I don't have enough information, but I'd appreciate it if you were around this weekend."

"Isn't it the big barbeque?"

"Yep, seems to be a nesting ground for snakes. I could use a sharp set of eyes around."

Buck crinkled his eyebrows. "Sir?"

Charles chuckled. "That young woman I was just with, seems she is going to put herself right in the middle of the den of deadly snakes. I would appreciate it if you could keep your eyes open and make sure nothing happens to her. It would kill Emily and Kennedy if anything happened to her."

Fuck! "Can I ask who she is?"

Charles laughed, looking at Buck. "You mean, she beat the shit out of you and you have no idea who she is?"

Buck busted out laughing. "I forget that about you, that you know things. And, for the record, she didn't beat the shit out of me."

"Well, that split lip and black eye say differently. She is special, tough as nails, but very special to us. That is our Kennedy's childhood friend. She grew up down the road, in the house you renovated for us."

"You bought her family farm?" Buck was learning a hell of a lot more than he wanted to.

"Not only bought it, overpaid for it. The girl had just lost her parents, and she was in a fancy college that cost a fortune. She didn't deserve to have that debt, so I bought it for an obscene amount of money so she could pay for school and still have money to live off while she found a job she loved. Then I renovated it, so she would have a place to come home to. I didn't think she would ever move to the big city like Kennedy. She is a farm girl at heart."

"Charles, who is she? What's her name? What does she do that she is going to step into the den of snakes?" He was curious about her now, and about this conversation.

"Her name is Lyssa Dawn, and she is our lawyer."

Buck sat there in silence. "A lawyer? Charles, what would you need a lawyer for?"

"Not sure yet. Lyssa is working on it. But this weekend could prove to be an information extravaganza. I'm just a bit worried about her. If what she has uncovered, is in fact, the truth, she could get herself hurt, and I don't want to have Emily bear the guilt for that. Not to mention, it would kill Kennedy if anything happened to her."

They pulled up to the gate, and Buck jumped out to open it up. When they drove through, he stopped. "Charles, where does Lyssa live?"

Charles looked at him and smiled. "In the town south of ours."

"Do you have her address?"

"I do. What are you up to, Buck?"

"I think it's time we had a talk."

"I don't think Lyssa would want me to give her address out."

"Well, then could you call her please and ask her to come out here?"

"That I can do," Charles said. Buck jumped out and shut the gate. They drove to the house in silence. When Charles got out of the truck,

Buck just sat there letting everything Charles had said to him sink in. Maybe he misjudged her; maybe she wasn't like most women. He knew he was going to have to eat shit, but for some reason, he didn't seem to mind eating this particular plate. Climbing out of the truck, he headed to the house. It was time to come clean.

Knocking on the door, Emily walked up. "Hello, Buck," she said as she opened the screen door. "Come on in."

"Thank you, Emily. I was wondering if I could talk to you and Charles."

She smiled. "Of course, come on in and have a seat."

He thought she would go into the living room, but instead, she headed to the dining room. Charles was sitting at the table with a folder in front of him. Buck sat down.

"My name isn't Buck, it's Callen McCabe. I used to be an investment broker in Chicago, a corporate raider. I was engaged to be married to a woman I thought was in love with me. She maxed out my credit cards, took every piece of expensive jewelry I bought her, emptied our bank account, and then left me. I'm afraid I didn't handle it well, and I sold my company, my penthouse, and my cars, then I bought my truck and drove. This is where I landed, I'm afraid, outside your gate."

Charles smiled at him, pushing the file toward him. "I was wondering why it took you eight years to tell me that."

Callen opened the file. Everything there was to know about him was right there. Looking up, he said, "Why didn't you tell me you knew who I was? How did you get this?"

"You were unconscious for three days, so I looked in your wallet. I thought I should call someone. I asked a friend of mine to look into you, and this is what he gave me. The way I see it, if a man who is worth nearly a billion dollars wants to work as a ranch hand, something pretty terrible must have happened. It wasn't my place to ask. I needed the help."

He laughed. "Yes, you did. I'm sorry I lied to you."

"You didn't lie to us, son. I only had you checked out because I wasn't sure who you were. I knew I couldn't handle the day to day anymore. I probably should have gone with one of the boys, but to be honest with you," he leaned in to whisper, "I'm not sure they are smart enough. You owned a billion-dollar company, I needed the help, and I needed to know I could trust you. You have a very impressive resumé. I figured you could handle it."

"You can trust me, sir. I'm sorry I kept it from you. It was more than a bit humiliating. I guess I'm still working through it. I would appreciate it, though, if you wouldn't tell anyone who I am. I like the anonymity."

"You've been Buck for nearly eight years." Charles smiled. "Perhaps, the question I want to ask you now is a bit uncomfortable for me. But Lyssa didn't do that to your face because you did her wrong, did she?"

Buck smiled. "Not in the way you think. I'm responsible for her face. I let my ego get in the way, and I suppose my pain and anger is still buried inside of me when it comes to women. I misjudged her by her appearance and assumed she was like *her*. My mistake."

Charles laughed. "Be careful, Callen. That girl is tough as nails."

His hand reached up to his lip. Smiling, he said, "Don't I know it." Just then, they heard a car door shut. "Do you mind if I talk to her alone?"

Charles shook his head. "I've got some ice in the freezer. You know, just in case you need it."

Callen laughed. "Here's hoping I don't." He stood and walked to the door just as Lyssa was walking up the steps. He pushed the door open and walked out, meeting her on the porch.

She stood there looking at him. "Excuse me," she said, going to step around him.

He crossed his arms over his chest as he stood in her way. "We need to have a talk."

She laughed. "Fat chance in hell. I've got absolutely nothing to say to you."

"Well, I have a great deal to say to you. Now, you can come with me willingly or I can make you. Your choice."

She laughed, looking up into his eyes. *Fuck, she's beautiful.* "What, getting your ass kicked once wasn't enough?"

Charles sat at the table chuckling, listening to the two of them.

Callen laughed. "You were lucky I was being a gentleman. I won't make that mistake twice."

"Somehow, sweetheart, I don't think you have a gentlemanly bone in your Neanderthal body. Now, if you will excuse me, I have an appointment."

"Yeah, you do. With me."

"In your dreams, big boy." When she went to move around him, his hand came out and wrapped around her waist. His whole body went into shock.

She pushed his hand away. "Don't fucking touch me."

He chuckled, bracing himself as he scooped her up in his arms, tossing her over his shoulder, and headed off the porch toward the barn.

"Put me down!" she yelled, hitting him in the back.

He smacked her pretty damn hard on the ass. "Stop fighting with me."

"Oww, are you fucking kidding me? You're going to spank me like a child?"

"You're acting like a child."

"Put me fucking down!" she screamed as she hit him again, kicking her feet.

His hand cracked against her ass again, his arm acting like a vice grip pinning her legs to his chest. Then, out of nowhere, she was flying through the air, landing on a pile of freshly tossed hay.

"What the fuck is your problem?" she yelled as she got up. "What are you, like, five?"

"It would seem I owe you an apology for hurting you," he said gently. She froze, looking at him. He was stunning. His eyes softened as she gazed at them. He stepped forward, his hand coming up to touch her lip, her eyebrow, then trail along the light bruises on her face. "I didn't know I did this to you. I'm sorry I hurt you," he whispered.

He watched as Lyssa licked her lips, her eyebrows coming together in thought. "I'm not sorry I did that to your face," she said, her voice bitchy. She wasn't backing down.

He chuckled softly. "I deserved it and more. You didn't deserve this." His thumb padded across her bottom lip.

She stared into his eyes as he continued to touch her cracked lip. Slowly, he bent his head closer to hers. He could feel the heat of her breath on his lips, when she spoke up, snapping him out of the trance. He'd been about to kiss her.

"Please, don't," her voice barely audible.

He smiled and slowly pulled back, dropping his hand from her face, and taking a step back. "Charles filled me in on a few things and asked me to keep my eyes open this weekend."

"What did he tell you?" she asked all breathy.

"Just that this weekend is going to be an information extravaganza, and that you are going to be walking into a den of snakes. He wants me to make sure you don't get hurt."

She laughed. "Well, Charles is overreacting. Nothing of the sort is going to happen to me. I'm a big girl. I can take care of myself. So, thank you, but it's not necessary." She moved to walk away, but he stepped in front of her.

"Tell me why Charles and Emily need a lawyer," he said softly.

She looked up at him. "If he didn't tell you, then I certainly cannot. Attorney-Client privilege."

"I might be able to help you."

She moved to his left to walk around him, but he stepped in front of her. "I know men like you. What you are offering me, trust me, I don't want it."

He laughed. "What do you think I am offering?"

She jerked her head up, looking him right in the eyes. "You're not the staying kind. A fuck is a fuck." She shoved past him.

His eyes closed. She had spit his words back in his face. She was halfway across the drive before he snapped his head in her direction. Her perfect ass was his view. His feet were moving. Wrapping his arm around her waist, he picked her up and carried her back to the barn.

"Are you fucking kidding right now? Put me down, you beast."

Down she went, back into the hay. "I wasn't done talking to you."

She got up, dusting herself off. "Listen to me, you fucking asshole, I am not some horse you can break. Keep your fucking hands off me."

Her feet were moving, but his hand snaked around her neck, pulling her to him, and his mouth crashing down on hers. He couldn't stop himself. She pushed on his chest, even hit him a few times, but slowly, she let him kiss her. Slowly, she let him lead her. Slowly, she began to respond to him. When her tongue touched his, he groaned deep in her mouth, fueling his body into some kind of frenzy he'd never felt in all his experience.

His hands moved to her face, through her hair, his body moving flush with hers. His erection pressed against her stomach, and she broke their connection. Pulling his head back, his eyes slowly opened to see her looking at him with wide eyes.

"What the fuck," he whispered on her lips.

She stood there blinking at him, so he bent to kiss her again. This time, she responded with not only her mouth but her body as well. She was pressing herself against him, and when he moved his hands down to her ass and then her thighs, lifting her, she surprised him by wrapping her legs around his waist. He moved them further inside the barn, pressing her back against the wall.

He let go of her legs and moved his hands to her hair, pulling it off her face. It was when he pressed his erection against her core that she lost her mind. He pulled back, his breaths ragged, looking at her. "What the fuck was that?"

When she shook her head and pulled her lip between her teeth, he gently pulled them off the wall and set her down on her feet. She stood there visibly shaken by what took place.

"I need to go. Please, don't do that again. I am not some plaything for you to play with." She walked out of the barn and got in her car.

He just stood there, his mind clouded over with lust and something different. Something he wasn't sure he understood. He heard her car pull away, and he was out the door going after her. Jumping in his truck, he flew out of the drive. She was stopped at the gate, opening it up.

Slamming the truck into park, he moved toward her. Picking her up, he crashed his mouth down on hers, sitting her on the hood of the car.

Pulling back, he looked at her. "You are not a plaything. You could never be a plaything. What the hell was that back there? First, you push me away, then you… I don't know what the hell you did to me."

He watched as her eyes filled with anger. "I don't want to do this. I have a job to do. I just can't…" She stopped talking and pushed on his chest, trying to get away from him.

"No, talk to me. Tell me what the hell that was?"

She managed to get off the car, so he grabbed her arm, fixing himself to his spot, ready for her backlash. She spun around. "I don't know what the hell that was or what the hell I did to you."

He chuckled. "You're a liar. What are you trying to accomplish here?"

She ripped her arm out of his grip and took off running. *Fuck!* He took off after her. She was fast, making it out into the field before he caught up with her. "Stop," he said as he wrapped his arm around her waist, pulling her to him. "Stop."

She was crying. "What the hell do you want from me?" She looked a mix of terrified and pissed. "You're nothing but a taker, an egotistical asshole, who thinks he can just take what he wants. Well, I'm not for the taking. I'm not your next fuck-and-go chick. Just leave me alone," she screamed at him.

He smiled, turned on, despite her tirade against him. "Go on, get it all out so we can have a real conversation."

Oh, she was so pissed. He took a deep breath when her tears stopped and she continued yelling at him. "There aren't any real conversations to be had between us. That in there," she pointed to the barn, "was your way of trying to fuck me. I hate to tell you this…" She paused. "What the hell is your name anyway? Never mind, I don't care. You aren't going to fuck me. Not now, not ever. I'm not that girl."

He stood looking at her. Every fucking word out of her mouth was the truth, and it hurt. It hurt badly. "You're right. You are absolutely right. I am that guy. I didn't use to be that guy, but I am him now."

"Oh, I know you are. But you won't be him with me."

"No? You sound so sure of yourself. I think that kiss says otherwise."

And there it was. Her fist came out of nowhere, connecting with his face. "Fuck!" he yelled, letting her go.

She took off, running across the field. He watched her go; he let her go. "What the fuck? What the fuck?" he yelled as he watched her get in her car and take off down the gravel road. He sat down in the grass then laid back to look at the sky. "What the fuck was that?"

He finally got up and headed back to the barn. His fucking cock hurt so bad. She was dangerous; that he knew. He stood there looking at the spot on the wall where he'd pressed into her, his mind on nothing but her. *Who the hell is this woman?* Shaking his head, he got back to work. The tractor wasn't going to fix itself, and they needed it to be ready in the next few weeks.

He finally managed to get the engine apart and found the broken piece. Looking at his watch, he figured he could still make it to the parts store before it closed, so he put the part in a box and headed out to his truck. Charles was sitting on the porch when he walked out. He waved him over.

"So, that went well." He chuckled. "The girl has a wicked right hook."

Buck chuckled, rubbing his jaw. "She sure does."

"I might have a piece of advice for you."

"A piece of advice would be nice."

"I've known her most of her life. Not once have I seen her with a boy, or a man. I think my advice to you would be to stop scaring the shit out of her, and you might not keep ending up with bruises on your face."

Buck sat there letting his words sink in. Slowly turning his head, he spoke softly and slowly. "Charles, are you saying what I think you're saying? She's never had a boyfriend?"

Charles shook his head. "None that I know of."

"No fucking way," Callen whispered.

Charles laughed. "I told you she was special. Smart, beautiful, and well, yeah."

"Jesus, no wonder she freaked out on me in the barn."

"Why? What happened in the barn?"

"I sort of kissed her, and well, I think I pissed her off."

The laughter that bellowed out of Charles echoed through the yard. Buck smiled and chuckled. "Yes, that would explain a great deal. Buck, I know you've been hurt, and I know now why you are here. But she isn't that girl. She is the kind of girl you respect. She's the kind of girl you search for all your life. She is special to us for other reasons, so I am asking you to treat her respectfully. Don't play her, and please don't use her like you have those other women. You have a not so good reputation around these parts with women. I know they give and you take, and they agree. But not her, not Lyssa. If you aren't going to give her everything she deserves to have, then please respect me enough to not try."

"Well, sir, that's the thing. I can't seem to get her out of my head. When I kissed her… I don't know, something clicked inside of me. Like the missing piece that made me this asshole was out of place, but now it seems to be back in place. Please trust me at my word. I even told her she isn't a plaything. She could never be a plaything. But having this knowledge you bestowed upon me, well, I'm pretty sure she is never going to talk to me again."

"I wouldn't be so sure about that. You wouldn't have walked out of that barn if she didn't feel something. Trust me, I've seen her beat the shit out of boys twice her size defending Kennedy. She may be tiny, but she knows how to take a man down. Just don't pressure her. I'll talk to her, see how she is feeling. But that's all I'm going to do. You were once a good, decent man; you just had a bad thing happen to you."

"Charles, no offense, but I made this mess. I'll fix it. Even if I have to take a few more to the jaw. Yes, it was a bad thing, but it's been eight years. I think it's time I man up and deal with myself. Thanks for understanding and not throwing me out on my ass."

Charles laughed. "You're the best manager I've seen. Some of the other ranchers wanted to know where I found you. I'm surprised they haven't tried to steal you away. Now, go on, get out of here. I've got some pie to eat."

Buck laughed. "See you tomorrow."

"Yep, you and the guys have some tents to put up. Saturday is only a few days away."

He nodded and got up and headed to the parts store. He had a great deal to think about. This woman was under his skin, and he needed to get his shit straight if he wanted to ever stand a chance in hell of having her.

CHAPTER FOUR

Lyssa pulled over once she reached the blacktop. She didn't understand why she was crying. Was it because he kissed her, or because she liked it and it scared the shit out of her? She couldn't act like this. He was just a man. A fucking gorgeous man. Wiping her eyes, she put the car in drive and headed home.

Her phone rang, scaring the shit out of her. Pulling over, she dug it out of her bag. It was the law offices. "Hello."

"Lyssa?"

"Yes, this is Lyssa. Who is this?"

"It's Katie."

"Katie, why are you calling me?" She was confused. She didn't think Katie liked her, let alone had her number.

"Listen, I got your number from your personnel file. I called your house, but there was no answer. I'm not sure what happened or why you quit, but there's some stuff going on here that I think you need to know about."

"It's really not any of my business anymore. Katie, I wasn't aware you even liked me."

"That's not it at all. Like I said, there are things going on here that you need to know. Can we meet somewhere? I'm not comfortable talking here at work."

"Sure, there's a place down on Main Street, a little diner. Meet me there in, say, an hour."

"Great, I will see you there." The line went dead.

"Well, that was weird." She sat there looking at her phone. All of this was weird.

She dialed the phone. "Mr. Greenvale, I just got the strangest phone call from a girl at Slate Law Offices. She said she had some information for me. I set up to meet her at a little diner I know on Main Street in the city. I'm heading there now. I guess I just wanted you to know where I'm going."

"Lyssa, please, be careful. I know you can take care of yourself, but if what you told me is the truth, someone at that law firm knows what's going on. Should you go alone?"

"That's why I set it up in a public place. I'll call you when I'm done."

"Please, be careful."

"I will." She disconnected the call and started driving.

Mr. Greenvale hung up and dialed the phone.

"Yeah," Buck answered.

"Well, it seems you might be able to redeem yourself."

"Charles? What are you talking about?"

"Lyssa. There's a meeting that is going to happen in an hour in the city. A diner on Main Street. Maybe you could go check it out, make sure everything is on the up and up."

"Charles, I'm going to do this because you asked me. But I am going to need you to tell me what is happening."

He chuckled. "How about you do this and then call me? I'll have Lyssa tell you."

"You've got a deal." He hung up and put on his boots then grabbed his keys and left. He had no idea what the hell was going on, but if

Charles called him to intervene, then he was more than worried about her, which in turn, for some strange reason, made him concerned.

The drive wasn't as bad as he thought it would be. He found the diner and made his way inside. Lyssa hadn't arrived yet, so he found a place in the back and got comfortable. He ordered coffee and a piece of pie. A few minutes later, he saw her walk in the door and find a table to sit at. He had a perfect view of the back of her head. He sat there looking at her. *What the hell is it with this woman? Why can't I let her go? She obviously wants nothing to do with me. But, then again, I was being a dickhead.* He chuckled to himself as he watched a woman walk up to her table.

Lyssa sat at the table, looking at her cup of coffee but not drinking it. She couldn't for the life of her understand why Katie wanted to talk to her. Ten minutes after she sat down, Katie walked in and sat across from her.

"Thank you for coming," Katie said. "There is so much weird shit going on. Did you take one of Knox's accounts?"

"I did. Why?"

"Well, after you left yesterday, Knox and Mr. Slate got in a huge shouting match. Knox wanted to know why Slate sent you out to that ranch account."

"I don't understand why it should matter. I was sent out there because I know the Greenvales. Mr. Slate thought I could settle Mr. Greenvale down."

"Exactly what he said. What was weird was that Knox knew that you knew them. He's been watching you."

"Who, Knox?"

"Yep, that's why he never made a move on you. Apparently, some guy named Hugh, from what I can understand, that's Knox's partner, he told him if he touched you he would lose everything. But when you came back to the office and asked for the account, and then quit when Mr. Slate wouldn't give it to you, Knox went batshit crazy."

"How do you know this Hugh guy is his partner?"

"Well, I was at Knox's, and before you say anything, yeah, I know. Disgusting. Anyway, I was there in the bedroom when that guy Hugh came over. They were talking in whispers, but Hugh was pissed off that whatever they were doing was taking so long. He has no intention of getting married to secure this deal." Lyssa's heart sank. Kennedy was being used again. "Anyway, he was talking louder than a whisper. He told Knox to make sure you weren't made aware of the account, that if you found out, that Knox would pay the price. When I heard the door shut, I got back in bed and pretended I was sleeping. Knox woke me up and told me I had to leave because he had somewhere he needed to be. Who the hell has something to do at nearly one in the morning? Anyway, I got dressed and left, only I didn't leave. I waited outside, and when he drove off, I followed him. He went to your house, Lyssa. He has a key to your house. I don't know if you were home or not, but I watched him walk into your house. He was in there for about fifteen minutes before he came out."

"Why didn't you tell me this? That shit is just creepy. When did this happen?"

"Last week. I overheard Knox talking to some guy, who I assume was that Hugh guy. He told him he needed to hurry, that the two-month deadline was becoming a problem."

"Are you fucking kidding me? So, Knox has been following me around?" She looked out the window. "Katie, you need to forget about this. You need to take a vacation or go visit your mom."

"Hmpht... Why? It's not me Knox is after. You should have just slept with him like everyone else. Listen, I need to go. I hope everything works out for you, and you should change your locks."

Lyssa watched her get up and walk out the door. She stood and dropped some money on the table and walked out. She needed to make sure all her notes were in her bag.

～

Buck got up and followed her out. As she was walking to her car, he watched some guy walk up to her and grab her by the arm.

"You fucking little bitch," he whisper-shouted to her.

She ripped her arm from his grip. "Don't fucking touch me, Knox. What the hell is your problem?"

He slammed her against the car, knocking the wind out of her. "You. You're my problem. I want my fucking account back. You have no fucking idea what you are doing. Stupid fucking…"

Lyssa brought her knee up, landing it in his groin. Callen watched as she grabbed the guy's head and slammed his face into her knee. "I told you, asshole, not to fucking touch me."

Callen was moving and fast, as Knox stood up, his fist in full swing. Callen caught him by the throat and threw him on his back on the ground. Turning, he looked at Lyssa. "Get in my truck now."

She stood there looking at him, then at Knox. "What?" She couldn't believe he was there.

Knox was getting up. "Now, Lyssa. Get in my fucking truck." He turned and swung, hitting Knox right in the face, knocking him out. Spinning around, he grabbed Lyssa by the arm and pulled her away. He opened the truck door and picked her up, putting her in the seat. When he got in, he started the truck and took off. "Where do you live?" She just sat there, staring out the window. "Hey." He touched her arm. "Where do you live?"

Turning her head, she looked at his hand. "It doesn't matter."

"What do you mean, it doesn't matter?"

"He has a key to my house."

"Was that your boyfriend?" His heart slammed in his chest. He didn't want him to be her boyfriend.

"No, I don't have a boyfriend." Her voice was distant.

He knew she was in shock, so he just took her to his place. He pulled into the driveway and turned off the truck. Turning, he looked at her, seeing she had tears dropping on her cheeks. He climbed out and carried her into his house, sitting her on the couch. He pulled his phone out of his pocket and called Charles.

"She's safe. I've got her at my house. Charles, some guy attacked her in the parking lot. What the hell is going on?"

"Let me talk to her."

He put the phone to her ear. "Lyssa."

"Mr. Greenvale," she whispered.

"Lyssa, you stay with Buck. He will make sure you're all right. You tell him everything, all right, sweetheart?"

"All right."

He took the phone from her ear. "Charles, what the hell is going on?"

"I told her to tell you. I will see you both in the morning." He hung up.

Callen set the phone down and then sat on the coffee table in front of her. "Hey, what is going on?"

Her eyes moved up to meet his, and she sat there looking at him. "Someone is trying to steal Mr. Greenvale's land, and I think my boss, that man by my car, and Kennedy's fiancé are doing this."

He sat there looking at her. His hands reached out and landed on her knees. "And you've been investigating this all on your own?"

"Yes, they sent me to talk to Mr. Greenvale, so I could calm him down while the time ran out. They have two months left to divert the taxes before they can buy the land outright. His daughter's fiancé is doing this. Kennedy is in New York setting up the company whose name is on the paperwork. That man, Knox, the one at my car, he was the lawyer appointed to this case. He has a key to my apartment, and the only place he could have gotten it from was Hugh, and he got it off Kennedy's keychain."

"Would Kennedy have given it to him?"

She shook her head. "She is going to be devastated when she finds out what Hugh is doing. I'm not so sure he loves her, not like you're supposed to love someone when you are getting married. I think the wedding is part of the scam. They are all coming to the barbeque on Saturday, and I'm sure it's to scope the land. Brody Buckingham is the best man, and he's also the C.E.O. of the Alexander Corporation, which is owned by Brody and Hugh."

"Will you excuse me for a minute?" He grabbed his phone and walked outside, then dialed a number he thought he would never dial again. "Tom, it's Callen."

"Holy shit! What the fuck? We all thought you were dead."

"No, not dead, just gone. Listen, I need a favor."

"Yeah, sure, anything. What's up?"

"I need you to find me everything you can on some guys—Brody Buckingham and Hugh Bell."

"Not a problem. So, how have you been?"

Callen laughed. "I've been good. I'll call you in the morning. Oh, and can you not mention this call to anyone? Not yet anyway. I'll know more in the morning. We'll talk then."

"You got it."

Callen hung up and stood there looking at the sky. "Mother fucker," he whispered. He was about to do some things he didn't want to do. He didn't want to be that man anymore. He liked being Buck. He liked working on the ranch. He didn't want to be a corporate raider, but he was good at it. If these fuckers wanted to play, then he was going to play. That fucker was trying to hurt her, and there is no way that was going to happen again. Today was Tuesday, so he had four days to do this. Could it be done? He knew it could.

His door opened, and he turned his head. "You all right?" Lyssa asked.

"Not really. How about you?"

"I'll be fine. How did you know where to find me?"

He smiled. "Charles called me."

"So, what are you trying to do? Redeem yourself?"

He chuckled. "Yeah, something like that. I think we need to talk."

"I think you might be right."

He pushed off the wall and followed her back into the house. "Do you want a beer?" She shook her head. "First of all, I want to apologize for my behavior at the ranch. Not for kissing you," he smiled, "but for the things I said to you and the way I treated you."

She sat there with a smirk on her face. "I forgive you."

He laughed. "Good. I think it's time I told some truth myself. My name is Callen McCabe, but everyone here knows me as Buck. I was burned badly by a very beautiful woman. In the end, she walked away with five million dollars of my money. It pissed me off so bad that I sold my company, sold my penthouse, sold my cars, and disappeared. I drank myself into a stupor and fucked anything that looked at me the wrong way across the country, until one night eight years ago, when I ran into the post outside Charles' ranch. He and Emily took care of me, and about a week later, he had a heart attack. Emily asked me to stay and help around the ranch until he was better. Charles didn't get better. So, I stayed. I like it here. I'm nobody, and nobody expects a thing from me. I still drink and womanize because I'm embarrassed that a woman like *her* got the best of me."

"You loved her."

He laughed. "Yeah, I did. It crushed me when she walked out the door. I'm not sure I've recovered. Well, I was sure I would never recover, until today."

Her eyes locked on his. He watched as she drew her bottom lip between her teeth. Shaking her head, she told him, "I'm not what you want. I'm not her. I am not just another warm body for you to fuck."

"I know, but I'm still not sorry I kissed you."

Her smile made him catch his breath. "That was some kiss."

"Yeah, it sure was."

"So, what was your business eight years ago."

He wiggled his eyebrows at her. "I was, in a way I suppose I still am, a corporate raider. So, you're a lawyer?"

She chuckled. "I'm an unemployed lawyer. I always wanted to be in a courtroom. I like to argue with people."

He busted out laughing, something he hadn't done in a long time. "Don't I know it."

"I'm also very observant," she admitted, and he looked up at her. "I see things most people don't. I probably should have been an investigator or something, but part of being a good lawyer is seeing things that aren't obvious to others." She stopped talking. Callen didn't say anything, just sat there. "Oh my God."

"What?"

"Mr. Slate wasn't in on this, not to the degree that I thought. Maybe he was being blackmailed or something. Hugh knows me. Well, he thinks he knows me through Kennedy. She would have told him these things. That's why Knox was so pissed off at Mr. Slate. Hugh told Knox to keep me away from this case because he knew I would put the pieces together. That's why Knox had the key to my house, so he could check to see if I knew anything."

"Where are all your notes?"

"In my car." She looked at him. "We need to get my car. My bag is still in the back seat."

"I'm not so sure it's still there. But come on." He stood up.

"Seriously? Don't you have some philandering to do?" She was being a smart ass.

He stopped walking and turned to look at her, his hand moving to touch her face. "I think my philandering days are over," he said softly, watching her swallow.

"Don't go changing because of me. I'm not that girl, Buck. I'm not a fuck-and-go girl." She turned her head away from him.

He just smiled. "No, I suppose you're not. But I'll grow on you."

She laughed. "Yeah, I don't think that's going to happen anytime soon. I'm sure, once this is over, you'll be back out there doing what you do. Come on, it's getting late and I'm hungry." He watched her open the door and walk out.

Closing his eyes, he thought, *I'm not going anywhere, sweetheart.* He followed her out. The drive was quiet. He was in his own mind, thinking about how nice it was to kiss her, to touch her. If what Charles told him was true, he was sitting in his truck with a rarity in life. A woman a man only dreams of having. His eyes moved from the road to look at her. She had the perfect profile. God, she was beautiful.

"What?" she smarted.

"Nothing."

"No, it's something. Please, stop thinking about me as if I'm your next conquest." Her voice was soft.

"Not my next," he countered.

She smiled. "Not your anything."

He just smiled as they drove. Pulling up to her car, he could see that all her windows were intact. They got out of the truck together. Callen stood by her while she unlocked the door and grabbed her bag out. Then he helped her back in the truck. Getting in, he locked the doors and they were moving again. "Should we stop by your house, maybe get some clothes?"

"That might be a good idea. I mean, unless he has a gun, I'm pretty sure I can kick his ass."

He busted out laughing. "I'm pretty sure you could as well. Where do you live?"

She directed him to her house. Putting her bag on her shoulder, she crossed it over her chest. Together, they went up to her apartment. When Lyssa opened the door, they walked into a destroyed house. All of her things were smashed and destroyed.

He put his hand on her arm, pulling her behind him as he moved into the room. It didn't sound like anyone was in the apartment. Callen pulled his phone out and dialed nine-one-one, handing the phone to Lyssa.

When she was done, she gave him the phone back. "I should get some clothes."

"Come on, I'll go with you."

Once she gathered enough clothes to last a week, they moved back into the living room, just as the police knocked on the door. The whole experience took over an hour, and they were back on the road again. Knox had been implicated in the destruction, and Callen felt a bit better that she was with him and not out there alone. She didn't say a word on the way back to his house.

When they got there, she said, "Do you have a pillow and a blanket? Where is the bathroom so I can change? I think I'm tired and want to go to bed."

"Aren't you hungry?" he asked softly.

She shook her head. "Not anymore. I'd like to just go to sleep."

"You can sleep in my bed. I'll take the couch."

She shook her head again. "I don't want to sleep in your bed, where…" She stopped.

He moved toward her, pulling her into his arms. "No woman has been in that bed, beautiful. I promise you."

She half-chuckled, half-sobbed into his chest. He thought he was going to lose his mind when she dropped her head on his chest. "I'm the guest. I should sleep on the couch."

He kissed the top of her head. "I don't really sleep in there a great deal. You go." He pulled away from her, showing her where the bedroom was and the attached bathroom. "I'll be on the couch if you need anything." She nodded, and he walked out, pulling the door closed. He leaned against the door. "Fuck," he whispered.

His head was swimming. *What the hell is happening to me?* He pushed off the door and walked to the kitchen to grab a beer. This was all too complicated. He needed to make sure she was safe now. No more of this shit. His phone vibrated in his pocket, so he pulled it out and swiped the screen. A message from Tom.

Got your info, call me.

He dialed the phone. "Hey, buddy. That was fast."

"Yeah, well, I don't know what you're after with this, but if you are going to tear this guy's company apart, now would be the time. He is completely invested, no money to spare."

"Interesting, can you email me the shit?"

"It's already there. Hey, are we getting the band back together?"

"I think we might have a reunion performance, a one-time thing."

Tom laughed. "I'm in. I'm sure the guys would be as well."

"I'm going to go over what you sent me, and if it's doable, I'll let you know after I make some calls. I think I might have a little ass to kiss."

Tom laughed. "No, you don't. We all understand what happened. We never got the chance to say how sorry we were. We weren't very good friends."

"Apparently, you talked about it," Callen chuckled.

"Hey, when your friend and business partner walks away from a good life and leaves everything behind, friends talk. We support you no matter what. You just didn't give us the chance. But we understand. We know how much you loved *her*."

Callen felt his heart lurch. "Thanks, man. Yeah, *she* was it for me."

"And now?"

"Now, I think I might be on the mend."

Tom laughed. "What's her name?"

"No name, just some stupid shit I pulled. I hurt someone, and now someone else is trying to hurt them. You know me. I can't sit by and let the people I care about get hurt. Listen, I've got some reading to do. I will be in touch in the morning. Do your job, Tom. Find out how much. We have four days."

"You got it. Talk soon."

Callen disconnected the call and fished his laptop out of the cabinet. It's been eight years since he turned this baby on. Plugging it in, he let it all load. He needed to piggyback off his phone to get wifi, but the email came. He opened the email and got comfortable.

Three hours later, he had a plan and some ass kissing to do. Closing the laptop, he got up and went to check on Lyssa. Quietly, he opened the door and walked over to the bed. She was so small he could barely see her. His smile was automatic as he reached to move the hair off her face. Taking a deep breath, he moved his hand away and turned to go back into the living room. He needed some sleep.

Pulling the door closed, he heard her say, "Don't go." He stood there for a minute, thinking he had imagined it until she sat up. "Callen." Her voice was soft.

"You all right?"

"I'm not sleeping very well. Could you stay in here with me? I think I might be a bit freaked out."

He chuckled, looking around. This would be the reasoning behind having a chair in your bedroom, he thought. "Let me drag the chair in here." He turned to walk out.

"No." Her single word stopped his heart. "Here." He heard the blanket move; it was that quiet. Slowly, he turned to see the space she had made for him in the bed.

"Lyssa…" Her name was a hiss on his lips.

She didn't say a word or move. The silence was so loud that the only thing he could hear was his heart beating.

~

Lyssa laid on the bed for hours. She could hear him out there talking. Her eyes closed, and she tried to sleep, but everything that happened was rolling around in her brain. *Why would Knox try and hurt me? Is the Greenvale ranch that important? What is this going to do to Kennedy? Does she know? Who the hell was Callen talking to? Was it a woman? Was he cancelling a date?*

She was getting tired of herself. It is what it is. He wasn't an option for her. Men like that want one thing, and there is no way she was giving it up to someone like him. Then she kept thinking about that kiss in the barn, the feel of him pressed against her. She was positive she had an orgasm. She wasn't sure what one of those really felt like, but damn it felt fantastic.

When the door opened, she closed her eyes, sure he was just getting something to change into, but then she felt his fingers on her face. He didn't say anything, just took a deep breath then walked away.

Lyssa didn't want to be alone, and it was obvious to her that he wasn't sleeping either. She invited him to sleep with her. She was more than a bit freaked out. Three days ago, she had a boring research job at a law firm that paid damn good money, and now, she was unemployed, inviting the hottest man she had ever seen in her life to share a bed with her.

She sat on the bed, watching him slowly move toward her. Her heart slammed in her chest when he climbed on the bed. Laying down, he pulled her to him, keeping the blanket between them.

"Come here, beautiful. Get some sleep," he said softly, maybe too softly, but she was so tired and freaked out.

Laying down, her head on his chest, he wrapped his arm around her, and she felt his lips press against her head. Lyssa closed her eyes and was asleep nearly instantly. When she woke, she was alone, but she could smell coffee and soap. Lying on her back, she kicked the covers off and stretched.

Callen had woken before the sun, as he did every morning. Gently, he got out of bed. His cock was so hard he needed to relieve himself, so he headed into the shower. It just took a few pumps of his hand, and thoughts of the warmth of her body, and he was spilling all over the place. He groaned. *What the fuck is my problem?* He grabbed a pair of boxers and jeans and went to the kitchen to make coffee.

Walking back to the bedroom with a cup for Lyssa, he had just walked through the door to see her stretching in his bed. Her back was arched, her nipples erect and poking through her t-shirt. He lost his breath, as well as the grip he had on the cup.

When it hit the floor, she turned her head, looking at him. Her smile grew slowly when she saw his chest and realized he was staring at her. His body moved, and he was on the bed, his body over hers. He didn't touch her, but fuck if he didn't want to. Every fucking neuron in his body was hyper aware of her. She just laid there staring at him, then she licked her lips and he lost it. His mouth slowly and gently covered hers. He was totally prepared to get slapped, punched, or kneed in the balls, but that didn't happen. She kissed him back. It was when her hands came to rest on his shoulders that he felt his arms tremble.

Pulling back, he whispered on her lips, "What are you doing to me?" His eyes traveled to her lips, dark pink and wet from his kiss. "I'm not sorry for this," he whispered as he kissed her again, gently lowering his body onto hers. Her hands moved over his shoulders, her fingers in his hair.

His mind had nothing in it but her. There was so much danger brewing around her, but the only thing he felt, saw, or heard was her. When she moved her leg and wrapped it around his thigh, he rolled them over. He pulled out of the kiss. "I can't do this," he whispered to her, his hand cradling her face. His thumb tugged at her bottom lip. "I can't do this, beautiful. Not now."

She smiled and nodded. "I know. I can't do this either. I don't want to do this with you. It's just… I think I'm scared, and for some reason, I don't feel that way with you."

He chuckled. "You're scared?" She nodded. "All the more reason we can't do this. I want to do this with you," he pressed his erection into her hip, "but not like this. You don't trust me. Hell, I don't trust me. But I'm not sorry for kissing you, past, present, and future."

He pulled her to him and kissed her again. When he was done, he got off the bed, fixing his erection in his jeans before turning around. "Get in the shower. I'll clean up the mess."

She giggled and got up, moving to the bathroom. When he heard the water turn on, he put his hands on the dresser. "What the fuck is going on?" Shaking his head, he cleaned up the coffee and the mug, then went to make something to eat. It was going on six in the morning, and he needed to make some phone calls.

Breakfast was done so he headed to the bedroom to let Lyssa know. He knocked, but there was no answer, so he opened the door. She had her back to him, pulling up her jeans. If a human being could lose their mind just from looking at someone, it happened to him at that moment.

She was wearing black lace panties that sat just high enough to see her perfect heart-shaped ass. He was instantly hard. He watched as she pulled up her jeans, his eyes traveling up, her back bare. He stepped back and pulled the door closed. He felt his knees shake.

His hands came up, and he leaned on the wall, trying to get control by taking deep breaths. She was perfect, just like he knew she would be. He needed to get this feeling under control. She made it perfectly clear to him that she was not an option for him. He was just horny and needed to get himself under control. He couldn't have a cloudy mind.

This was about saving the Greenvale ranch and keeping her safe. Nothing more. He pushed off the wall and knocked a bit harder on the door. "Hey, I made breakfast," he yelled.

"Be right there," she yelled back.

He went back to the kitchen, and she was only a few steps behind him. "You all right?" she asked.

He chuckled. "Yes, why?"

"You're a bit flushed." Her hand reached up to touch his forehead. "You don't have a fever. You sure?"

He laughed. "Oh, I'm sure. Come, let's eat. I've got some phone calls to make and some shit to eat."

She laughed and sat down. It didn't take long for either of them to scarf down the food. They didn't have dinner last night.

"I'll clean up while you make your calls," she said, grabbing his plate.

Callen went outside to make phone call after phone call. It took him more than an hour to get the ball rolling and to transfer some money around. He was going to take fucking Hugh Bell down and his little friend Brody Buckingham.

When he walked in, Lyssa was sitting at the table. He noticed she had her phone in her hand. She made a phone call herself. Not one she ever thought she would make.

"Hey, you ready to go? We need to go see Charles." She nodded and got up, giving him a strange look. "What's going on in that head of yours?"

"I don't think you want to know the answer to that question," she smarted.

He put his hand on her stomach, stopping her. "Believe me when I say that I do."

She looked down at his hand, then up to his eyes. "Yeah, no you don't. Come on, let's get moving."

She walked away, so he chuckled and followed her out the door.

CHAPTER FIVE

Lyssa was in her own head, and thoughts of the man sitting next to her were in the forefront of her mind. The way he held her all night long. The way it felt to sleep in a man's arms. The way he kissed her. The look in his eyes when he looked at her.

"Do you think I'm cute?" she blurted out. "I was just wondering."

He chuckled. "No," he said. "I don't think you are cute. Isn't that a word girls in, say, grade school would use?"

"I suppose."

"Why would you ask me that?"

"I don't know, I was just wondering."

He tried hard to hide the smile forcing its way across his lips. They didn't talk the rest of the way to the ranch, but he could feel her looking at him every now and then. Pulling up, Callen turned off the truck and just sat there. Lyssa opened her door, "You coming?"

He nodded, turning his head to look at her, "I'll be there in a minute. You go ahead."

She smiled at him as she jumped out of the truck. He sat and watched her walk away. Something caught his attention out of the corner of his eye, a flash of light. Pushing open his door he called out for her to run. Lyssa took off toward the house just as he took off for the barn. Running in he grabbed the rifle from his office and headed up to the hayloft. Looking through the scope he could see a man sitting on the side of the road with a pair of binoculars. His heart started beating again.

Rolling over on his back he took a deep breath, "Fuck, what is wrong with me?" He climbed down and made his way to the house. Knocking on the door, she pulled it open.

"What the hell is wrong with you?" She shouted, "You scared the shit out of me."

He opened the screen door and walked in, "That guy from last night is sitting in his car down the road. He has binoculars. I thought, well, you don't want to know what I thought. Where is Charles?"

"In here," he heard from the dining room.

He walked into the room and shook Charles' hand. "We've got a great deal to discuss."

Charles smiled. "We do, indeed."

Callen looked down then back up at Charles. "We haven't eaten breakfast. Would you two care to join us?" Callen said.

"We," Lyssa started, but Emily put her finger to her mouth, silencing her.

"We would love to have breakfast." She smiled at Lyssa.

"Great, let's do this."

They piled in his truck, and Lyssa and Emily sat in the back. About halfway down the gravel road, Charles touched Callen's arm and nodded. He pulled over, and everyone got out, walking out into the field.

"Charles, what was in your hand?" Lyssa asked.

"I believe they were listening devices. Emily found them while she was cleaning." He looked at Callen. "I don't know what is going on in this world anymore. I'm an old man, and it seems my future son in law is trying to steal my land."

"Charles, that is not going to happen. I am going to ask something of you, and I need for you to trust me." Charles nodded. "Let me buy the ranch from you until this is over. It's the only way to not give you another heart attack. I will sell it back as soon as I am done."

"Done? What do you mean, done?" Lyssa asked.

Callen took a deep breath. "I am going to destroy Hugh Bell and Brody Buckingham. I used to be a corporate raider. I am going to buy their companies and tear them apart. I've already started the process. Come Saturday, they won't even know what hit them until Monday morning. I had a great team when I did this years ago, and I spoke to all of them this morning. I moved some money around, and it's already started. Seems Mr. Bell is maxed out; he doesn't have a penny to spare. Mr. Buckingham is strapped as well. All of their money is invested in this new company. I am simply going to walk in the door and take it all."

Lyssa stood there looking at him. "Are you fucking serious?"

He chuckled. "Very. Last night, that guy was going to hurt you. How many times has he been in your apartment watching you sleep? He isn't going to get the chance to do it again. Bell won't even see me coming. Hell, the financial world thinks I'm dead." He turned to Charles. "You and Emily have been nothing short of family to me. You took me in and took care of me after I crashed my truck, and then you gave me a job. I haven't failed you once, so I'm asking you to trust me. I know what I am doing. I'm sorry, though, that Kennedy is going to get hurt by all of this. But do you really want her to marry an asshole who would steal your land?"

Nothing was said for quite a while. Lyssa just stood there staring at him. Charles looked at Emily, and Callen knew she was worried. She was afraid her husband would have another heart attack. "You have a deal," Charles finally told him.

Callen smiled. "I'll have my guys move around the state and I'll write you a check. How much is a reasonable amount?"

"Well, let's see, we have thirty thousand acres of a working ranch. Fifty million would be reasonable."

"Done," Callen said.

"Wait a minute," Lyssa interrupted them. "You have fifty million dollars?"

Callen smiled, enjoying her surprise. "Breathe, Lyssa. Breathe. Can you draw up the paperwork and make this legal?"

She just stood there looking at them both. "This is crazy. This is batshit crazy," she said and walked away.

Charles chuckled when Callen went after her. He and Emily walked back to the truck.

"Hey," Callen called out to her.

She just kept walking, shaking her head. Then she just stopped and turned to look at him. "Seriously?"

"Yes, I have fifty million dollars. I have a bit more than that, actually."

She shook her head. "How much more?"

"I'm not sure, but more."

"Do you know how crazy this is?"

"Do you know they aren't playing with all their cards on the table? That guy was going to hurt you. I won't let him hurt you."

She laughed. "You did, so what makes him any different?"

"I was being a dick. He is out for blood. There is a big difference. Come on, we can take them back to the ranch and you can draw up the paperwork so they can relax. This is stressing Charles out. Please, we can argue about this later. Let's get this done so they can relax. We have a barbeque in three days." He wiggled his eyebrows at her.

Shaking her head at him, she headed toward the car. "This is sick. You know that, right?"

"Yeah, I know."

They didn't talk on the drive back, and no one said a word while Lyssa drew up a purchase agreement between Callen and Charles. They both signed it, Lyssa witnessed it, and then Callen handed him a check for fifty million dollars. When it was said and done, they took all the paperwork into town to the county clerk's office and filed it. Then they drove to the bank where Charles deposited the check. After, they went to eat.

When they got back to the ranch, Callen and the guys, along with Lyssa, began the process of setting up the tents. When the day ended, they were both exhausted. Emily had made everyone dinner, and it was odd how they all ate in silence. When they finished, thanks and goodbyes were had and they got ready to leave. Callen was in the truck while Lyssa said goodbye to Emily and Charles.

He couldn't take his eyes off her. She knew about him now; she knew about his money and who he was. His heart raced with fear. He was terrified, more now than before. *Will she turn out like all the rest of them? Will she let me get close to her now?* Closing his eyes, he could see her stretched out on his bed, her back arched. She was beautiful, and he wanted her. Hell, what man wouldn't want her? *But, will she let me have her now, now that she knows I'm rich?*

The truck door opened, and his eyes snapped open. "You sleeping in here?" she smart-mouthed him.

Laughing, he said, "Nearly, I didn't get much sleep last night."

She sat down, putting on her seat belt. "It's a wonder with all your corporate raiding and conniving."

"I do not connive."

She cocked her eyebrow at him. "What you did today was very well planned out. Buck, are you really going to give it back to them?"

He felt a sharp pain sear through him at the sound of her distrust. Not knowing what to say, for fear he would say something stupid, he didn't say anything at all. The closer they got to town, the more agitated he became, unsure why he didn't like that she didn't trust him. Turning onto his street, his phone vibrated in his pocket. He pulled it out, setting it on the seat.

He watched her eyes turn toward the phone, a look of disgust on her face. She probably expected it to be a woman. He still didn't answer her, leaving her to make her own assumptions. Like every other rich man she'd probably ever met, he figured she thought him a liar.

When the truck stopped in his driveway, he grabbed his phone and got out, opening the door for her to go in, but she just sat in the truck looking at him. He turned his back to her, not wanting to see the doubtful thoughts crossing her face. She didn't know him any better than he knew her, so he could only imagine what she was thinking.

Callen turned to look at her then glanced at his phone. Two messages, one from Tom:

It's all happening. Damn, I missed you.

Callen smiled. The next message was from Stu, his number one when he played the game.

We need to talk. This is too easy. I thought you were going to challenge me. Give me a call.

This caused him to laugh out loud. Too easy. These guys still had the same bloodlust he remembered. He could feel the excitement bubbling deep inside of him. The best part of what he used to do was the kill shot. When he would tell the owner of whatever company that he had simply walked in the door and now owned everything. It made him very arrogant, very full of himself.

It suddenly dawned on him, his head lifting to see her piercing blue eyes looking at him, that he lived his life like this, even now. Even now, he was an arrogant bastard, and she knew it. It dawned on him that she saw him; she could feel him. Not sure he liked that, not sure he didn't. She wasn't like *her.* She wasn't like most women. She didn't give a shit about that stuff. Charles was right.

His feet were moving. He opened the truck door and pulled her out and into his arms, his mouth covering hers. She pushed on his shoulders, pulling her head back. "No," she said. They stood there staring at each other. "No, Buck. This can't happen. I'm not her. Trust me, I'm not her."

"I know." He knew deep in his heart that she wasn't *her.* "My name is Callen. I would like it if you called me by my name." Callen sat her down, her hand on his chest, and he could feel those piercing eyes looking into his soul. He knew she would never be with him. He had never felt so defeated in his life. Nodding his head, he let her go. She turned out of his embrace and went in the house. Callen shut the truck door and called Stu.

"Hey, man, what's up?"

Stu laughed. "This is like taking a walk in the park. What are you up to?"

"Some people I know are being railroaded and it pissed me off."

"Where are you?"

"Yeah, you wouldn't believe me if I told you." His voice softened. "I think I'm on the edge of getting past the past."

"Ahh," Stu said with a laugh. "Met a woman, did you?"

"Something like that."

"Cal, I know what *she* did to you. I know how invested you were. I can only imagine how you felt when *she* walked. I mean, come on, you were on top of the world, and *she* took you down."

"I think the world shifted for me recently. I'm learning to let it all go." He looked at his house.

"So, she's beautiful?"

Callen smiled. "It's not that. The people I'm trying to help, they are so real, so genuine that I am finally seeing the man I want to be."

"So, she's not beautiful."

"Oh, she's beautiful, genuine, real, and I hurt her."

"You've got it bad."

Callen laughed. "Not yet. It's a long road to redemption. I've got eight years to make up for. Not that I regret any of it, but it's a huge amount of shit to swallow at one time."

"Well, we are moving along. This should all be done by Saturday."

"This is a good thing. I'd like if you guys could be here when it happens."

"Oh, I would love to hear the story and see this guy's face when you break it to him."

"Let me see what I can do. I might be able to make that happen. I think I might miss you guys."

Stu laughed. "Does this mean you're coming back?"

"No, man, I'm not coming back. Not now…" he paused.

"She isn't the big city type?"

"Not sure. Not sure, my friend. Not sure."

"Well, you let us know when and where. I'll make sure the guys don't have any plans for the weekend."

"Sounds good to me. Listen, I'm going to go. I think I have a fight waiting for me."

"A fight?"

"Oh, hell yeah, and let me just say, I think I like fighting with her."

"Can't wait to meet her."

"Yeah, we'll talk soon." He disconnected the call and headed into the house.

When he walked in, Lyssa was sitting on the couch. Kicking off his boots he sat on the coffee table in front of her.

"I'm not sorry I kissed you," he said softly.

She sat there looking at him. "What is it you want from me?"

He smiled. "Not a thing."

"You're a very good liar, Callen." She said his name with a bit of disdain. He didn't like it. It cut deep. "You look at me like you want me. The way you kiss me, well, I don't have anything to compare it to, but it feels like you want me. You press yourself into me, so I know kissing me excites you. So, I am led to believe, from the facts mind you, that your ultimate goal here is to get me naked in your bed."

His eyes didn't waver; he could see the fear in hers. "All of the above is fact. But not like you think it is. I look at you the way I do because you are beautiful. It's a guy thing. I couldn't explain the way it feels when I kiss you, but I will say you taste so damn good." He watched a slight blush cover her cheeks. "You do excite me. Hell, sweetheart, I think you could excite a dead man. And, yes, at one time, I did want you naked in my bed. I still want you naked in my bed, under me, on top of me, all over me. Who wouldn't? But it's not what you think."

"How could fucking me not be what I think? I'm not that girl, Callen." He didn't like the way she spit his name out. "I'm not a fuck-is-a-fuck girl. I don't play the game, I refuse. Too much internal pain to waste my time."

"It's not what you think. I am learning that you are not that girl. When and if it gets to that point, where you are naked and in my bed, I will be the only man who ever touches you," he said softly.

She swallowed, shaking her head. "It will never happen," she whispered.

"Why? What makes you so sure?"

"Because I know men like you. I'm not a plaything. I'm looking for the rest of my life, not until you are bored with me. I'm not ever going

59

to find what I am looking for, so I stopped looking a long time ago. I am better than the game, and I deserve what I want out of life. My father told me that, and I believe him." He watched her stand. "I'm going to take a shower. Do you want to go first? Because when I am done I'm going to sleep. Do you want me to sleep on the couch?"

He laughed, his hands coming up to her thighs, pulling her toward him as he stood. Moving up her body, he pushed them into her hair, capturing her lips with his and he kissed her. When he finished, he let her go and walked toward the bedroom. "I'll go first. You can sleep in my bed."

She just stood there, her hand reaching up to her lips. *Why would he do that?* She didn't want this with him. Not with him. She smiled. Who was she kidding? The man was fucking gorgeous. But he was a player, he said so himself. He was not the type to stay, a fuck is a fuck. He wanted to fuck her. She wasn't stupid. Well, in the ways of men she was, but she knew what an erection was and why men got them. He always had one when he kissed her. She felt it, more than once.

But this wasn't about them. This was about the Greenvales and what was happening to them. When her wits came back to her, she was moving across the living room and into the bedroom, but she stopped short when she realized he was standing with his back to her naked. Her breath hitched in her chest. She had never seen a man naked before, not in real life, and he was stunning. Every muscle in his back and ass were flexed. He was still wet from his shower. She felt something stir inside of her, and something changed at that moment. Her mind swirled with emotions she didn't know how to handle. Her heart raced, slamming in her chest so hard she could hear it in her ears.

"Lyssa, what are you doing?" His voice was soft but sounded like a cannon.

Her eyes closed, and she turned around to walk out of the room, completely and utterly embarrassed. "Oh my God," she whispered to herself.

He came out a few minutes later in just his jeans, no shirt, walking up behind her. He didn't touch her, but she could feel the heat rolling off his body. "What are you doing?" he whispered, his breath on her head.

"I... I... I came in there to tell you to stop kissing me. You're a player, Callen. This, whatever this is, can't happen. Mr. and Mrs. Greenvale need my help. They need our help. I'm just what is in front of you now. When this is over, I'll go back to my apartment in the city and you'll go back to doing whatever it is you are doing, and it will be over. I cannot be an option for you. This... you kissing me all the time is confusing me, and I'm the one who is going to be left in the dust when you get what you want."

"What is it you think I want?"

"Me. To fuck me, and it's not what I want."

"What if I said it's not what I want?"

"Then we are on the same page. Then you should stop kissing me."

Neither of them said a word. She slowly turned, making sure not to look at him, and walked into the bedroom. Shutting the door, she let out the breath she was holding.

Callen stood there with a smile on his lips. He didn't want to fuck her and leave her. He wanted all of her; he was sure of it now. She didn't care about what he had, only about who he was, and who he was, wasn't the type of man she wanted. It was ironic if he was being honest with himself. Here he was, this man, this man who could fuck a woman into oblivion, and now the one he believed he wanted, wanted nothing to do with him. Shaking his head, he chuckled and made his way to the couch. Shutting off the light, he dropped his jeans and got comfortable.

Lyssa was shaking as she took her shower. She was shaking as she dressed in her sleeping clothes. She was shaking as she climbed into bed, her mind going in a million different directions. What she didn't know was that Callen laid on the couch thinking and feeling the same way she was.

She was changing him, mending his heart. Sealing his fate. *Have I found her? Have I found the woman who can and will be my equal?* He knew he would protect her. He knew that he never tasted a kiss like hers. He knew, looking into her crystal blue eyes, that his breath caught in his chest each and every time. He knew he would never hurt her again. He knew she was innocent and totally unaware of her effect on him.

When this was over, he wanted to prove to her how wrong she was. Yes, he was a cad, a player, a one fuck kind of guy. He knew what women wanted from him; none of them cared enough to stop his advances. They just let him fuck them, so he did. But now, now he had found the one who wanted nothing to do with him. *Is that what is making her so appealing? We always want what we can't have.* He thought with a smile on his face.

Closing his eyes, he tried to sleep. But knowing she was in there alone, he was having a hard time. *Can I let her believe that all I want is to fuck her?* It's probably best. She told him repeatedly that he wasn't what she wanted. He made a promise to himself to make her understand that he was a kind and decent man, and he was worth it. She was worth it to him, to make her understand.

He finally fell asleep. However, Lyssa couldn't sleep. She sat on his bed with her back against the headboard looking at the door. She was so confused. *Is that what he wanted, to confuse me? Is that how he works, kissing a girl stupid? Make her think he wants her, then taking and leaving?* With her knees pulled up to her chest, she laid her head on them, closing her eyes. *What is it about this man that makes me crazy?* For hours, she sat like this, wondering, speculating. She was a smart person, so why is it that everything about this man confused her?

She heard the handle on the door turn and watched as it opened. He was standing there in his boxers. He was checking up on her, making sure she was all right.

Callen woke up feeling strange. He got up and went to check on her. When he opened the door, he saw her sitting with her knees drawn up to her chest. Stepping into the room, he moved slowly to the bed, climbing on. His natural instinct was to pull her into his arms.

"What's wrong, beautiful?"

She didn't fight him; she came willingly. "Why are you doing this to me?"

He smiled. "Doing what?"

"Being so nice to me. Kissing me all the time. Confusing the hell out of me."

"I don't mean to confuse you. I like kissing you, and I'm generally a nice guy. It's just that I've been hurt very deeply, and I have taken that pain out on many people. You shouldn't be one of them. I'm sorry for being an asshole to you. You should be sleeping."

Lyssa didn't know how to react to his body wrapped around hers. He didn't have any clothes on. His chest was hard but soft. The muscles in his arms were huge and tight as he held her, his breath warm on her head. Her eyes closed as she breathed him in, his scent hypnotizing her, lulling her to sleep. She felt him shift his body and lay down, but he didn't let her go.

Callen held her like she was a life jacket in a rough sea. She fit in his arms like she was made to fit there. It had been such a long time since he held a woman like this, like he meant it. Closing his eyes, he fell asleep.

It was Lyssa who woke him long before the sun came up. Her hand moved up his chest, setting him on fire. Her head moved off his chest. Turning his head, he was met with her fingers touching his lips. "Why do you kiss me?" she whispered.

He scooted down the bed so he could see her face. "At first, it was because you are so damn beautiful," he said softly. "So beautiful." His fingers touched her face.

"And now?"

"Because once I tasted you, I couldn't stop."

She pushed up, pulling her knees to her chest. "See it's things like that, that confuse me. I don't have much experience, well, none actually, but isn't that what men say to women to get them all goosy inside?"

He put his arm behind his head and laughed. "I suppose they do."

"Have you ever said that to a woman to get her into bed?"

He shook his head. "No, I have not. To be honest, I've never really had to say anything to get a woman in bed."

She looked at him. "No, I suppose you wouldn't have to do that."

"Lyssa, what is wrong?"

"I'm confused by you. I'm sure of the fact that you want to fuck me. I just don't understand why you are going through all this trouble to achieve that when it's so easy for you to just go out to the bar and get yourself laid."

"Well, for a lawyer, you are very observant. But your facts are a bit off."

"How so?"

"When I first saw you walking into the house, I thought 'oh, hell yeah, nice ass'. Then I saw you standing by the fence and had the same thought. But when you picked your head up and I looked into your eyes, you took my breath away. I think I was more afraid than anything. I think it freaked me out so bad that I did this to your face. I was so pissed at myself for having any kind of emotion, and it projected out to you when you didn't do a thing. I formed an opinion of you, based on what had happened to me before."

"With the woman you loved?"

"Yes, I have been bound and determined to never feel anything for another woman. When she left me, she gutted me. I couldn't, no, didn't want to ever feel like that again."

"So, what's different now?"

He didn't say anything for a long time. "I suppose, I'm different now."

She smiled at him. "Why now, after all this time? If it's been working for you so well, why change?"

"Do you want the truth? Because I'm pretty sure the truth is going to make me look like an asshole."

Giggling, she said, "You already do."

"Well, that's true. So, why now?" She nodded. "I cared about her to the point of obsession. I'm not sure if that is what happened, maybe I suffocated her. But she was my world. Everything I did, I did to make her smile, to make her happy. I invested my soul in her. When she left, when she took as much from me as she could take, it left me empty and unfeeling. I didn't even have the thrill of my work anymore. I struggled to open my eyes in the morning. So, I ran, and I suppose I've been running ever since. The least amount of my emotions I allow out, the least amount of pain I feel.

"When I realized that I was responsible for hurting you like that, it gutted me. I am not a brutal man. I would never intentionally cause a woman any sort of bodily harm. The fact that you stood up to me and gave me as good as you got made me think about the type of man I was. I actually laughed when I pulled away from the ranch that day. But when it hit me that I did this to your face, I felt ashamed. My mother would have been disappointed in me for hurting you and laughing about it. Every time I look at your face, I feel ashamed. I don't like that feeling. I don't like feeling period. But it's happening to me."

"So, the kissing me thing you keep doing, is that because you feel ashamed that you hurt me? Are you trying to make me feel better? Or are you just trying to fuck me?"

He sat up, looking her in the eyes. "I kissed you the first time because you are so fucking beautiful. I'm surprised you haven't been kissed like that before. I am not in any way what so ever trying to make myself feel better. I don't think I will ever feel better for hurting you like this." His fingers touched her face. "I have no intention of fucking you. At least, not yet, and certainly not until you ask me to."

"So sure of yourself, Mr. McCabe," she whispered.

"No, I'm not really. I'm hopeful. But I don't deserve to have a woman such as yourself. Not yet anyway, but I am hopeful that one day I will."

Her breath hitched in her chest. "Why me?" Her voice sounded so quiet.

His face moved closer to hers, whispering on her lips, "Because you see me. You see right through me, and you taste so damn good." His mouth covered hers, his hand wrapping around her head, pulling her down on the bed with him, down on his chest. Callen pulled back, tucking her into his side. "Sleep, beautiful."

Lyssa wrapped her arm around him, her leg coming up over his. Callen rolled onto his side, wrapping his leg around her and pulling her into his cocoon, holding her close. He decided he wasn't going to fight this feeling. He enjoyed the feel of her in his arms. Her total honesty with him just blew his mind.

They woke gradually as the sun was coming up. She pulled away from him and rolled onto her back, stretching. Callen's eyes couldn't stop from taking her in. His mouth watered when his eyes landed on her breasts. Even laying down, they were perfectly round, her nipples poking through her tank top. He moaned as her back came to rest on the bed. "You are making it very difficult for me to be a gentleman."

She busted out in giggles. "I don't even know what to say to that." Her head turned to look at him.

He moved quickly, getting up on his hands and knees and hovering over her. "If I didn't know better, I would say you are tempting me. But somewhere, somehow, I know you don't have a single clue what that means."

He kissed her slowly, growling deep inside when her hands touched his stomach and skirted around the waistband of his boxers. Pulling back, he bored his eyes into hers, seeing the lust in them. Innocent lust, new emotions for this beautiful woman in his bed. He pushed back and sat on his heels, trapping her leg between his.

She didn't feel uncomfortable while he looked her over; just the opposite, she felt alive. His eyes stopped on her stomach where her shirt had pulled up and the skin was showing. She watched as he dipped his head, pressing his lips to her skin. His hands moved to her sides, his thumbs nearly touching in the middle.

She felt them move up her back, under her shirt, his thumbs catching the material, pulling her shirt to the bottom of her breasts. Her eyes closed as his mouth explored her stomach, his nose touching the underside of her breasts. She could feel herself getting warmer, her lower body getting hotter. There was a vibration in her core, something she had never felt before.

When he finished tasting her skin, he lifted his head, his eyes drawn to her nipples. They looked so big under the cloth, he felt his cock move. He nearly lost his mind when her hands touched his. "Lyssa," he hissed as she moved them up, pulling her shirt up and over her breasts. His eyes darted to hers. He saw fear in them and shook his head. "No, beautiful."

"Yes," she whispered. "Look at me. Touch me."

He watched as the pink flush covered her whole body. She was stunning. He wanted to draw one of her perfect nipples in his mouth, but he couldn't do it. He just looked at them. Pink, they were so pink. He had never seen nipples as big as hers. So hard, so big. The words came out of his mouth, so full of passion, he shocked even himself. "Lyssa, you've never done this before, have you?" She shook her head. "You're still a virgin, aren't you?"

"Yes," she sputtered out as her back arched.

He knew she wanted him. His head moved on its own. He needed to make sure she enjoyed it, his lips brushing her nipple. God, he was going to come. The tip of his tongue gently flicked the peaked tip, then he moved to the other one and did the same thing. Her whole body lifted off the bed. His hand moved, wrapping around her and pulling her off the bed into his chest. He kissed her as she came undone at his touch. He lost his mind when her bare chest pressed into his, her nipples like little daggers.

Her kiss was deep and forceful, and she let out an almost-sob as her breath shuddered. He laid her down and laid with her, touching her face, wiping her tears. "Talk to me. Tell me what happened."

Her eyes opened, sedate with her experience. "What was that?"

He smiled big. "That, I believe, was an orgasm," he said sweetly, his thumb running along her bottom lip.

"That felt incredible."

"I need to know something. Why are you still a virgin?"

Her face changed, her whole body changed. Shaking her head, she moved away from him, pulling her shirt down, then she got out of the bed and just walked out of the room.

She paced the living room talking to herself. "Shit, what the hell are you doing? He's a player. He takes what he wants, and here you are giving yourself to him on a fucking silver platter."

Callen grabbed a pair of jeans and a t-shirt and made his way into the living room. "What just happened?"

She stopped and looked at him, and he fought his instincts to step back. She had fire burning in her eyes. "I can't stay here anymore. I can't do that again. I don't know what the hell kind of game you are playing with me, but that..." she pointed to the bedroom, "can *never* happen again. I am falling right into your plan. Yes, I'm a virgin, and I plan on staying that way. You will not have me. You will never have me to use like that."

"Stop," he shouted.

She snapped her eyes up, shaking her head. "You are nothing but a player, Callen." The venom in her voice when she said his name made him jump. "You asked me if I was a virgin and then you took complete advantage of me. Yes, I pulled my shirt up. I asked you to touch me, so that is on me, but believe me, it will never happen again. If you were any kind of a gentleman, you would not have done that."

She was moving, and she was right. Moving past him, she went to the bedroom and slammed the door. "Fuck," he said. It took him a minute to get his bearings, and he was moving. Opening the bedroom door, he didn't even notice that she was topless.

Turning, she started to yell for him to get out, but he picked her up and walked to the wall. She raised her hands to push him away, but he captured them in his and raised them above her head, pinning them to the wall. His mouth crashed down on hers, his kiss deep and fierce.

"Stop this," he said as he pulled away. She went to open her mouth to talk, and he just kissed her again to stop her from talking. "Stop this," he whispered. She went to say something, and he kissed her again. Pulling back, he said, "Let me talk." She nodded. "I am not playing you or playing with you. Not now. But you are right, if I was a gentleman, I would have stopped myself. You are so fucking beautiful, and the way you look at me makes me feel alive again. My cock is so fucking hard all the time. I fucking jack off in the shower twice a day. That's how crazy you make me. Your nipples are so fucking perfect, so fucking huge, like little beacons calling me. I just touched them, and I was being a gentleman because I wanted to devour them. To suck them until they were raw. I want to pinch them between my fingers, bite them with my teeth. I want to feel them drag down my chest. I want to palm them and make you scream with pleasure. But because I am a gentleman, I did none of those things. And just for the record, I've wanted to fuck you so hard for so long I am losing my mind. I saw you yesterday, pulling up your jeans with your black lace panties sitting perfectly on this ass. If I wasn't a gentleman, my hands and my mouth would have been all over this perfectly fuckable ass of yours. But I'm not that man anymore. I don't want to be that man anymore. So, I'm sorry, but it's a bit difficult to keep my hands off you. I don't want anyone else. I want you. I can have any woman I want, but I want you. Don't you see, beautiful, no one else will do for me. So, I am being a gentleman. I am waiting for you to realize, for you to see that you can trust me. That I am not going to play you. I know it's going to take a long time for you to be there with me, but you know what?"

She shook her head.

"I can wait. I will wait. I asked you if you were a virgin because I don't want to do what just happened. I don't want to freak you out. I don't want you to run." He lowered his voice. "I don't want you to walk away. I would rather fight with you than make love to anyone else."

Her tears just came. "I'm so scared," she whispered.

"I know, and it's all right. It's all right."

She nodded and leaned into his lips. He kissed her, pulling her off the wall and into his chest, letting her legs go. She dropped them to the floor as he ended the kiss. Putting his forehead on hers, he whispered, "Don't run."

"I won't."

Callen turned and walked out of the room. He needed to gather his thoughts. He just disclosed a great deal of information to her. He said things he didn't think he would ever be capable of saying again. Once in the living room away from her, his hands landed on his knees and he bent over nearly hyperventilating. "Fuck."

His mind raced a million miles a minute. The feel of her against his chest, her body, her skin so white, so soft. Her scent, the way his cock jumped when he pressed into her. "Fuck," he whispered. He was going to earn her trust, and by God, he was going to respect this woman. She isn't like anyone he had ever met. Charles was right; she is so special.

His whole body tensed up before she touched him, running her hand up his back. "Hey," she said, bending down to look at him. "You all right?"

He chuckled. "I don't think I'm ever going to be all right again. I shouldn't have said those things to you."

"Yes, Callen, you should have. I need to know these things, and I need you to tell me time and time again. You're right, I don't trust. I've never trusted." He stood up. "I watched guy after guy use Kennedy and then just drop her. It was all about sex. I made this decision to not do it. And now, she believes she is getting married. She believes he loves her. You cannot expect me to just surrender to you. I can't do that. But, hearing you say these things to me in a consistent manner in which you have been, helps me to relax. I'm sorry if I am being impossible."

"No, never impossible. A woman like you deserves nothing but the greatest respect. The man you met is not the man that I am in here." He touched his chest. "He has been lost and muted for a long time. Not until you trust me completely and I feel that I am ready. Trust me, beautiful, I want to rip your clothes off and take you on every surface of this house." He watched her blush. His voice softened. "I want to be the only man that ever has that privilege. Okay?"

She nodded. "Thank you for being honest with me."

"Thank you for believing me. Now, come on, we have work to do. There are only two days left until the big party."

They didn't say much on the drive out to the ranch. They didn't say much while they worked or when they ate lunch together. Charles came out, and they walked into the field to talk.

"So, the check cleared." He chuckled.

"I was hoping it wouldn't bounce," Callen countered.

"What's going on?"

"I talked to one of my guys. They wanted to know if they could come and watch the fireworks. I told them I would let them know, but it's going to be easy. Everything should be in my name by Friday afternoon. Neither Mr. Bell nor Mr. Buckingham will have a clue when they get here Friday night."

"When are you planning on telling them?"

Callen smiled. "I'm not. I was thinking about this. Maybe you should just casually work into the conversation that you can afford to throw a huge wedding now, and that you and Emily are going to do some traveling. When Kennedy asks how that is possible, just casually tell her that you sold me the ranch. Or that you sold it. Then we can gauge all the reactions around the table. My guys will be there, and then I will tell Mr. Bell and Mr. Buckingham who I am because I can guarantee you that they have heard of me."

"Well, we won't need any fireworks, that's for sure," Charles said.

Callen looked at Lyssa. "I don't know, I could stand to see some fireworks."

She smiled at him. "Dream on!" she snapped.

Charles chuckled. "All right then, that's the plan. Let the day go on, and when the evening comes and most of the guests have left, then the real show begins. I like this plan, Buck. I like this plan. Oh, and yes, of course, your guys can come. It will make everyone wonder who the hell they are. I'll just tell people they are business associates." He nodded his head, chuckling as he headed back to the house.

When he was out of earshot, Lyssa said to him, "You're setting up Kennedy."

He smiled. "Don't you want to know if she is in on this?"

"I don't believe she would hurt her parents like this."

"Sweetheart, you would be surprised what people will do for money." He had a bitter edge to his voice.

She stood there looking at him. "Is that what this is about?"

"What?"

She raised her eyebrows. "You're testing me. You want to know if I'm interested in your money. Oh my God! Oh my God." She spun around, looking for the quickest way to get away from him. "You fucking liar. Oh my God. That was all bullshit, everything you said about fucking trust. Do you really believe I am this fucking stupid? Holy shit. Oh my God." Callen stood there looking at her freaking out. She was right. "You are a lying fucking bastard. I let you see my boobs. Oh my God, I'm such an idiot." Shaking her head, she started walking.

"No," he shouted.

Her legs took off, and she was running toward the house. "No fucking way." Callen took off after her. He caught her, taking her down in the grass. "Get off me," she yelled, hitting him in the back. "Get the fuck off me."

"No!" he yelled.

It was the only word he could get out. She slammed her knee into his crotch, and searing pain jolted through his body. Rolling off her onto his side, he threw up. She took off running into the house. "Charles, can I borrow your truck?"

He already had the keys on the table. "He is a nice guy," he said as he handed them to her.

"He's a fucking liar. He is setting Kennedy up," she said as she moved to the front door. It was what he said that stopped her in her tracks.

"I know."

She just stood there, looking at the keys as they became blurry in her hands. She heard the back door open, and her feet were moving. She was out the door and across the driveway and in the truck in no time at all. As she drove past the house, she saw him standing in the doorway.

Charles stopped him from chasing her down. "Let her go. She'll be back."

Callen froze, watching her drive away in tears. "Why are women so complicated?"

Charles laughed. "They aren't once you figure them out."

Walking back into the dining room, he said, "It's been a long time,

Charles, since I gave a shit about a woman. I don't think I'm doing a very good job of it."

"Sit down, son. That woman is falling hard for you."

"I might have to argue the point, Charles. I can't seem to keep my foot out of my mouth."

"Keep in mind that she has been protecting my daughter most of her life. I don't want my daughter to be a part of this, but I have a feeling she is. It's going to kill Emily, but there is nothing that can be done now. The plan is in play."

"Charles, I'm so sorry all of this is happening to you and Emily. You don't deserve this. I hope we're wrong, for your sake as well as Lyssa's."

"It will be what it will be. I don't see any bruises on your face." He chuckled.

"Yeah, she got me in the balls this time."

Emily walked out with a bag of ice. "This should help. I saw her take you down. That girl has a lot of spirit in her. I saw her beat up two boys in that field out there, and she was a tiny little thing."

"Thank you." He took the ice and sat on it, making sure his balls were right on the ice pack.

"Buck?"

Callen put his hand up. "I think you can call me Callen if you want. I only told you that name because I didn't want to be myself anymore."

She smiled at him, nodding her head. "I'll try, but you've been Buck for as long as I've known you. I know that Charles has spoken to you about Lyssa. But I wanted to say something to you. If she didn't care for you, she wouldn't waste her time fighting you. She is scared. She has always been afraid of getting hurt. Kennedy has been hurt so much by men, so Lyssa knows what it feels like second-hand. She's always been a little independent like that. Just have patience with her."

Callen smiled. "I'm not going anywhere any time soon. As each day goes by, I fall a little bit further under her spell. It was an instant thing, I think. I'm just trying to get over myself."

She patted him on the hand. "Good, she needs a good strong man who is going to love her like she deserves to be loved."

Callen smiled at her. *Am I falling in love with her? Is that what is happening?*

Emily went back in the kitchen, and Callen laid his head on the table. His fucking cock hurt. He must remember to not tackle her again.

"It'll get better," Charles said with a grin as he walked by.

He just sat there, his head on the table, with his eyes closed. When his balls felt numb, he got up and headed out back to finish his work. They had one tent up and the dance floor put down. So, they had one more tent which was half-way up and then they needed to set up tables and chairs, along with two huge buffet tables. The headcount was about a hundred or so.

Callen and the guys stayed until the light was nearly gone from the sky. Calling it a night, he headed to his truck. He was worried about Lyssa, unsure what he should do. But he opted to just go home and leave her to her space. As he was driving down the long drive, he noticed that the lights in the little house that she used to live in were on. As he pulled up, he saw Charles' truck parked outside.

He sat there, not sure if he should go in or just leave her be. He decided to just leave her be and turned to go home.

CHAPTER SIX

As Lyssa drove away from the ranch, she was crying. *Why should I believe him?* Because he was so good looking it took her breath away. *Doesn't every girl want, or wish for a man that looks like him to want her?* She was so confused, so pissed off.

Her eyes landed on the house she spent her childhood in. Pulling in, she was sure Charles had the key on his key ring. Sure enough, she opened the door. She was stunned at how different it looked. Different but the same. All the details were still there, but they were all redone to look brand new. "Who did this?"

She walked from room to room, seeing there was furniture in each room. The dining room table had been refinished, the same one she sat at nearly every night of her life. It was beautiful, all shiny and new looking. The kitchen was state of the art but still had its character. The shelves with her mother's cookbooks still on them were refinished to look like new. The crown molding was still there. Someone took great care in refinishing it.

When she walked out onto the back porch, she saw there was now a mud room with a laundry room fitted with a brand new washer and dryer. The back porch had been rebuilt, and somehow it felt bigger to her. Shaking her head, she went back in, shutting and locking the door, and headed upstairs, which had been refinished as well. The railing and the spindles were the same as when she was a child. She couldn't help but smile when the fourth stair creaked. "Still creaks," she whispered to herself.

Every room she walked into was furnished and redone. All the crown molding up here was refinished as well. The ceiling in her old room was fixed; she couldn't even see the crack. She sat in the makeshift bay window and looked out over the fields. She could see the tent in Kennedy's backyard.

Why would she do this to her parents? Why would she? How could she? These questions wouldn't stop rolling around in her head. She had changed so much from the girl she grew up with. *Is that what sex does to you? Does it change you? Make you a horrible person? It must, because look at Callen. He was, maybe he still is, a horrible person.* She hurt him really bad this time, but he lied to her. He didn't trust her enough to tell her what he felt, what he thought about Kennedy. The worst part about it all is that she might think and feel the same way. *How would Hugh have known which key was mine unless she told him?*

Everything was so confusing, especially Callen. *Could a man like him, be happy with a girl like her?* She didn't want anything more than what she already had. Okay, maybe she wanted a job. Maybe when this is all over, Mr. Slate would give her job back. No, that's not what she wanted.

Lyssa climbed on her bed, which wasn't her bed, but the frame and headboard were hers. Lying down, she closed her eyes and fell asleep.

When she finally woke up, it was dark. Reaching for the light, she didn't expect it to turn on, but it did. She wondered what Charles was up to. *Why would he do this?* Turning off the light, she made her way downstairs. She was hungry, her stomach growling, so she headed into town. The only place that had a decent burger was the bar. She was sure no one would remember who she was, so she parked and went in. Ordering a burger to go, she sat down at the end of the bar while she waited, sipping on a pop.

It didn't take long for her food, and she paid and thanked the bartender. As she was walking out, she turned her head to some woman laughing. Sitting in a booth at the other end of the bar with a blonde on his lap, was Callen. Her whole body started to shake. She was frozen to the spot she stood in, watching as he kept trying to remove her from his lap. Her heart was slamming in her chest, her vision blurred. She felt her hand reach out to grab something, anything. Then it all went black as he picked his head up to see her fall to the floor.

Callen went home and took a shower. He wanted to go back to the little house and talk to her, but he knew she had to come to him. So, he wrote her a note and pinned it to the door in case she came back, letting her know he went to have a beer. He needed a beer after the day he had.

Walking into the place was probably not the best choice he could have made. It never failed that when he came in here, he had women all over him. Apparently, he and his cock were well known. Shaking his head, he found a booth in the back, with a perfect view of the door in case she came. He was just sitting there minding his own business, watching the door every time it opened. His heart sped up every time headlights crossed the mirror behind the bar. He wanted to see her, to talk to her.

A woman came over and started hitting on him. He was politely explaining to her that he was waiting for someone. She was drunk and really didn't care to listen. Somehow, she managed to get on his lap. He was having a hell of a time getting her off. When she happened to move as he pushed her off him, he saw her.

She was standing still, looking at him. "Fuck," he growled at the woman.

"Yeah, baby, that's what I want to hear."

His eyes not leaving Lyssa's, he started to stand up when he watched her eyes close and she hit the floor, slamming her head on the half wall. People were running over, but he didn't want any of them to touch her. "No!" he shouted. She belonged to him.

He was moving. By the time he got to her, some guy had her in his arms. It took everything he had not to punch the guy when he said, "I got you, beautiful."

Callen looked at him, nodding to him. "She's my girlfriend," he said to the guy. He handed her over to him, and Callen took her to his truck. She weighed nearly nothing, so getting her in was easy. He ran around and jumped in, started the truck, and rushed home.

It took a few minutes for her eyes to flutter. He had ice on her forehead where she had a huge bump. "Lyssa," he whispered. "Come on, sweetheart."

She opened her eyes. "Please don't touch me." She pushed his hand away and tried to sit up. "Owe, shit," she said when she put her hand on her head. "What the fuck?"

"You fainted." His voice was soft.

She turned her head and looked at him. "I need my things," was all she said, getting up. He watched her walk into the bedroom. When she came out, she had her bag full of clothes and her other bag. She didn't even look at him; she just walked out the door, slamming it behind her.

There was a note hanging on the door, so she pulled it off she read it, then dropped it on the ground. Her feet carried her back to the bar. She was still hungry, so she put her stuff in the truck and went back in. Her food was sitting on the counter. Picking it up, she left and headed back to her apartment. It didn't matter anymore; nothing mattered anymore. She couldn't do this with him. She couldn't trust him.

"What a fucking fool I am. How fucking stupid?" She understood now, all those times Kennedy was hurt by a guy. Never again. When she got back in the city, she called a locksmith. She would pay for the late-night call. He met her at her apartment. An hour later, she had a new lock and a deadbolt.

After eating her burger, she went about cleaning the place up. Knox did a number on it, that was for sure. It took her hours to get it all clean. She took her bags into her room and plugged her phone in.

She needed a shower. When she finished, she crawled into bed and crashed.

When her alarm went off, she was wide awake. Going through her routine was somehow boring. Laughing, she grabbed the phone book and called a towing service to have her car towed home. It took two hours, but at least it was there. Then she climbed into Charles' truck and headed out to the ranch. It was Thursday, and she needed to make sure everything was all right with Charles and Emily. Kennedy would be home tomorrow for the weekend, possibly for a longer time than that after everything came to light.

Pulling up at the farm, she didn't see Callen's truck, which just made her even more angry that he wasn't there. He probably went back to the bar and then home with the blonde who had been on his lap. *Isn't that what men do? They can't have one, so they just move on to the other.* At least, that was her experience with Kennedy.

Charles was sitting on the porch when she walked up. "Everything all right?"

She smiled. "Just fine. Charles, why would you spend all that money refinishing my childhood home?"

"Lyssa, I needed to put the boy to work. He had his own issues for wanting to be alone. So, I had him do it. He does good work."

She looked at him. "Who?"

"Buck."

"Callen did that?"

"Yep, took him the better part of a year. Emily bought the furniture. We wanted you to always have a place to come home to. I know, at least I think I know, that you were never going to move up to the big city. It was your home."

"Well, thank you, Charles, but it wasn't necessary. I'm fine in the city. Do you think one of the guys can give me a ride back home? I had my car towed over to my apartment this morning."

"So, you went home last night?"

She smiled. "Yes, where else would I go? Knox is in jail. Apparently, his fingerprints were all over my apartment, so he isn't getting out until he goes in front of a judge. I'm going to talk to Mr. Slate, see if I can get my job back now that this is all done. Everything will be fine now. Callen has seen to it."

"I think Tiny is in the shed. He'll give you a ride back to the city. You're still coming on Saturday?"

"Charles, if Kennedy was a part of this, I'm not sure I can be here to see it. I've loved her my whole life. I don't know if I can handle knowing she would do this."

"Sweetheart, you are a part of the wedding party. You have to be here."

"No offense, Charles, but you and I both know there is not going to be a wedding. I'm just tired of playing games with people. I haven't been this exhausted in a long time, not since college." She chuckled. "I just want my boring life back. I want to live in my world, do my job that I love, and read my books. Nothing more. I'll see how I feel, but don't expect me. I'll tell Kennedy I'm not feeling well." She stood. "I hope everything works out for you."

"Lyssa, can I say something?"

"If it's about him, then no. I can't care. I don't want to care. He's a liar and a player, and I'm not playing." She paused, turning to look at him. "I think I might have feelings for him. I'm just afraid. I know I shouldn't be. I know I should just go with them, but it doesn't feel right. He doesn't trust me, and well, I can't handle that. I know he has problems with trust as well." Shaking her head, she started off the porch. "Goodbye, Mr. Greenvale."

She walked off the porch and headed to the shed. Tiny was more than happy to take her home. As they were driving down the highway, she saw Callen drive by. What was he doing this far from home? Then it dawned on her that he was coming from her house. Mumbling under her breath, she said, "Asshole."

Tiny chuckled. "You know he has been a bear all morning. Mr. Greenvale told him to go take care of whatever was bothering him."

"Can we please not talk. I'm appreciative of you taking me home, but can we do it quietly, please?"

"Sure," he mumbled.

Pulling up to her building, she thanked Tiny and got out. She just wanted to sleep. Tomorrow, she would go talk to Mr. Slate and try to get her job back. Walking up to her apartment, she saw an envelope stuck to her door. She laughed as she opened the door. Opening it up, she began to read. When she realized it was from Callen, she crumpled it up and tossed it on the table. "Asshole."

After changing, Lyssa crawled into bed and crashed. She didn't want anything to do with the outside world. As she slept, she dreamt. His touch, his kiss, the warmth of him. When her eyes popped open, she was so warm, so disheveled, her nipples hard. Her core ached. "What the hell?" she whispered. Hearing pounding, she jerked her head toward the door.

Scrambling to get up on her shaky legs to make her way to the door, she heard him. "Lyssa, open the damn door."

"Go away," she said breathlessly. Her body was still tight from her dream.

"I'm not going anywhere. Please, open the door."

There was no reasoning in her head as she flung open the door. His eyes traveled up and down her body, pausing at her chest, her protruding nipples. His eyes shot up to hers. He didn't wait for her to invite him in as he pushed past her. "Who's here?"

She just stood there, her mind still foggy, and watched him barrel through her house. She managed to push the door shut and lean against the wall while he tore through the place. When he appeared in front of her, she giggled. "What is your problem?"

"Who has your cheeks so pink and your eyes looking so sedate?" he asked softly as his fingers touched her cheek.

She closed her eyes. "You," she whispered, licking her lips as she pushed off the wall and walked away from him.

He reached out and grabbed her arm. She turned, and he picked her up, kissing her. She had no control, her body still in tune with her dream. Her arms wrapped around his neck, and God help her, she kissed him back. Pulling her head back, licking her lips, she whispered, "I can't do this with you."

"It wasn't what you thought."

"I know, but I can't do this with you. You have the ability to hurt me now. I can't handle the way I feel now."

"How do you feel?"

"Like I've been gutted."

"I'm so sorry for what you saw. It wasn't what you thought." Tears formed in her eyes. She didn't want to be this girl. "No, beautiful, don't cry. I was waiting for you."

She shook her head. "I can't feel this way. I don't want to feel this way."

He was starting to panic. "What way?"

Shaking her head, she pushed away from him. He let her go, sliding her down his body. She moved away from him and into the living room. Callen scanned the room, seeing his note crumbled on the table. She was shaking, and he had no idea what to do. "I think I realized I might have feelings for you. But you don't."

He toed off his boots, moving toward her. Standing right behind her but not touching her, he whispered, "Yes, I do."

She spun around, looking at him. "You just want me because of what you know about me. All men want that."

He shook his head. "I would want you either way." His voice was soft and raspy.

She stood there with tears falling from her eyes. His hands moved to her face to wipe them away. "Don't cry, beautiful. I'm not going anywhere. It's here I want to be, with you."

"Why did you think someone was here?"

He smiled. "This beautiful flush on your skin. I want to be the one who makes you look like this. The way your nipples are so hard. I want to be the reason that happens."

"You were. I was dreaming about you," she whispered.

His mouth came down on hers hard. She wrapped her arms around his neck, and he lost control. Picking her up, he walked her to the bedroom and laid her on the bed. He pulled his shirt over his head and dropped his jeans on the floor. Climbing into bed with her, wrapping himself around her, he pulled her into his embrace.

"No more dreaming, you have me. I'm not going anywhere. I'm here."

Lyssa relaxed against his hard body. Closing her eyes, she fell back asleep.

As Callen held her, he couldn't believe how she felt in his arms. He wanted to belong to her. He wanted her to belong to him. This is where he wanted to be. Finally, his body relaxed as her warmth filled his soul, healed him. He belonged to her.

It was the middle of the night when her hand moved up his chest, waking him. She pulled herself up his body, kissing him. His hand moved to her hair, his other hand on the small of her back. "Callen," she whispered on his lips. "What is happening to me?"

He smiled. "I think the same thing that is happening to me."

Giggling, she asked, "What's that?"

"I'm not sure, but it feels incredible."

She rolled away from him. He watched as she slid out of her pants. His heart stopped in his chest when she crossed her arms over her chest, lifting her shirt off. Laying back down, she pulled herself against his body, making him hiss and groan. "Are you mine?" she whispered, touching his lips.

His heart burst. "I am," was all he got out before she kissed him.

It was a kiss that lasted a very long time, a kiss he never wanted to end. She tasted so fucking good on his lips. Her tiny, perfect body was wrapped in his arms. He knew at this moment that he would die for her. She had been waiting for him, and he was honored to be this man. He was honored to be here with her. Pulling out of the kiss, she tucked her head into his neck, whispering, "I'm yours."

Closing his eyes, he held his breath. He had been given a second chance at getting all that he wanted. Never would he do anything to hurt this woman. Together, they fell asleep.

He woke before the sun as he had every day for the past eight years. His fingers roved slowly up and down her back. Her soft skin felt incredible to touch. He could feel her body change as she slowly woke from her slumber.

"Callen," she moaned, setting his skin on fire.

"Mmm, I'm here," he moaned.

"You said you were mine."

He smiled. "You said you were mine."

"I've never wanted someone before. I think I've been so angry because I want you to be mine. I don't want anyone else to have you."

His hand wrapped around her back, his fingertips touched the side of her breast as he maneuvered her onto his body. Slowly, he moved his hands up her side, touching her. "No one else will ever have me." His eyes closed as she brought her legs along his side. He kept them close as she pushed herself up to sit on his stomach, his hands coming to rest on her thighs.

"Callen, open your eyes."

Slowly, his eyes opened. She was a vision sitting on him, her hair cascading down her chest. Her nipples were hard and peeking through her beautiful hair. "Lyssa, what are you doing?"

"I saw you, in the bedroom. You are so beautiful. I thought it only fair that you see me," she whispered shyly.

He sat up quickly, wrapping his arms around her, and she slid down his body, her core rubbing along his cock. His mouth crashed against hers. Pulling back, he looked at her. "I am not rushing this. One night of talking is not trust. In time, beautiful. In time. I plan on looking at you for the rest of my life. No rush." She giggled, pressing her core into him, then moving slightly. "Do you know what you are doing to me?"

She shook her head. "No, but I like the way your eyes look when I do this." She moved along him again.

"Lyssa," he moaned. He was going to lose his shit. Slowly, he pulled her back, shaking his head. "Stop."

She looked down at him. "You're so big," she whispered. He felt her hands move to touch him. The back of her hand ran along his cock. "It feels like steel," she whispered.

His hand covered hers. "Please stop," he moaned.

"Why?" she whispered, kissing him.

His tongue gently touched her lips. "Because, beautiful, I'm going to lose my mind."

She giggled, laying backward and forcing him to let her go. She landed on the bed between his legs. He closed his eyes and laid back. He felt her roll off him and get off the bed. Then he heard the bathroom door shut. "Fuck," he moaned, rolling over onto his stomach. *What the hell is wrong with me?* The bathroom door opened, and he felt her climb onto the bed, then he felt her very naked body lay down on top of him.

"Callen," she whispered, kissing his back.

"Yeah," he moaned.

"Were you serious?"

"Yes, beautiful. I'm positive."

Giggling, she got up. He wanted to look at her, but he didn't move. He needed to get rid of this erection. "You can get up, I'm dressed now. I'm going to make some coffee. Are you hungry?"

"I am," he said, rolling over. He felt her eyes move to his cock.

"You are so big. Is that normal?" Her innocence made him blush.

"Yes, it's normal," he chuckled as she walked out of the room.

Callen got dressed, and after they had breakfast, they headed out. "I'm going to drive my own car. If we are going to pull this off, we can't be together. Kennedy will be there by the time we get there."

"My buddies will be here soon as well. I need to go pick them up when we get back. I won't be able to stay with you tonight," he said as he pulled her to him, kissing her.

"I know, I'll probably stay with Kennedy, hence the overnight bag."

"This is weird." He smiled.

"I know. Are you my boyfriend?"

He laughed. "If you want me to be."

"Do you want to be?" she questioned him.

His smile nearly broke his face. "With all that I am. Yes."

She nodded. "Good to know," she said as she got in the car.

She couldn't wipe the silly smile off her face the whole way there. Callen stopped at his house while she continued to the ranch. When she pulled up, she heard her friend squealing. Lyssa was out of the car, running up the sidewalk. The two girls collided, landing in the grass hugging and laughing.

"Oh my God, I've missed you so much," Kennedy said as she moved the hair off Lyssa's face.

"Right back at you. How have you been?"

They lay on the grass looking at the sky. "God, Lys, I've been so busy. I like New York, but I miss home. I miss being here." She turned her head. "I miss my best friend. Won't you move to the big city? Now that you are unemployed, I'm sure Hugh will give you a job."

When Kennedy spoke those words, her heart broke. She didn't tell Kennedy that she'd lost her job. Hugh must have told her. She played the part. "I got my old job back. It's all good. Besides, you know me, I'm a small-town girl."

"I know, but I had to ask. Hey, you want to go for a ride? Hugh and the guys won't be here until later today."

"Oh? They're coming tonight? I thought they weren't coming until tomorrow. But, hell yeah, I haven't been riding in forever."

"Hey, Daddy has a new ranch hand. His name is Buck. He's pretty fucking hot."

Lyssa laughed, wondering why she would bring him up. "Kennedy, you are getting married in three months."

"Yeah, but I'm not dead. He's smoking hot."

The girls laughed all the way to the stables, walking arm in arm. They saddled the horses and took off across the back field. They rode for hours.

Callen jumped in the shower and then headed to the airport to pick up the guys. It was good to see them all. Tom was the first one off the plane, grabbing him in a bear hug. "Fuck, it's good to see you alive."

Callen laughed, and before he could talk, Stu had him in another bear hug. "Looking good. Jesus, what the hell? You feel like a rock."

Callen patted his stomach. "Good food and hard work."

Slade and Mitchel were next. "So, what the hell have you been doing?"

"You wouldn't believe me if I told you. Did you bring the paperwork?"

He laughed. "Is the Pope Catholic?"

"Good, I want to get this finalized before we head out. I need this to be taken care of."

They all walked out to his truck. "No shit, a pickup." Tom laughed. They got in and Callen signed all the papers.

He looked at Tom. "Do it. Hit the button so I can bury this fucker."

"We stand to make a huge profit from this, should send you over the billion-dollar mark," Stu said.

"It doesn't mean much to me anymore."

They all just looked at him. "She must be something else for you to say that," Slade said.

Callen just chuckled, thinking in his head, *You have no fucking idea how much.* They sat and watched the computer screen as they did with every deal they did together. When it was done, Callen let out a deep breath. "Now, let's go. Listen," he said as he drove, "this is a casual thing, so just be yourselves. The pretense is that you are business associates of Charles Greenvale. No more information than that. The big reveal comes after the barbeque. For now, I'll take you to the hotel so you can drop your shit off, and then we'll head out to the ranch. It's where I work."

"You're a billionaire ranch hand?" Stu asked.

"Nope, I'm Buck the ranch hand, and let's keep it that way. I'm happy. It's good work, and the Greenvales are wonderful people. You can all give me hard time about it later. Right now, we have roles to play in order to pull this off. So, when we get to the ranch, you are there to work. And please be respectful and not arrogant assholes."

"Who us?" they said in unison. They all laughed.

"You are just guys. So be ready to work."

By the time they got back to the ranch, Kennedy and Lyssa had been out riding for a good few hours. When Callen saw her car, his heart sped up. He knew the black car at the end of the drive belonged to Kennedy.

They all piled out of the truck just as Charles was walking out of the house. Callen introduced them all. "The girls should be back in a bit. They've been riding for a few hours now." Then he looked at the guys. "Any of you city slickers know anything about horses? Their horses are going to need a good wiping down when they get back. Those girls ride them hard."

Just as he finished, all heads turned to the field when they heard the girls yelling at each other. Lyssa came flying around the house into the driveway. Callen's breath hitched in his chest when he saw her face.

"Fuck me," Stu whispered.

"Holy shit," Mitchel moaned.

Kennedy came flying out from the side of the house a few seconds after Lyssa, who turned in her saddle. "Beat your ass again, bitch."

"Oh, yeah right, you fucking cheated, bitch." They both busted out laughing.

"You'll never figure out how to jump if you don't try it," Lyssa said, knowing damn well Kennedy knew how to jump that particular fence. She was the one who taught Lyssa how to do it.

"I know how to jump. I'm just not crazy enough to jump a four-foot fence."

Lyssa laughed as she climbed down from her horse. Callen heard Stu moan when she landed with her back to them. Kennedy climbed off hers, and Lyssa took the reins. "Go on, you wuss, and rest your perfect ass. I'll take care of these two." When she turned around to walk away, she saw them. "Wow," she whispered. Smiling, she said, "Hi, I'm Lyssa. That's Kennedy, the bride to be."

One by one, the guys introduced themselves to both the girls. "Jesus, Dad, you keep hiring guys that look like this, I might have to rethink getting married."

Lyssa blushed at her friend's boldness.

"Well, you're not married yet," Stu said to her.

"No, I most certainly am not." She turned on her heels and headed toward the house.

Lyssa began walking to the stables. Charles cleared his throat, and all heads turned to look at him. "Gentleman, I'm sorry to say that both of those lovely young ladies are spoken for. So, mind yourselves." He winked at Callen.

Callen chuckled. "Come on, guys, there is still plenty to do." They headed to the barn. For hours, they hauled stuff to the backyard—grills, chairs, tables, glassware.

Just before dusk, a car pulled down the drive. Kennedy ran out the front door, Lyssa not far behind her. When the car pulled up and the men got out, there were four of them. Callen knew who Hugh was only because of the way Kennedy threw herself at him.

Lyssa walked up behind her, and Hugh grabbed her, pulling her into a hug. Callen had to stop himself from moving across the lawn as he and the guys walked out from the back of the house, his eyes on her. A man walked up to her. "Hi, I'm Brody. Best man." He reached for Lyssa, and she stepped back, making Callen smile.

"Lyssa, maid of honor," she said, squaring her shoulders. Then she looked at Kennedy. "I'm going to go. I will see you first thing in the morning."

"Don't go. Hang out with us," she said to her.

"Yeah, don't go, beautiful. Stay and hang out with us," Brody said to her.

"No, thank you," she said to Brody. Turning, she looked at Kennedy. "I'll be back early." She kissed Kennedy on the cheek.

Callen's eyes watched Brody; the guy was salivating, checking out Lyssa. Leaning over, he said something to Bell. Stu put his hand on Callen's arm. "Let it go," he whispered.

Callen ripped his arm away from Stu. "Like fucking hell," he growled as he watched Brody run after Lyssa.

Standing there, he watched the interaction between the two of them. Brody leaned in and whispered something in her ear. It was her response that had them all laughing. She slapped him across the face and then slammed her hands into his chest, pushing him to the ground. "You fucking asshole," she yelled.

"What? Come on, with an ass like that…" Brody said, laughing.

Lyssa turned, and when she did, her fist connected with his face. "Don't think it is ever acceptable to talk to me like that." Brody landed on his ass.

"What the fuck is your problem?"

"Men like you are my problem. Just because you're rich, you think you can treat someone like this. Well, guess again, asshole. Come near me again and you won't walk right for the rest of your life."

Kennedy ran up to her, hugging her. Callen saw her lips move, saying, "I'm so sorry." Lyssa shook her head and got in her car. Brody got up and called her a bitch, and Callen was moving across the driveway.

Charles stopped him. "Buck," he called out. Callen looked up. "Can I have a word?"

Lyssa looked at him as she pulled away. Callen walked up on the porch. "Don't blow this. She can take care of herself. Now, go on, we have a hell of a day tomorrow. Leave these assholes to me. I'm supposed to tell you she will meet you at your place. Now, go on, don't keep the lady waiting."

Callen shook his hand and headed to his truck. The guys piled in. "Care to explain that out there?" Tom asked.

Callen laughed. "Not yet."

"Well, let me just say this, those two could stop fucking traffic on a highway in Chicago. Wow," Stu said.

Twenty minutes later, Callen pulled up in his driveway. Jumping out of the truck, he made a beeline to Lyssa who was getting out of her car. "Are you all right?" he asked, his fingers touching her face. "What did he say to you?"

She leaned into his fingers. "You don't want to know."

He laughed. "Yes, I do."

She leaned into him, pushing up on her toes. "He wanted to know what my ass tasted like." He looked at her, and she blushed. "You said if you weren't a gentleman you would have had your mouth all over my ass."

"I did," he whispered back.

A voice cleared, and Callen smiled. Turning his head, he saw his friends standing there watching the two of them. "So, spill it," Slade said.

Callen turned. "Guys, this is Lyssa."

"Yes, we met earlier."

"She's the lawyer I told you about, who uncovered all of this."

"Yes, and?"

She giggled. "And I suppose I'm his girlfriend, but no one can know."

Tom slapped him on the back. "I wouldn't come back to the real world either."

She turned to him. "You're thinking of going back to Chicago?"

He shook his head. "No, beautiful, I'm not going anywhere." Without looking away from her, he said, "Guys, can you give us a few minutes?" They all walked away. When he knew they were far enough away, he leaned further down. "I'm yours, remember? I'm not going anywhere. You asked me if I wanted to be your boyfriend this morning. Do you still want me to be?"

"Yes, please."

"Good, do you want to come in for a while?"

"No, I need to get home and take a shower. Tomorrow is a big day, an exhausting day of lies. I hate lies, Callen."

"I know, me too. But look at it this way. It's only ten hours of lying and then we can watch the fireworks. I really want to kiss you right now."

She smiled. "I know, me too. But we have to be careful. I will see you tomorrow." She put her hand on his chest. "Good night, Callen."

"Good night, beautiful."

He walked her to the car and opened the door for her. She paused and looked at him one more time. Touching his chest again, she got in the car and headed home.

Callen stood on the street and watched her drive away. He wanted to go with her, but they needed to get their plan straight. When he walked in, the guys were all sitting around looking at him.

Stu started, "She's fucking gorgeous. Why didn't you tell us?"

"Because this is new. We've been overcoming some shit."

"Is she the reason for the black eye?" Tom asked.

He chuckled, touching his face. "Yeah, I spun out with her behind my truck. I'm responsible for her face as well."

"So, she beat the shit out of you?" Slade chuckled.

"More than once, I'm afraid. She has a hell of a right hook."

"Is this serious?"

He stood there looking at them. "I hope so. We are just learning to trust one another. You all know what *she* did to me. I've spent the last eight years drinking and fucking anything that moved. When I hurt Lyssa, she was dressed in this damn pencil skirt, tight across that ass, and she reminded me of *her*. I judged her, and I was so wrong. But, yeah, she has watched men hurt her friend, Kennedy, all through high school and college. She isn't very trusting of men. When she uncovered all this shit that is happening now, she clocked me in a field when I suggested she was the same way, in it for the money."

"And now?"

"Now, we are learning."

"Well, don't hit me for saying this, but she is one fine woman," Mitchel said.

Callen nodded his head. "Don't I know it."

"So, I'll be the one to ask, seeing as how you all are chicken shits," Tom said. "What's she like in bed?"

"Well, she doesn't snore if that's what you're asking."

"You know it's not."

Callen looked at them all. "I wouldn't know. We haven't gotten there yet. Hell, I haven't had sex since I met her."

"Shit," Tom said. "You losing it or what?"

"No, man, she just isn't that kind of girl, as she keeps reminding me. She's the kind of girl you wait your whole fucking life for. My money doesn't mean shit to her. She's a good, kind, smart woman."

"Fuck you. You're in love with her," Tom spit out.

"Not yet, but I think I'm on my way." After a minute, he asked, "Are you guys done?"

They all sat there looking at him. It was Slade who spoke. "We're just giving you a hard time. Partly because we are jealous, but mostly because if anyone deserves happiness in this world it's you. We are happy for you."

"Thanks."

They sat and hashed out the plan and how things were going to go down. An hour or so later, Callen took them back to the hotel. He didn't go home but headed to Lyssa's house. He needed to make sure she was all right.

When Lyssa got home, she locked her door and slid down it, shaking her head. "What a fucking asshole," she said. Her phone started ringing, so she pulled herself up and headed to the dining room, grabbing the phone off the wall.

"Hello," she said.

"Lys, oh my God. I am so sorry for what happened with Brody," Kennedy said.

"Yeah, the guy is an asshole, that's for sure."

"What did he say to you?"

"He told me I had an incredible ass and he wanted to know what it tastes like."

"Are you fucking kidding me?" Kennedy sounded pissed.

"Yeah, no, I'm not kidding you. It's fine. It isn't anything I couldn't handle, and it certainly isn't anything I haven't heard before."

"But still, he's supposed to be a businessman, a gentleman."

Lyssa laughed. "You know better than that. The more money they have, the more arrogant they are."

Kennedy laughed. "I wish you would have stayed."

"Why? So I could fight that asshole off all night? No thanks. Besides, this is the time that your parents get to know Hugh. That's what this is about. So, it's better that I'm not there, and besides, I'll be there first thing, and you better be ready because I feel like dancing."

Kennedy laughed. "Oh, you are so on. I love you, you know."

"I know, I love you, too. I'm so happy you finally found him." She was shaking her head. They all had a part to play.

"Thanks, that really means a lot to me."

"I'm going to go. I need to take a shower. I smell like a horse. I love you."

"I love you. See you tomorrow, bitch."

"See you tomorrow, bitch."

They hung up, and Lyssa headed to the shower. She grabbed a t-shirt and didn't bother with any pants. As she climbed into bed, she paused to smell her sheets. They smelt like him. Her smile locked on her lips. *Does he really care about me? Could I be falling in love with him?* The way her body felt, she had never felt like this before. She'd met gorgeous men before, spent time with them, but none of them made her blush. None of them caused her heart to beat faster.

Closing her eyes, she let the memory of him take her to sleep.

Callen burned up the miles between towns. Shaking his head, he hoped she would move into the house on the ranch when this was over. He spent a year restoring it. Granted, at the time, he had no knowledge what for. He considered asking Charles if he could buy the place, but then he would have known about him.

It felt like it was only a few minutes until he pulled up to her place. When he thought about her, time seemed to move quickly. He knocked a few times on the door, but she didn't answer. He knew she had to be sleeping, but the reality of what is happening settled in, and he banged on the door.

When he heard the lock turning, his heart started beating again. The door opened and there she was, wearing only a t-shirt and her panties. Her nipples were puckered and pushing through her tiny shirt.

"Why are you opening the door in that?" he asked, a bit upset.

She scratched her head, looking at him. "Why are you interrupting my dreams?"

Letting go of the door, she turned and headed back to bed. Callen stood there, looking at her perfect ass covered in red lace. He locked the door and toed off his boots, following her to the bedroom, where he was privileged to see her climb into bed. He stood there stunned.

She laid down. "You coming?" she whispered. Walking to the bed, his clothes came off and he climbed in next to her. She snuggled to his side. "I'm so tired," she moaned as he wrapped himself around her.

"Come here," he whispered, pulling her to him. God, he was instantly hard. He should have taken care of his erection before he came here. Chuckling, he thought it wouldn't have made a difference. Closing his eyes, he breathed in her scent and fell asleep.

Sometime close to morning, he felt her move out of his arms. He didn't say anything as she got up and headed to the bathroom. Taking a deep breath, the only thing he cared about was that she was all right. When the door opened, he heard himself moan as his cock got harder. She looked like heaven, so tiny, so strong, and her nipples were still hard.

Climbing back into bed, she snuggled into him again. "You're so warm," she whispered.

He chuckled. "You're so beautiful."

Tilting her head up, she kissed his jaw. "Why are you here, Callen?"

"I was worried about you," he whispered, kissing her forehead.

"Liar." Her breath was hot on his jaw.

He chuckled. "I was. I still can't believe that asshole."

She rolled onto her back. "I've dealt with men like him my whole life. They are arrogant and single-minded."

"I know, I've been that guy for the past eight years."

She turned her head, looking at him. "Callen, are you that guy now?"

"If I was, you wouldn't be wearing any clothes."

She turned onto her side. "To be honest, I don't want to be wearing any clothes."

"Lyssa," he whispered.

"Callen, I think I have some serious feelings for you. You are all that is in my mind, all the time."

He rolled over. "Yeah?"

She nodded. "Brody didn't bother me. You bother me."

"Why do I bother you?" he asked, moving her hair off her face.

"You make me feel strange. Like I want, no, need to be near you all the time. I didn't want to come home last night. I wanted to stay with you. I'm glad you came here."

"Yeah?"

She nodded. "Yeah." He leaned in and gently kissed her. She wrapped her arm around his neck, pulling herself to him. His hand landed on her side, his thumb pressing against her chest. She pulled back. "Why are you so careful with me?" Her hips moved along his thigh.

"Because I want so much more with you. But I'm afraid you will think that sex is all I want from you."

She smiled, moving her hand from his neck and onto his. Her eyes not looking away from his, she moved his hand up. "Lyssa, what are you doing?"

"I want you to touch me. I want to feel you touch me," she whispered as his hand covered her breast.

He thought his mind would explode when her breast filled his hand. It fit perfectly, her nipple so hard. "God, beautiful, you feel so good," he moaned as his hand closed around her.

"Touch me, Callen. My body aches, and I need it to stop. I can't think straight. Please, don't stop."

His mouth came down on hers as he kneaded her breast. He pulled her shirt up so he could feel skin on skin. He felt himself come a little when his fingers found her nipple, gently pinching it in his fingers.

Smiling, he looked down at her, at her nipple in his fingers. His mouth watered. Pressing on her, she laid on her back. Callen rolled with her, pushing her shirt all the way up. He knew he was going to come when his mouth wrapped around her nipple.

"Ahh," she called out at the feelings coursing through her body.

"Just relax, beautiful, and feel me," he whispered, taking the other one in his mouth.

She squirmed and pressed into him time and time again. Her moans and cries were etched in his brain. She let it all go. When he had his fill, he pulled up, sitting back on his heels. "Look at you. Never have I ever..." he whispered as he looked at her. Her back slightly arched. Her nipples were so fucking hard he couldn't handle it. "I need to use your shower." He got off the bed and headed to the bathroom.

Turning on the shower, he pulled off his boxers, his cock so hard it hurt. It was less than a minute he was under the water that his release came, three strokes of his hand. Just the image of her fucking perfect body pulsing under him took his breath away.

His hands on the wall, he felt like an asshole. He was so embarrassed by his actions. He got out, dried off, and put his boxers back on. There was a wet spot on them, but he didn't care. He sat on the bench at the foot of her bed, resting his arms on his knees and hanging his head in shame. *What the fuck is wrong with me?*

He felt her before she touched him. "Hey, what's wrong?"

He shook his head. "I'm so sorry."

"Why are you sorry? Callen, talk to me."

"I'm such an asshole," he whispered.

She moved around him, maneuvering herself to sit on his lap, her hands coming up to his face, forcing him to look at her. She was fighting back tears. "Please, Callen. Please, don't hurt me."

He wrapped his arms around her. "It will never happen. I can't ever hurt you. I think I'm falling in love with you," he whispered.

"Then why are you an asshole?"

His hands moved up and down her back. "Because I can't control myself. What I just did was such an asshole move. Please, Lyssa, forgive me."

He felt her body tense up. "I don't understand."

"I shouldn't have done that to you and then went in your shower to come."

"Is that what you did in there?"

"Yes," he whispered. "I lost control. I wasn't a gentleman."

She giggled. "Well, I think the asshole move would have been to whip it out and come all over me. So…"

He laughed, pulling her back a little and kissing her. "You think?"

"Oh yeah, because that would have freaked me out big time. I mean, someday, I'm sure I might enjoy watching you touch yourself, but not today."

He kissed her. "No, I suppose not." They sat like this kissing for a few minutes. "Lyssa, baby." She smiled a sweet smile at him. He knew she didn't have a clue what she was doing. "I'm having a very difficult time not touching you."

"Callen, you can touch me if you want," she whispered on his lips.

His hands flew to her head, his fingers threading through her hair, and he deepened the kiss. He needed to keep his hands away from her body. "Not like you think. I want to touch all of you, and the gentlemanly thing to do is move you from this," he looked down her body to her core, to her red lace panties, "very tempting position." Licking his lips, he looked up at her.

She smiled her shy smile. "Yes, perhaps you are right. I'm sorry." She started to move. "I didn't realize."

"Hey." He pulled her to him. "Don't apologize. I want to do this right. I want to do this right, beautiful. You need to trust me. You need to know that you are all I want. All right?"

She smiled. "What would be the ungentlemanly things you want to do?"

He chuckled, running his tongue along her lip, whispering, "I want to rip these ever so sexy panties off your body and touch you there. I want to feel your release. I want to grab your ass, lift you up, and slide you down on top of me, pushing deep inside of you. Don't you for one minute think I don't want this with you, but I'm not an asshole anymore. Not with you, beautiful." He watched her face and body blush a near crimson color.

"Oh," she peeped out.

He laughed, standing up with her wrapped around him like a monkey. Turning, he set her on the bench, kissing her. "Come on, we have a long day today."

She swallowed the lump in her throat, nodding at him as he grabbed his jeans and pulled them up. Her eyes never left his cock. When he zipped his jeans, he kissed her on the forehead. "I'll make some coffee."

She licked her lips and smiled at him.

When he walked out of the room, he let out the breath he was holding and leaned against the wall. He knew what he was doing, and what he did was the asshole move. So much shit was going to happen today, and he fucking started it off like this. It wouldn't end well. He knew it was too soon. This woman was it for him. He was terrified he'd just fucked it all up.

Lyssa sat on the bench feeling odd. She looked at the door, her eyes filling with unshed tears. *What the hell is happening? Why would he do that? Why is this so hard?* Kennedy made it look easy. She was with lots of guys. She got up and changed her panties and got dressed. A nice tight pair of jeans should make him crazy. Maybe a tight t-shirt as well. Yes, she smiled as she got dressed.

Grabbing her boots out of the closet, she headed out to the kitchen. She didn't talk to him while they ate. There was a plan brewing in her head. If he wanted her like he said he did, she was going to make him crazy today. Maybe, by the end of the night, he would be ready to do more than jump up and come in her shower.

They left together, kissing in the parking lot. Lyssa got in her car, and Callen in his truck. The drive was weird, with him behind her. She kept looking in her rear-view mirror. He had a small smile on his face. He turned at his street, and she continued on to the ranch.

Pulling up, she met Charles in the driveway. "What are you doing up so early?" she asked as she got out of the car.

He chuckled. "I'm up because I knew you would be here at the crack of dawn. I overheard a few conversations last night that I think you need to be aware of. Where's Callen?"

"He turned off the road toward his house. He needs to pick up his friends at their hotel, too. Why?"

"Can you take me over there?" he asked.

"Of course, come on, get in." She pulled out onto the road. "Charles, what is going on? Are you all right?"

He chuckled. "I'm fine, just an old man working it."

Lyssa busted out laughing. "Working it?"

"What, that's not the slang you young people use?" He chuckled.

"Charles, you are not old. By far."

Lyssa pulled up in the driveway behind Callen's truck, and they got out. She walked behind Charles as they made their way to the door. He knocked, and she stood looking out at the street.

Callen opened the door. "Charles, what are you doing here?"

"We need to talk. Are your friends here?"

"No, I was just going to get them."

"I'll do it." Lyssa looked down the street.

He nodded his thanks then stepped around Charles, looking at her. "What are you looking at?"

"I don't know, something doesn't feel right." Her voice was softer than usual.

"They can walk over. I don't want you going alone. It's just two blocks away." He pulled his phone out of his pocket, dialing it. "Hey, Tom, can you guys get over here right now? Hike it." He told them where to go.

"Yep, on our way. Be there is five."

He disconnected the call. "Come inside," he said, putting his hand on her arm.

"No. Something's wrong, Callen. I can feel it."

Callen looked at Charles, who nodded to him. Fear filled his heart. *What the fuck is going on?* Charles moved into the house. Callen stood behind Lyssa, looking down the street. A few minutes later, Tom, Stu, Slade, and Mitchell came trotting down the street.

"Hey, what's going on?" Mitchell asked.

"Not sure, come on in," Callen said. He put his hand on her arm. "Lyssa, come on."

She shook her head. "No, you go. Leave the door open."

He stood there freaking out. Stepping back, he leaned on the door frame. His eyes not leaving her, he said, "Charles what's this about?"

"Well, I heard a few conversations last night. They suspect you to be a problem today. They have some plan to isolate Lyssa from you. They believe you and she are together. Whatever they are going to do, they are planning on doing it today. She cannot be left alone."

Lyssa spoke. "Is Kennedy in on this, Charles?"

"Unfortunately, she is the one that figured it out."

"Figured what out?" she said softly.

"That you and Callen are a thing. She told Hugh that the easiest way to get him under control and out of the picture was to remove you. Sweetheart, she knows you haven't, well, you know."

"Of course, she knows, she is my best friend. But what does that have to do with anything?"

"Brody has staked his claim to you. Apparently, he likes it rough, and you gave him just what he wanted when you beat his ass yesterday."

Mitchell looked at Callen, mouthing, "She's a virgin?"

Lyssa laughed. "Yes, Mitchell, I'm a virgin. And trust me when I tell you this, I'll cut the fucker's dick off before he has a chance to use it."

No one said a word, but Charles started chuckling. "You should see your faces. Listen, the object here is to not leave her alone. Never. One of you needs to be with her every second. Can you do that?"

They all nodded. "She won't be alone."

Lyssa pulled out her phone and sent a text, "No, you know what?" She pushed her phone back in her pocket and started talking. "The plan has changed. I'm not going to let some rich assholes scare me or threaten you. Come on, let's go. Time to make some noise." She went to walk off the porch, and Callen reached for her. Turning, she looked at him. "You've been testing me to see if I'm worthy of your love, of your heart. Well, this is your test from me.

Let's see what you are made of, Mr. McCabe. My parents didn't raise me to be anyone's pawn. Now, let's go. Charles, are you coming?"

He busted out laughing. "Right behind you."

"Mitchell, Stu, you guys come with us. I know I can kick some ass, but just to be safe." She headed off the porch toward her car. They all followed her.

Callen, Slade, and Tom got in the truck. "That chick has spunk."

"I'm glad you find this funny. She is scaring the shit out of me. She is one determined woman. You guys better watch her. Do you have all the paperwork?"

"Got it right here." Tom patted his jacket. "Is she always this bossy?"

Callen chuckled. "Yes, she is fierce in protecting herself."

"You're going to marry her, aren't you?" Slade asked

"I'm hopeful. Listen, she is so special, it's a wonder she isn't married. She isn't afraid of a damn thing. She calls me out on all my shit. And smart, she is so smart, she sees shit that others miss. She has this weird sense about her. She can hear you lie in your voice. She has this thing about looking into your eyes. She can see your soul."

"Wow, you do have it bad." Tom chuckled.

"Yeah, but what I just said is the truth. Just watch her. You're going to freak out when you see it. Oh, and she has this thing about body language. She has like this sixth sense about her. It's unreal and so fucking sexy it makes my head spin. Total honesty with her, or she will not hesitate to call you out on it."

They all laughed as they pulled up in front of the ranch house. Together, they walked in and sat down at the table. Emily was up and had made breakfast for everyone. Lyssa helped her serve it. When they were finished, she helped clean up. While in the kitchen, Emily whispered to her, "Be careful today."

Lyssa hugged her. "Today may not happen like we planned. I'm not going to let them hurt you. I don't care if Kennedy is my best friend or not."

Emily smiled at her. "She always thought the world of you. I can't imagine she is doing this because she wants to do it."

"I know, something isn't right. We'll figure it out," Lyssa whispered.

She left Emily in the kitchen and wandered into the living room. Stu followed her, sitting across from her. "It's going to be all right," he said sweetly to her.

She just looked at him. "Tell me about her. What was she like?"

He sat there looking at her. "She was beautiful. Smart. Conniving."

"Why do you think she hurt him like that?"

"We don't know. She played a good game of pretending. He was so in love with her. Kind of like he is with you."

She shook her head. "No, he's not. I can feel it. He doesn't trust me. He's afraid, and I think it's because he hurt me, so he feels guilty." She reached up to touch her eyebrow. "He told me that he laughed when he left me in the dust."

"Do you love him?"

"I don't know what love is. I thought I did, but I don't. I've never been in a relationship before, and the only ones I know are Charles and Emily and my parents. But my parents fought a lot. I don't think they loved each other like you should. I think my perception of love is something that doesn't exist. People are just... I don't know." She paused. "He makes me feel different. He makes me want to do those things. But he won't. He keeps telling me he's not ready. I've never met a man like him. Not sure where this is going, but I feel him wanting to go back to his business."

"Would you go with him if he did?"

She shook her head. "No, I'm happy with my life. I'm okay being alone. It is what it is. After I lost my parents, I got lost in school. Then I came into some money that paid for my school and left me with a nice chunk of change. I don't have to work if I don't want to but being focused on anything other than what my life really is, makes me happy."

"And what is your life, really?"

She giggled. "Dull, boring, quiet, happy. I like myself, so being alone isn't a problem. I watched so many people hurt Kennedy. She just wanted everyone to like her, but no one did. She's too beautiful, if that's a thing. She doesn't know how to be happy on her own."

"You seem to have it all figured out."

"No, not really. What I have is myself. I can't hurt myself. As long as it's just me, well..."

He sat there looking at her. "He's falling in love with you if he hasn't already."

She smiled. "He thinks that, yes, but I don't feel that from him."

"Give it time." He smiled.

"He'll go back to Chicago now that he's tasted that life again. And that's fine, that's why I'm not getting attached to him. He won't be happy here anymore. He hasn't been happy here at all. Who can be happy with a different girl each time? Working, drinking, and fucking, that's not being happy."

He laughed. "I could probably find twenty guys who would argue with you."

"Perhaps, but at the end of the day, when they look in the mirror, they are still alone and unsatisfied. Because if they were satisfied, they wouldn't need to go out and do it again."

He just sat there looking at her. She turned her head when she heard footsteps on the stairs. Whispering, she said, "Showtime." Standing up, she walked out into the dining room. Stu stayed in the living room.

Kennedy walked up to her and hugged her. Lyssa didn't want to hug her, but she did. "Can we go out on the porch and talk?" she whispered to her.

Kennedy nodded. Holding hands, they walked outside. Mitchell and Slade walked out behind them and sat on the steps, while Lyssa and Kennedy sat in the rocking chairs.

"I love it here in the mornings. It's so quiet," Kennedy said as she looked around.

"Tell me what happened to you," Lyssa whispered.

"Nothing happened to me. What are you talking about?"

"Kennedy, I know. I know everything, except for what happened to you."

She sat there looking at Lyssa. Her eyes filled with unshed tears. "Nothing happened," she whispered.

"Yes, it did," Lyssa whispered back.

Her lip quivered as a tear fell on her cheek. "I can't."

"Yes, you can. I love you. I've always loved you. Tell me."

"I can't," she said as another tear fell on her cheek.

"I'll fix it, don't worry."

"You can't, Lys, not this time. This time, you can't."

Lyssa just smiled at her and grabbed her hand, squeezing it. They sat there in silence until Hugh came out the door.

"There you are. I was wondering where you got to." Kennedy squeezed her hand hard. "Good Morning, Lyssa. You guys are here early." He was so sweet.

Lyssa smiled at him. "We've got a lot to do, don't we, guys," she said to Slade and Mitchell.

"We sure do, we should get to it," Slade said as he stood up.

Lyssa let go of Kennedy's hand and walked into the house with the guys, leaving Kennedy and Hugh on the porch. Walking into the dining room, Lyssa caught Callen's face. His eyes told her he was worried. She just smiled at him. Turning her head, she came face to face with Brody. He put his hands on her shoulders, and she brought her knee up, slamming him in the balls. "I told you yesterday not to fucking touch me."

"You fucking bitch. What the hell is your problem?" He was bent over.

"You, you're my problem. Don't touch me again, Brody, or I'll make sure you never have children," she whispered to him. Moving out of the way, she found a seat away from Callen and sat down. Stu was still in the living room, and Mitchell and Slade joined him. Brody moved into the hallway, holding his crotch, mumbling how much of a bitch she was, and how he was going to teach her a lesson. She just sat there looking at him.

When Hugh and Kennedy came in, they sat down, and Emily served them breakfast. Hugh's other two friends came down a few minutes later and ate in the kitchen with Brody. Lyssa waited for them to finish. She waited for Kennedy to take the plates into the kitchen.

"I'm going to take a shower," Kennedy said as she headed for the stairs.

"Can you wait a minute? I need to talk to you two before everyone gets here," Lyssa said. She saw the fear on Kennedy's face, her eyes begging her not to do this. Lyssa tried to convey to her that it was going to be fine.

She sat down next to Hugh. "What's this about, Lyssa?" Hugh asked as Brody and his other two friends came in.

"Well, I was wondering why you are forcing my friend to betray her family. What is it, Hugh, that you have on her that would make her do something so horrible?"

He chuckled. "Lyssa, you do indeed have a wild imagination." Turning, he looked at Kennedy. "You were right, sweetheart. She is a bit out there." Lyssa watched as Kennedy put on a huge fake smile. Looking back at Lyssa, he said, "I am nothing but in love with your friend, and that's why we are here. To celebrate that love and to get to know her parents."

Lyssa leaned forward as Tom stood up and moved around the room until he was standing behind her. She saw Mitchell come out of the living room. "You're a liar," she said in the sweetest of voices. "You know that I know you're a liar, that's why your boy Brody keeps assaulting me. You are trying to shake me up. No man is that aggressive with a woman."

Hugh chuckled and leaned forward. "Like you would know."

Her eyes looked at Kennedy. "Oh, trust me, Hugh, I know." Her eyes moved back to his. "You know I know," she whispered. "You know a great deal more than you are saying, a great deal more than even Kennedy knows. But, Hugh," she smiled at him, "I know a few more things than you know."

He chuckled. "Lyssa, have you lost your mind? I have no idea what you are implying here."

No one said a word; all eyes were on her. Hers were on her friend and Hugh. "I'm implying that you are hurting my friend to gain access to her parents, to this land. I'm implying that you don't love her, that you aren't going to marry her at all. You see, Hugh, and I'm not sure if Kennedy told you this about me, but I see things that most people don't. I was sent here to calm Mr. Greenvale down because he kept getting letters saying his taxes hadn't been paid, that they were going to foreclose on the land in two months, thanks to your friend Knox. But that isn't going to happen."

Hugh sat there staring at her. She could see the fear in his eyes, even as he smiled at her. "Lyssa, what are you talking about? If Mr. Greenvale is going to lose his land, I will certainly help him out. He is, after all, going to be my father in law."

Shaking her head, she told him, "No, really, he's not. You see, Mr. Greenvale sold this ranch, for a nice profit I might add." She saw it all in his eyes.

His head whipped to Kennedy. Lyssa saw her flinch, and she knew he was hurting her friend. Lyssa's eyes moved to Mitchell, who walked up to Kennedy. "Miss Greenvale, can I speak to you please?"

Kennedy looked at Lyssa, and she nodded. She went to stand, and Hugh grabbed her arm. "Stay here, sweetheart." He was having a hard time keeping his temper in check. Kennedy ripped her arm out of his grip and went with Mitchell.

Hugh stood up to go after her, when Lyssa said, "Hugh, please stay. There is so much more to be said."

He turned around, slamming his hands on the table and leaning into Lyssa, but she didn't flinch. Callen stood up, and Slade came out of the living room. "You don't have a fucking clue what you are talking about. Kennedy was right. You are fucked in the head with your wild fantasies. No wonder no man wants you. No man could ever live up to the fucked-up world you have made up in your head."

Lyssa stood up. "Now, Hugh, there is no need to lash out at me because you can no longer blackmail my friend to get this land. I did the legwork. I know it was you and your friend Brody who did this. There is no denying it. But you know what? It isn't going to happen. Nothing is ever going to happen again for you or your asshole friend."

Tom reached into his pocket and tossed the paperwork on the table in front of Hugh. He looked down at it. Brody stood up, slamming his chair on the floor, then Stu came out of the living room to stand a few feet behind him.

Lyssa didn't take her eyes off Hugh's. He was scared. She couldn't help the smile on her face. Callen hadn't taken his eyes off her. Charles just sat there with a huge smile on his face.

"You see, Hugh, I know my friend better than you do. She isn't in love with you. She's afraid of you. Did you think I wouldn't notice that she is in pain? Did you think I wouldn't notice the look of fear in her eyes? Did you think I wouldn't notice that she refused to jump a fence that we have been jumping for fifteen years? You are hurting my friend, and now I'm going to hurt you. You think I'm some insipid girl? Well, Kennedy did a fantastic job of making you believe that I am. Did you really think I wouldn't figure out that Knox had a key to my house, and the only way he could have gotten it was from Kennedy? It's over now. I didn't do this for anyone but her. I've always been the one to pick up the pieces when she self-destructed. You don't know me, Hugh Bell, but I can guarantee you will never forget me."

She was pushing him to blow up, but she had to admit, the man had some serious control. As calm as he could manage, he said, "You run a good bluff, but there is no way he could have sold this land. I made sure of it."

She laughed. "Have you met my boyfriend, Hugh?"

He laughed at her. "You, with a boyfriend?"

"He's in this room. You might know him, or know of him. I'm pretty sure you do. He's notorious. You see, Hugh, he bought this ranch. Mr. Greenvale no longer owns it. I made sure of that. I drew up the paperwork myself. I even filed it with the county and state. All back taxes have been paid in full, twice I might add." She watched in the background as Brody looked at all the guys, trying to figure out what she was talking about. "Even Mr. Buckingham is scared," she whispered. "You should be scared too."

"Why would I be afraid of you? You are nothing to me."

She giggled. "Oh, Hugh, that's where you are wrong. I'm the one who is going to send you to prison. You and your friends here. I wanted to give Kennedy this day so she could have some fun, but you needed to have control over me, so you pushed your disgusting friend at me to throw me off. But when you decided to hurt my friends, and to try and hurt me, well, I took offense to that. I have friends too, Hugh, friends who are F.B.I., friends in the State Department. You want to believe that I'm too afraid to live in the big city, but you forget, we went to Harvard."

"You are delusional. What the hell are you even talking about? You really should be locked up. Lyssa, you need some serious help."

She busted out laughing. "Go on, Hugh. I know you're dying to know who my boyfriend is."

"A ranch hand? What the hell could a ranch hand do to me?"

She leaned closer to him, too close to him for Callen's taste. "He can take everything you own." Pushing back, she stood straight; she stood tall. "My boyfriend is Callen McCabe." She watched Brody swallow hard. "He now owns Bell Industries and The Alexander Corporation. He is going to give all that land you stole from those people back to them. He is going to take your companies apart and sell them off." She pushed the papers Tom threw on the table at him. "You're done."

Callen watched as she started to move away from the table. Hugh was fast, but she was faster when she slammed her fist into his throat. The door opened, and three men walked in. She looked at the lead guy and smiled. "He's all yours."

Callen was in shock. He looked at his friends who all had smiles on their faces. He watched her walk out the door. No one moved. Hugh and his friends were arrested and hauled out. Callen ran out the door to find her, but she was nowhere in sight.

"They took off on the horses," Mitchell said to him. "Did you know she was going to do this?"

"Not a fucking clue."

~

When Lyssa walked out the door, Kennedy was standing in the drive with two horses. Mitchell was with her. She had tears running down her face. Mitchell was going to ride with her, but Lyssa told him they would be fine.

They rode across the field. Kennedy stopped and just sat there. "I'm so sorry," she whispered.

"I just wish you would have come to me."

"You couldn't help me."

Lyssa smiled. "I just did. It's over. Please tell me what happened?"

"He's a master manipulator. I didn't know, but he made me his submissive. He's been hurting me for a long time. He forced me to do this. He has pictures of me, video of me," she got very quiet, "with multiple men."

Lyssa reached for her friend, wrapping her in her arms. "Aww, Ken, what happened to you? What happened?"

They got off the horses and sat in the grass. "He was so sweet, so cute, and so very rich. I've always wanted to be anything but what I am." She looked around the field. "Inside, I think I'm better than all this. How do you find happiness here?"

"Sweetie, you have to be happy with who you are. You are a wonderful woman, a fantastic friend. Why would you want to be anything else?"

"I'm so arrogant, so conceited. Look at me. Women who look like me shouldn't be stuck on a farm out in the middle of nowhere."

Lyssa laughed. "I guess you were never really happy here. I suppose I hoped you would be. I miss you, I miss this. Kennedy, I'm sorry that you aren't happy, but life isn't about material things. You should know that. You hurt your parents."

"And you saved them. You saved me, again. I don't deserve a friend like you."

She bumped shoulders with her. "Yes, you do. I will always save you. I love you."

"So, tell me about Buck."

"There isn't anything to tell. His name isn't Buck, it's Callen McCabe."

"Shit, not the Callen McCabe? I used to swoon over him. He's changed. I think that beard changed his looks, but he is so fucking hot. I can't believe he has been working on this ranch for eight years. Are you two serious?"

"I don't think so. You know me, I'm not going to get my hopes up. He's far too rich and far too experienced for me I think."

Kennedy laughed. "Don't sell yourself short. You're a remarkable woman, with your talented mind. So, what's holding you back? Because I would have done him many times over."

"You are such a slut," Lyssa said laughing. "I just don't feel it with him. He's been hurt deeply, which is why he's here. He's a player, and I just get the feeling he's playing me. Don't get me wrong, he is the perfect gentleman, too perfect. He plays this guilt card very well."

Laughing, she said, "Lys, you always did that. You always tore everything apart. People are just that, people."

"Says the girl who found herself at the mercy of a sick fucker."

"Yeah, I suppose I'm not the best one for giving advice. You do what is best for you, like you always have. I'm so glad you are my friend. How am I going to face my parents?"

"They know what's going on. Your father is not a stupid man."

"Did he really sell the ranch to Buck, I mean Callen?"

"It was the only way to stop Hugh."

Kennedy laughed. "I should have come to you. I should have known you could fix this. I was so embarrassed, so defeated." She looked at her hand. "This ring is fake. He made me do this." She took it off her finger and threw it into the field. "I feel so humiliated."

"Ken, we all make mistakes. Hell, even me." Leaning in, she said, "I let him touch me."

Kennedy busted out laughing. "How was it?"

"Fucking fantastic. I got lost in the feeling, but that's all it was, was a feeling. There weren't any lasting emotions once it was over. I thought there was, but he just walked away acting like he did a horrible thing. That's how I know he isn't serious. I can't give myself to a man who doesn't want me that way. I'm not a plaything. I want it all."

"Sweetie, he's a fool if he doesn't realize how special and precious you are."

"I know, right?" Lyssa laughed. "Well, we should head back. I'm sure your parents want to talk to you."

"Will you stay?"

She shook her head. "No, you need to do this on your own. Let them help you. Let them help you heal. Stop fighting with yourself and be you. Be the girl I once knew. She's pretty wonderful, you know?"

"Thank you, Lys, for helping me. For getting me out of this mess."

"I love you. Call me when you've come full circle. I don't have a job, so I'll be around."

They got up and climbed on their horses. "Are you going to tell him how you feel?"

Smiling, she said, "I don't know how I feel. Besides, you know I'm not about to give him anything he doesn't deserve. He isn't ready for me. His ghosts still hold him down." She shrugged her shoulders. "I think we were thrown together because of you and this mess. It's the only reason I would have been out here. When we get back, can you take care of the horses? I'm just going to go. I've got some stuff to think about."

"You sure?"

"Yeah, I'll come by tomorrow."

They rode hard through the field. When they came around the house, no one was around. Lyssa got off her horse and got in her car and left.

∾

Callen and the guys were in the house with Charles when Kennedy came in. Callen just looked at her, waiting for Lyssa to walk in behind her. She looked at him. "She's gone."

He looked at his friends. Stu said, "Go, we'll be fine."

Then he looked at Charles. "They can take my truck. Go, tell her how you feel."

Kennedy looked at him. "She is my only friend. Don't you dare play her."

"I'm in love with her," he said standing up.

"She doesn't believe that," she said to him.

"I know, but she will. Did she say where she was going?"

She shook her head. Callen shook hands with Charles. "We'll take care of the ranch on Monday."

Charles laughed. "Go, it's fine."

With that, Callen left, his heart slamming in his chest. She was running from him. He felt it this morning at her house. He made a mistake, and he was going to do everything in his power to fix it. She was who he wanted. He wanted her for the rest of his life. As he drove down the gravel road, he saw her car parked at her old house. Pulling in, he turned off the truck and got out. His hands were shaking. Knocking on the door, he waited patiently. When she didn't answer, he walked around to the back. There was a key under the mat. As he turned the corner, he saw her standing in the field. He wanted to go to her, but he didn't. He just leaned against the house and looked at her.

He knew in his heart that he loved this woman. She was beyond incredible. Her hand moved to her face, and he watched as she wiped her cheek. His heart lurched, but he didn't move. She turned around and headed toward him, not looking up. When she was about ten feet from him, she looked up and stopped moving. They just looked at each other.

"What's going on in that beautiful head of yours?" His voice was soft.

"I'm not sure this is the best idea."

"Stu told me about your conversation."

"I figured he would."

"I can't, nor would I ever tell you how to feel. How to think. Lyssa, I'm not broken. Not anymore. I'm in love with you." He watched her face, but she gave no indication at all to her feelings. "Meeting you, getting to know you, has changed me. I want you; I want this life with you. I'm not going back. That's not who I am anymore."

She smiled a small smile. "No, now you're a player. Callen, how could you possibly change in a week? How could you possibly go from a different woman every other night to just one? To me? I am nothing like that blonde bombshell on your lap the other night. I'm not aggressive. I'm not experienced. I'm not anything."

"I have been trying to forget, trying not to feel humiliated, trying not to let a woman in. Acting and doing the things I've been doing has left me void, left me with the same problem I started with. Do I like who I have become? No. You, you filled that void. You, knowing you, fighting with you has made me realize that I'm worth something. That I matter again. Doing this with you has made me realize that I don't have to live this life alone."

"I can't be the reason you change. I don't want to be anyone's reason. It's only going to come back at me. I'm the one who is going to lose in all of this. I'm going to lose myself. This morning, I wanted you to make love to me. But you so coldly walked away. You got up and did what you did in my shower. I can't... no, I won't give myself to you and have you treat me so disrespectfully. You changed me this morning. I suppose, in a way, it made me hyper-aware of what was going on. But I don't want to live like that. I don't want to make the mistake of giving my entire self over to you and then you crush me. I would rather be alone. Stay alone, live my life alone. Look at you, look what it did to you. Look what it did to Kennedy. It's not what I want." She moved to walk past him.

"Lyssa, I'm in love with you," he whispered. His heart was racing; he didn't want her to leave.

"I don't believe you. You're just realizing you have the capacity to love again. It feels like I'm just your first steppingstone. Goodbye, Callen, and thank you, for everything you did to help the Greenvales."

She dropped her head as she walked away from him, tears falling, and she didn't know why. He couldn't love her, he just couldn't. He was just the best-looking man who ever showed any interest in her. Her chest hurt; her whole body ached.

Callen stood there watching her walk away, watching her leave him. He couldn't do it. He was going to fight for her. Not again, not again would this happen to him. He knew what he had in her. His feet were moving, and he grabbed her up in his arms.

"No, no, beautiful. I'm not going to let you do this. I love you. I'm going to fight for you."

He nearly fell over when her arms wrapped around his neck and she burst into sobs, burying her face in his neck. "Why?" she managed to get out. "Why, Callen?"

"Because I can't breathe when I'm not with you. I can't think of anything but you. I love you, beautiful. I love you."

She nodded in his neck. "I think I love you."

"Then why would you walk away?" He set her down.

"Because I'm afraid you are going to leave me. I don't want to feel the pain. I want a happy life."

"Do you feel pain now?" She nodded. "Then don't leave. Stay, stay with me." His hands wiped her tears as she nodded. "Let me love you. Let me love you."

He pressed his lips against hers, and his heart flipped when she kissed him back. "Come on," he whispered, taking her hand. He led her to the back porch. Pulling the key from its hiding place and unlocked the door. Together they went in. Standing in the kitchen, he said, "This is my house until Monday. Share it with me."

She smiled a little smile. He led her through it and up the stairs. Walking her to her old room, he kissed her. "Can I love you now? Can I show you how much I want to be here with you? I'm not afraid anymore. I'm sure of what I want." He whispered, "I want you."

CHAPTER SEVEN

Swallowing hard, Lyssa looked at him, looked into his eyes. He knew what she was doing. She was making sure, and he was all right with that. His hands moved to her waist, fingers slipping under her shirt. Slowly, he moved them up, and as he moved over her breasts, her arms raised in the air. Callen kept going up, making sure to touch every part of her skin. She kept her arms in the air as he dropped her shirt onto the floor.

Their eyes locked onto one another's. He stood there as she brought her hands down to his waist, repeating his exact moves, only she couldn't reach the top of his arms. With a small smile, he pulled it off the rest of the way, dropping it onto the floor on top of hers.

When he saw her hands move behind her, he shook his head. She replied with a small smile, dropping her hands. Her breath hitched when his fingers trailed down her stomach to her jeans. Once he had them unbuttoned and unzipped, his hands moved along the waistband to her ass. She sucked in a breath when he pushed them into her jeans and continued down, dropping to his knees to remove them.

His hands touched her legs all the way up to the bottom of her ass. His eyes shifted from hers to look at her core. She was wearing white lace panties, and he could see everything. He inhaled deeply, catching her scent, his eyes closing, his body standing.

Dropping his hands to his side, hers moved slowly, copying his moves. On her knees in front of him, her head level with his cock, she leaned her head in and ran her nose the length of him as she stood up, dragging her tongue along his abs.

When she was standing, he turned her slowly, moving her hair over her shoulder. He unclasped her bra, slowly sliding it down her arms to join the pile of clothes on the floor. Leaning in, his mouth captured the skin on her neck just behind her ear. He could see her nipples harden.

His hands moved down her sides to her panties. When she turned her head to look at him, he kissed her. Pulling away, he moved back down her body, taking her panties with him, his mouth kissing her ass as she stepped out of them. Bringing his hands up to her hips, he pulled her into his mouth, kissing her where her thigh met her ass. Opening his mouth, he sank his teeth into her, not biting her, but letting her know how he felt about it.

Her hair brushed along his face as her head fell back and a moan came out of her. Slowly, he stood, his hands on her hips, his fingers just touching her hairline. She turned to him, her eyes boring into his. She could see his desire. She could feel his love. Her hands moved to his hips, turning him around, and she repeated his actions, biting him in the same spot. She didn't know what to do or how to do it.

When Callen turned, they stood face to face for the longest time just looking into each other's eyes.

"Do you trust me, beautiful?" he whispered against her lips.

"Do you trust me?"

He smiled. "Yes."

"Yes, Callen, I trust you."

Slowly, his arms wrapped around her and he kissed her deeply. When their bodies came together, nothing else mattered to him. Nothing but this beautiful, incredible woman in his arms. Picking her up, he climbed onto the bed. Once she was laying down, he pulled back, coming to rest on his heels. His eyes left hers and traveled down her body. She was perfect. When he reached her core, his mind went blank, and her legs parted slightly to accommodate his knee.

Moving his hands slowly up her thighs, his fingertips softly touching her hair, he watched her back arch. "Incredible," he moaned. Bending down, he kissed her stomach, wrapping his arm around her waist. He lifted her onto his thighs, covering her mouth with his.

His hands moved all over her, down her back to cup her ass, trailing his fingertips along her core. He could feel every part of her, her swollen bud so prominent. "Lyssa, so much. So much I want with you. All of it, for always."

With her wet, swollen lips, her eyes moved down his body. He watched her, knowing she had never seen a man before. He felt her slide off his legs, and he didn't want to let her go, but he did. Her fingers touched him, her eyes taking him in. He had some precum on his head, and she reached up with her fingers and touched it. She sat there looking at it on her finger, then picking her head up, she had a smile on her face as she put her finger in her mouth.

Callen smiled at the face she made, then she did it again. It was when she shifted her body to get on her knees that he really freaked out. He knew if she put her mouth on him he was going to explode. But this is what lovers do.

When he felt her tongue roll across his crown, he growled and closed his eyes. He wanted to stop her, but he didn't. He needed to trust and so did she. For what seemed like an hour, she licked and sucked him. Her fingers touched his balls, and it took everything he had to talk himself down. When she finished her exploration of him, she got up on her knees, her fingers touching his lips.

Callen opened his eyes. "So beautiful," he said as his hands cradled her head. Kissing her, he laid her back down and traveled down her body to her core. He made sure his mouth, his fingers, touched every single part of her. Looking up at her for any sign of hesitation, the only thing he saw was her sexy blue eyes filled with trust. Looking at her core, his mouth watered. Slowly lowering his head, he gently blew on her.

"Ohh," she whispered.

He watched the goose flesh appear on her skin. Slowly, he made contact with her, his first taste of pure heaven. She was exquisite. Her back arched as his lips closed around her sweet swollen bud.

"Oh, God," she moaned. He felt her body contract and then pulse. Pulling back, he watched her stomach tighten with each pulse. God, he loved this woman. Looking at her, she was heaven. His body moved up hers, his head pressing into her. He stopped, pulling himself onto her stomach, his mouth covering hers, and he released. Pulling her to him, so lovingly, they shared their first deep release.

Lyssa had no idea what was happening to her, to her body. Her stomach hurt from pulsing. "Callen," she moaned into his mouth as he held her close.

When they calmed down, with his hand on her face, he looked at her. "I didn't want to run away."

She smiled. "Thank you."

"I'm afraid I made a mess."

"It felt very warm, and there's a lot of it."

He laughed. "Yes, there is. You all right?"

She nodded. "Why didn't you?"

"It would have been over before we started."

"You do know I have no idea what that means?"

He smiled, his thumb pulling her bottom lip. Leaning in, he kissed her. "I know, but you will."

"Let me get a washcloth and clean you up."

She nodded and laid on her back, looking at her stomach. He moved off the bed to the bathroom, and when he came back, he stopped short at the sight of her lying on the bed. She was touching his release, almost like she was finger painting herself. It was when she picked her fingers up and brought them to her mouth that his heart flipped, and he felt himself getting hard again.

He watched as she slowly touched her tongue with her fingers, her head falling back on the pillow as she licked them clean. He could hear her little mews, his smile getting bigger. He gently wiped her clean, dropping the cloth on the rug and laying down, pulling her into his arms.

"Mmm, Callen, you taste wonderful," she whispered on his lips, kissing him.

"So do you, beautiful."

His hands moved, touching every part of her, finally coming to rest on her ass. His long fingers brushing the hair on her core, with each pass, he felt her shiver. With each pass, her kiss grew deeper, harder, her mews making his heart race, his cock hard as a rock.

Rolling her onto her back, pulling from their kiss, he looked into her sexy blue eyes. "Lyssa, I want to make love to you. I want all of you."

She smiled. "I'm scared, Callen."

"I know, and we aren't going to do it yet, but I want you to know. You are who I want. You are who I love."

She smiled, touching his lips. "I love you."

They spent the afternoon touching, loving, and experiencing one another. After another round of orgasms, they lay in one other's arms. They could hear the music from across the fields. Lyssa's stomach growled, and they started laughing.

"There isn't any food here. Do you want to get dressed and go over to the barbeque?"

She giggled. "Everyone will know what we were doing."

Laughing, he agreed. "Yes, they will. I'm okay with that."

She rolled over onto her stomach, propping herself up on her elbows. "You are? I'm not a prize."

"Hey, you are the greatest prize my heart could have ever won. And I'm not done winning yours. Not for a long time. Every day, I will win a little more of it. You are the greatest prize, and I am so honored to be the one who you give your heart to."

She smiled a whole-mouth, whole-face smile. "Yeah?"

"Oh, hell yeah." He leaned in to kiss her. "Come on, beautiful, let's go have some fun and get some food."

She nodded and pushed up on her knees as he sat up. She heard him hiss, and turning her head, found him staring at her. Smiling, he shook his head and they got up.

"You did a beautiful job restoring this house. Charles gave it to me."

"I know and thank you. I needed something to do with myself. I enjoyed it. I learned a lot. I didn't know at the time that it was your house."

She giggled. "How could you have known?"

"Are you going to live here?"

"I don't know, it's your house now," she smarted. "I guess I'll have to wait until you ask me to move in with you."

Grabbing her around the waist, he pulled her against his chest, kissing her shoulder. "It never was, nor will it ever be my house. This is Charles' ranch, not mine. This is your home, not mine." He drew the skin on her neck into his mouth. "And I'm going to make love to you on every surface in it."

Her head fell back on his chest. "Promise," she whispered as his hands came up to cup her breasts, gently pinching her nipples.

"I promise," he moaned into her mouth, kissing her. They stood like this for a few minutes, enjoying one another. "Let me feed you." His hands left her breasts, and he kissed her neck and shoulder. They continued to get dressed, and together they went over to the barbeque.

CHAPTER EIGHT

When they walked up to the ranch house, people were everywhere. Stu, Mitchell, Slade, and Tom were sitting at a table with Kennedy, laughing. Charles saw them walking up holding hands when he approached them.

"I see you two worked things out?"

Lyssa blushed. "I guess we did. But, somehow, I think you knew that would happen."

Charles laughed, pulling her in for a hug. "Sweetheart, I know love when I see it. He's a good man. A good man for you."

She smiled. "Thank you, Charles."

Kennedy saw them and came running over, grabbing Lyssa in her arms. "Come and tell me all about it." She pulled her away. Lyssa turned to look at Callen who just laughed and nodded to her. Kennedy pulled her to the fence in the back. "So..."

Lyssa laughed. "There isn't anything to tell."

"Bullshit, you've been gone for hours. Did you do it yet? Was he kind to you? God, he's so dreamy."

"Hey, how are you? You seem so okay with everything that has happened to you."

"To be honest with you, Lys, I'm good. I knew the wedding was just a farce. I mean, he did hurt me physically, but most of the time, it was fine. I know I sound shallow, but he gave me lots of things."

"Kennedy, I don't understand how you just, basically, sell yourself like that. I know you. You aren't this superficial."

"I was blessed with this body and these looks, and well, men want to use it, so they are going to pay for it now. You know that men have been using me for years."

"Yes, but you don't have to do that."

She smiled. "Lys, wait until you have sex. You're going to want it all the time. I can see it in your eyes that he has sparked something in you. Now, forget about me. I'll bounce back. I guess, now I don't have a place to live, maybe I'll stick around here for a while until all this mess dies down. So, tell me, did you do it?"

"No, we didn't do it yet, and yes, he is always kind to me. And I will have to agree with you; he is very dreamy."

"What do you mean, you haven't done it yet? I would have been all over him." She turned to look at Callen. "How the hell do you keep your hands off a man that looks like that?"

Lyssa busted out laughing as she felt her face flush. "Ken, I don't have a fucking clue what to do. Today was the first time he's really touched me." Her voice softened. "I tasted his cum. I think I like it."

Kennedy turned to her. "You gave him a blow job? Sweetie, that's huge."

She shook her head. "Not a blow job, I just kind of licked him and tasted him. No blow job, and why do they call it a blow job? You don't blow on it. And, yes, it's huge. I'm not even sure how it will fit in my mouth, let alone, well, you know, down there."

"Aww, Lys, you are so innocent. I don't know why they call it a blow job, but once you start pushing your head down on him, your throat will open up. At first, it'll feel weird. I remember the first time I took a guy all the way down. I was freaking out that I would choke, but just breathe through your nose. It's fantastic once you figure it out, and trust me, you can get a guy to do anything you want once you do it right."

"Ken, I don't want anything from him, except for him. I'm not sure I'm cut out for this sex thing."

"Lys, have you had a real orgasm yet?"

She blushed. "Yes, today actually, when he... Well, yes."

Kennedy smiled at her, touching her face in a loving way. "He put his mouth on you down there?"

Lyssa nodded. "I didn't think I would like it, but he was so gentle. It was unbelievable. My whole body felt like it was floating. My stomach hurt afterward."

"I'm so happy for you. It only took nearly twenty-nine years for you to do this. He loves you. I can see it in his eyes. He will be careful with you. I'm so happy for you, Lys. So happy. Jealous as hell, but happy."

Lyssa laughed as they hugged. "Ken, how does it feel when you lose your virginity?"

She smiled at her. "I'm not going to lie to you, it hurts, but only for a few minutes. Oh, and make sure you have a towel or something because there is going to be blood. My first time was brutal. The guy I was with didn't take his time, and he hurt me."

"I remember, I think that's part of the reason I never wanted to do it."

"I know, but Callen loves you. He will be careful with you, and if he's not, you better tell me because I am so going to kick his ass."

"One more thing," Lyssa said. "What about protection? Birth control or condoms?"

"No condoms, not your first time. I have an implant in my arm. Here, feel this." She took her hand and pressed it on her upper arm. "It's birth control. It lasts for five years."

Lyssa stood there. "Did it hurt?"

"No, it's like a shot, and it takes about a week before it starts working. Then, after you know it's working, you can have sex. You don't need an exam. Your doctor should be able to do it right there in the office. So, before you have sex, get this. Then you don't have to worry about getting pregnant."

Lyssa stood there looking at her, then turned to the field. "What if I want to get pregnant?" she said softly.

"You can just have the doctor take it out."

"So, it's not going to hurt me or hurt my chances of having a baby?"

"Lys, what's wrong?"

She felt the tears fall on her cheeks. Whispering, she said, "I'm in love with him, and I don't even know if he wants kids. Ken, I want kids, lots of them. I hated being the only child, so did you. What if he doesn't want them? I can't live without having children."

Kennedy pulled her into a hug.

Callen had been watching them and realized Lyssa was crying. With his heart slamming in his chest, he headed toward them. He was nearly there when she looked at him. He could see the distress in her eyes. *What the hell happened?* He moved a bit quicker.

"What's the matter?" he said softly as they pulled from their embrace.

Kennedy smiled at him. Grabbing Lyssa's hands, she squeezed them and said, "Tell him."

Lyssa nodded, and Kennedy walked away.

Callen moved closer to her. "Beautiful?"

Taking a deep breath, she let the words tumble out of her mouth. "I know we don't know that much about each other, but there are some things I want in my life, and I am falling in love with... hell, I am in love with you." He smiled. "Callen, I want children, lots of them."

His hands moved to her face, his mouth covering hers, his kiss deep and firm. "Yes, yes. Lots of them. As many as we can take care of. Yes, beautiful, I want children. I want them with you."

"Really?"

He laughed, pulling her into his chest. "God, yes. I thought my time was up. I'm going to be thirty-five. I didn't think I was going to find you in time. Yes." They held each other for a few minutes. "Come on, let's get something to eat."

Together, they headed back to the party where they ate, drank, and just were.

Kennedy and Lyssa danced the evening away. The guys sat and watched them. Callen was amazed at the way she moved, so much so that he stood up.

Stu shouted at him, "Watch out! He's going to burn the place down!" Laughing, Callen stepped on the dance floor, while Kennedy stepped off to watch the two of them.

He stood there for a minute to let himself absorb the music. It had been a very long time since he danced or wanted to dance. But this woman was pulling him back into the world, and he wanted to dance with her. Slowly, he opened his eyes to see her looking at him with curiosity in her eyes. Then he smiled and grabbed her, pulling her hard against his body, and started moving. She was laughing, he was laughing, and the people were cheering. Kennedy was screaming as they moved across the floor.

He felt alive, truly alive for the first time in his life. Free. With her hair flying around, her body moving against his, there was nothing better in this life than this.

They moved together like they had been doing it their whole lives. Not one time did either of them make a mistake. The music slowed down, and Callen pulled her to him, his mouth covering hers, their bodies swaying to the music while they kissed. When he pulled back, he watched as her eyes opened. Whispering on her lips, he said, "I love you." Then the crowd erupted.

Her face was already flushed from dancing, but her smile lit the place up. She laid her head on his chest, and he wrapped her in his cocoon and they slow danced. He didn't want to stop, but he knew she had to be thirsty, so he guided her off the dance floor and back to the table.

Stu was talking up a very pretty, young lady, whose attention was immediately directed to Callen when they sat down. "Wow, you sure can dance. Care to take a spin with me?"

Callen smiled at her. "No thank you. My dance card is full." He smiled at Lyssa.

"Susie, have you met Callen? Callen, this is Suzie. I'm surprised you haven't met yet." She was being a bitch. She knew she was going to run across women he had slept with. Even being unsure if Suzie was one of them, she didn't like the way she was undressing him.

His hold on her hand tightened. "Nice to meet you, Suzie." He sat down, pulling Lyssa down on his thigh and wrapping his arm around her.

Kennedy laughed and said to Suzie, "I already tried. His heart belongs to Lyssa."

"Hey, you can't blame me for trying. Excuse me." She got up and walked away.

Callen looked at Stu. "Sorry about that."

Stu laughed. "Hey, I'm used to it. Whenever you're around, we never get the girl."

Callen was drinking his beer when he laughed, and it came out of his nose, which sent everyone into roaring laughter. "That is so not true," he said, coughing.

Lyssa was laughing so hard. "Well, he's taken now, so your odds should improve immensely."

Callen pulled her to him, looking into her eyes. "You're fucking right I am, so you don't ever have to worry about that. You're it for me."

She managed to straddle him, her hands on his face. "Is that right?" she whispered.

"So fucking right." He leaned in and kissed her. Grabbing her hair, he pulled her head back to expose her neck to him, planting a full mouth kiss in the center of her neck. Mitchell cleared his throat, and Callen chuckled, letting go of her hair.

"Now, now children. Enough is enough," Mitchell said.

Laughing, she rearranged herself, a shy smile on her face as she looked up to see Kennedy with her bottom lip pulled into her mouth. Lyssa knew that look and busted out laughing at her. She was sitting next to Mitchell, who was just as good looking as Callen.

The night continued, and Mitchell and Kennedy spent a bit more time than most huddled together. Callen wasn't going to worry about that. Lyssa visited with nearly everyone there. Callen just enjoyed watching it all happen. He couldn't help but notice more than a few women checking him and his friends out. Chuckling, he got up and walked over to Lyssa, wrapping his arm around her. He didn't need this shit anymore, but he knew he was going to pay for his past transgressions with the women of this town, this county. They stayed until long after everyone left, the ten of them sitting around a table laughing and talking. Everyone relaxed.

Charles said to Lyssa, "I'm just wondering how you know F.B.I. agents."

She laughed. "Kennedy and I went to school with Jefferson, and we kept in touch. When this first started, I called him and we had a long talk about it. Apparently, Hugh and Brody have been under the watchful eye of the agency. Me giving them what I had uncovered gave them enough to get an indictment."

"Well, let me say this," Stu said. "You surprised the hell out of us. How did you know he was hurting Kennedy?"

"We've been riding horses since we could walk. Kennedy was the one who egged me on to jump that fence in the first place, so for her not to jump it, I knew something wasn't right. Then, when she got down, I saw her face grimace. So yeah, two and two make four." Her eyes were on Kennedy. "She's been my best friend since I was seven and allowed to wander around by myself. Hell, we were college roommates."

Slade just sat there looking at her, watching her. Callen was watching Slade. "What are you thinking, old friend?" he asked Slade.

He shook his head. "Nothing."

Callen laughed. "We've been friends for a long time. I know that look."

Slade smiled. "Lyssa, can I ask you a question?"

She smiled at him. "Yes."

"How long have you been able to gauge people like this? Feel them?"

She shrugged her shoulders. "I'm not sure, probably my whole life. I always knew when my dad was going to yell at my mom, so I would leave."

Callen chuckled. "Slade? What's going on in your head?"

"Well, Lyssa, would you consider moving to Chicago?" he said softly.

She sat there looking at him for a long time. No one said a word. The tension was so thick you could have cut it with a knife. A million things ran through her head, and she felt Callen tense up sitting next to her. Her eyes moved to Kennedy, who looked at her with want in her eyes. Mitchell had a very tight smile on his lips. Her heart broke. *Did he lie to her?* He told her he didn't want to go back there. She didn't say a word when she stood up. Callen's hand moved to her leg, wrapping around it. He was hanging on to her.

Reaching down, she removed his hand from her leg and moved away from him, her eyes on Kennedy. Her eyes always betrayed her, and she could see that this was a planned moment. They waited for her to relax; they planned this. Her eyes moved to Callen. *Did he know?* Without saying a word, she turned and walked away.

Callen stood up. "Fuck," he said, going after her.

She was moving fast toward the field. Kennedy got up. "Now was not the time for that," she said to Slade.

"Why? It was as good of a time as any."

"No, it wasn't. You just don't get her, do you? She is special." Turning, she took off running in Lyssa's direction. But Lyssa was gone, and Callen just stood there in the field looking for her.

"What the fuck was that about?" he asked Kennedy.

"I just want the best for her. She has such a gift. She could be a great asset to your company."

Callen looked at her. "I don't have a company. I don't want a company. I want this life here with her. She doesn't want that life."

Kennedy laughed. "She knows you want to go back, that in your heart you do. She knows she will never be enough for you. She's not stupid. Why do you think she hasn't slept with you yet? She doesn't want to get hurt when you leave here."

"Are you that fucking self-centered that you just don't see anything but yourself. That is not the life she wants. If I wanted to go back, I would have years ago." He walked away. Going to his truck, he headed over to her house. Pulling up, he saw her standing in the backyard.

Running out there, she spun around. "Is that what you want?"

He could see the tears in her eyes. "If I wanted that life, I would have gone back a long time ago. No, beautiful, it's not."

She didn't say anything, just stood there looking at him. "My sense is that deep inside, you miss it."

"I won't lie to you. Today was a fucking rush, but it wouldn't have been if you hadn't been there, if you hadn't been in control. Do I think we would or could make a fantastic team and make billions? Yes, I do. But, and beautiful, there is a but, I don't want that life. I don't want to be consumed with our next killing. I want to spend my days with you. I want to love you, marry you and raise lots of fat babies with you."

Her breath hitched in her chest; she felt like she was going to pass out. "You want to marry me?" she whispered.

He smiled, taking a step toward her. "One day, yes," he whispered. "I don't want that other life back. I want this one with you."

"What would you say if I said yes, let's go to Chicago?"

He smiled, taking another step toward her. "I'd say no."

"Why?" she whispered as he moved closer to her.

"Because," his hand moved up to touch her jaw, "I don't want to leave the place I found my heart."

"Uh…"

"I don't want to ever leave the place that I first tasted the meaning of love, the first place I tasted you." He moved up to her, his mouth inches from hers. "I want to live here with you, in the house that I made love to you for the first time, and every time after for the rest of my life." She tugged her lip between her teeth as his thumb caressed her jaw. "Don't you dare think about leaving me, Lyssa Dawn. I won't let you go." His lips touched hers. "I love you, beautiful." Covering her mouth, his hand moved to the back of her head.

Lyssa's hands moved up his chest, balling his shirt in her hands as she pulled him to her. Callen picked her up, wrapping her legs around him, her hair cascading around them like a halo of golden beauty. Her lust took control of her, and she devoured his mouth, biting his lip. He couldn't move; he didn't want to move. The moment was perfect. He never thought he would ever feel like this. Nothing in the world could or would ever compare to how he felt.

She slowly released her legs, sliding down his body, and his hands moved up to her face, pulling her away from his mouth. Without a word being said, they moved together to the house. Once inside, their boots came off, their bodies moving without notice to either of them. They slowly undressed each other, Callen picking her up and laying her on the bed to look at her.

"You are so beautiful, and I am so honored to have you love me," he moaned before he touched her. He took his time with his mouth on her body. He didn't move to her core, only brushed along it a few times with his fingers. "Roll over, beautiful."

She smiled a small smile, terrified at what he was going to do, but needing to trust him. She slowly rolled over, his leg between hers. He started at her shoulders, his fingers touching her, his mouth following the path down her spine. He covered every inch of her to her perfect ass. Her hips moved slightly up and down as she felt his touch, as she felt him love her.

The first kiss, his first taste of the soft skin of her ass made him moan. Nipping the flesh between his teeth, he gently sucked at it and kissing her. He made a long, slow meal of her. Her mews made his cock twitch as he got comfortable, laying on his side, slipping his hand between her legs. Laying it flat on her stomach, he lifted her up a bit, holding her in the air to smell her scent. "So beautiful," he moaned as his lips kissed her, his tongue trailing along her exposed crack.

"Ahh," she whimpered as tension coiled in her belly. Her hips pressed into his arm, and he felt her body tense.

"That's it, beautiful," he whispered, the heat from his breath on her. "Feel me love you."

Her ass raised a bit more, and he slowly rolled her over, his mouth at her core. His hands and fingers began their exploration of her. The fluff of hair was so soft it felt like angel's breath on his fingers. She was pure and so vulnerable. So perfect he was sure he was going to lose his mind.

He touched every part of her, feeling every sensation she was. Her body twitched as his fingers brushed her swollen bud. Taking his time, he could feel her release building on his fingertips, his tongue barely touching her lips, trailing sensations along her.

Flattening his tongue, he ran it from bottom to top, wrapping it around her bud. She cried out, her back lifting off the bed. Callen pushed up, lifting her onto his thighs, her body limp as her arms wrapped around his neck, her mouth coming down on his, her core on his lower chest. She slowly moved down his body.

He felt his head slip inside of her, his hands stopping her from moving as he kissed her. Her hands touched his face and his tongue as they kissed. He slowly let her move down, surrounding his head. Deeper and deeper, he moved inside of her until he felt her. Stopping her, knowing how big he was, he was only a quarter of the way inside of her.

"Lyssa," he hissed.

Her eyes told him all he needed to know. Wrapping his arms around her, she pushed down as he pushed up, tearing through her innocence. She didn't scream out; her mouth came down on his as he slid all the way inside her. Neither of them moved, they just held each other and kissed.

Pushing up on his knees, he laid her down, putting his weight on his elbows, his hands on her face, and her legs wrapped around him. They laid there looking at each other, not moving. She smiled. "I love you," she whispered.

Callen kissed her hard and began the greatest moment of his life—making love to the woman he chose, to the woman who chose him. He had never felt a woman like he felt this one. Her body conformed to him, his body being the only body she would ever know. This woman would be his wife. This woman loving him would be the mother of his children. This woman in his arms was now and forever his life.

He felt her come time and time again, but he bit his mouth to stop himself from releasing. He never wanted this moment to end. He would make love to her as long as his body would allow, his thrusts slow and long. His hips flicked when he reached her end. Her mews, her cries, her lips, the way her perfect breasts bounced when he flicked his hips, all of it drove him to hold out, drove him to make her feel his heart. To make her feel that she was his in every way, and he would not only love her until the end of his life, but even after his life was over. She was all of life for him.

He felt her tighten against him. "Callen..." Her voice was deep and hazy from their lovemaking, her back arched as she gripped him like nothing he had ever experienced.

His eyes locked on hers, his lip pulled between his teeth as he let it all go. It was the most intense orgasm he ever had. So much so that he bit through the skin on his lip. The blood dripped on her neck as the last pulse left him. He felt her tears, his hand touching her face. "I love you," he whispered. "I love you."

Her fingers wiped the blood from his lip. She lifted her body up, his arm wrapping around her back to hold her there as her mouth covered his. Gently, he rolled them over, still buried inside of her. He knew there would be blood, and he knew she was going to be sore. He made love to her for a very long time.

She laid her head on his chest, his arms wrapped around her. "So, you're staying?" she whispered, and he felt her smile.

He laughed. "For the rest of my life. Why? Did you want to move to Chicago?"

She laughed. "Not in a million years. Callen?" she whispered.

"Yeah, beautiful."

"I'm so tired."

"Sleep, baby, I got you."

"Mmm," she moaned. "Okay."

CHAPTER NINE

He laid with her in his arms, his fingers moving so softly and slowly up and down her back, closing his eyes. *God, how did I get so fucking lucky?* Slowly, his hand came to rest on her ass, as he fell into sleep holding her.

"Callen," she whispered.

His eyes closed, he smiled. "Yeah, beautiful?"

"I have to go to the bathroom."

Smiling, he helped her sit up. "Let me carry you like this." He moved his legs, so he was sitting on the side of the bed, with her on his lap. She wrapped her arms around his neck as he grabbed her thighs, then standing, he walked her into the bathroom and stepped into the shower. Leaning her against the tile, his hands reached up to touch her face. "There is going to be blood."

"I know, it's all right."

He smiled, kissing her as he lifted her off him. Setting her down, he looked at his cock. Her innocence was all over him. "Thank you, beautiful, for the gift of you." His voice was soft. His lips kissed hers.

Her smile was shy, as she moved around him to turn on the water and a mixture of him and blood ran down her leg. When the water hit her body, Callen watched as the pink water moved toward the drain.

His heart lurched, his eyes moving to hers to see she was watching him. Shaking his head, he smiled. "So beautiful. For the rest of my life, I will love you." His mouth crashed down on hers, the kiss long and intense. He felt so privileged, so honored.

Giggling when they separated, she washed and got out, drying off, then she used the bathroom. She flushed just as he got out. He didn't want to make her feel uncomfortable. Grabbing a towel, he dried himself off while she walked into the bedroom. His eyes never left her perfect ass. With a smile on his face, he quickly toweled himself off and followed her. She was on her stomach with her leg pulled up a bit.

Crawling on the bed behind her, he cocooned her. Giggling, Lyssa rolled over into his arms. "It was so wonderful," she whispered.

Chuckling, he whispered, "I couldn't agree with you more."

"Can we do it again?"

"Aww, beautiful, all day long." His hand moved to her hair. "Are you sore?"

She was laughing. "So sore. We have to get up soon and help take down the backyard."

"Do you want to go into town and grab some breakfast?"

"Mmm, yes, but I'd rather stay here like this."

"I agree," he whispered as he kissed her.

"Callen?"

"Yeah beautiful," he whispered on her lips.

"What happens now?"

Her body tensed a little. He pulled back to look at her. "What do you mean?"

"Was this... Is this..." She was finding it difficult to say what she wanted to say.

He touched her face. "That was me loving you. This is and always will be me loving you. I will never get enough of you."

She nodded. "We didn't use protection."

"I don't care, do you?"

"No, I suppose I don't. I want to be with you."

He smiled. "I want to marry you."

"Yeah?"

"Beautiful, you found my heart. You found me."

"I want to love you, Callen. Can you love only me?"

His smile stretched across his face. "I do love only you. There will never be a day in your life that you won't feel that love."

"What if I get pregnant from this?"

Still, he smiled. "Then we will have a baby. My life began a week ago. You woke me up that day you beat the shit out of me for hurting you. When I saw you, when you looked into my eyes, my heart woke up. It pissed me off and scared the shit out of me all at the same time. When I kissed you that day in the barn, I knew then that I loved you. But I had been an asshole for so long, it took a bit to get my head on straight. Last night when we made love," she nodded, "that was me sharing that love with you. I wouldn't have done that if I wasn't ready for you. If I wasn't ready for this life we are about to live together. If it wasn't insane, I would ask you right now to marry me."

She smiled. "It's not insane," she whispered.

His kiss was deep and long. "Oh, God, Lyssa, marry me." His mouth covered hers, their bodies melding together. He wanted to make love to her, to feel her.

Pulling her leg over his thigh, he gently rolled them over, slowly pushing into her. "I love you, beautiful," he moaned into her mouth as he filled her. "So beautiful." He was slow because he knew she was sore. Her nearly silent mews drove him insane. His mouth found her nipple, and it was all over for them both.

He felt her nails dig into his arms as she gripped him and pulsed around him. He felt her warmth encase him, and he let it go, his mouth finding hers. For what seemed like hours, they shared their mouths, their touches.

When they finished, the sun was up. "Come on, beautiful, let's get you cleaned up."

"Will there be blood again?"

He smiled at her, touching her face. "To be honest with you, I've never made love to a woman who was a virgin."

"Really?"

Chuckling, he told her, "Really, but from what I know, there could be, but shouldn't be. I think it's hit or miss. Do you want me to carry you to the shower again?" His lips brushed along her shoulder.

She giggled. "You can't carry me to the shower every time we make love."

"Why not?"

"Because that's just silly." She arched her back, and he moved, pulling out of her.

Looking down, he smiled. "No blood."

She rolled out of the bed, and he watched her all the way to the bathroom. He heard the water turn on. Laying back, he felt his life was complete. It wasn't long before she was finished in the shower. He got up and headed to the bathroom.

"I don't have any clean panties," she said.

"Neither do I. Don't wear any."

"You think?" she said as she dried off.

He turned on the water. "Yeah, let's go commando."

She was giggling as she walked into the bedroom. Looking at the bed, her smile was pinned to her face. She had made love for the first time, and the second. She couldn't help but wonder if he was that tender with other women. If he touched them like he touched her. His lips touched her shoulder, and she leaned into his chest.

"What's wrong?" he whispered.

"I was just wondering if you touched other women the way you touch me. If you were as tender with them."

He stepped around her, his hand tilting her face up to his. "What's this about?" He could see the turmoil in her eyes. He could feel the tightness of her body. "Lyssa, no. The answer to your question is no. I've never touched a woman the way I touch you. Not even *her*. I know now that I didn't love her, not completely."

"Is that how you love me?" Her voice was a bit shaky.

"Hey, come here." He pulled her into his arms. "I thought I knew what love was. I think I wanted what we had to be love. But it wasn't. What I feel for you is totally consuming me. The only way for you to believe me is for me to show you every day. Trust me."

137

"I do, Callen. I wouldn't have made love to you if I didn't. I think I feel you so deeply that I'm scared it's not real."

He picked her up, climbing on the bed with her, and made love to her again. As they came undone with each other, his mouth never left hers. They lay in each other's arms. "This is real, beautiful. What I feel for you is real. My past is just that, my past. It was just the road I needed to take to be here with you. I don't think I could love you so completely if I hadn't lived through what I did. I don't think you would be able to love me if you hadn't lived the life you lived. I don't believe that I've been here all this time, just hiding out. I've been here learning about the man I'm supposed to be, the man before you now, who can and will and does love you exactly the way you should be loved. I'm not going anywhere, beautiful."

The tears fell from her eyes. "I do love you. That's what this has to be. I can't breathe, thinking you don't want me forever."

"Don't think that way," he whispered. "I want you forever. Marry me, let me love you always."

"Yes, Callen, love me always."

They kissed for a while longer. Then Lyssa washed up and they headed over to the ranch. Getting out of the truck, Callen said, "You go in. I'm going to go get the guys."

She nodded and walked up to the house, where Charles was sitting on the porch. Callen waved and then left.

"Come and sit with me," he said to her. Smiling, Lyssa sat down. "I didn't get the chance to thank you for what you did to save this ranch."

"I was just doing my job. Besides, you and Emily were like my second set of parents. I grew up on this ranch."

He nodded. "I have something for you, and I don't want any arguments." He reached into his shirt and pulled out an envelope, handing it to her.

"Charles, you don't need to pay me. It's fine."

He chuckled. "It's just a little something for you."

She opened the envelope and gasped. "Charles..." Tears welled up in her eyes. "I can't." Inside the envelope was the deed to the land and to the house she grew up in.

"Yes, you can, and you will. That house belongs to you. Well, until tomorrow morning, it belongs to Callen, but that's just a technicality. It's yours. Now, take it and begin the life you've always wanted. That man loves you. He's been moping around here for eight years with a broken heart. You mended him. It's your new beginning. Take the money you have left over and start your own law office in town. I know lots of people who need a good lawyer. You, my dear, are a good lawyer."

She wiped her tears. "Thank you, Charles."

"It's the right thing to do. I know your momma and daddy weren't the greatest parents, but that was all they had, and it should and now does belong to you. Callen fixed it all up, so it can be the place you raise your children."

She sat there looking at him. "I'll take it under one condition."

He laughed. "No conditions. It's yours."

"Kennedy doesn't want this ranch. When it's time, will you sell it to Callen? He loves his job here."

"I planned on it. I've already spoken to Emily. He's been our first choice for a few years now. Kennedy will find her place in this world. She is my daughter, and I love her, but what she did here... Well, I'm going to have a hard time forgiving that."

"You're so sure of that." She smiled at him.

"That boy doesn't see anyone but you."

"I hope you're right."

He laughed. "Time, my dear. Time."

Just then, Kennedy came out of the house. "When did you get here?"

"A little bit ago. Did you just get up?"

Kennedy laughed. "Oh, no you don't. Let's go." She grabbed her hand and pulled her off the porch and out to the back fence. "Spill it. What the hell did you get so pissed off about last night?"

"Why did you set me up? Ken, you know I want nothing to do with the big city. I'm not you."

"Because you can't live your life in this small town. You are so smart, Lys, so smart. Jesus, you have a gift, and you should use it. Chicago is huge, and with Callen McCabe by your side, God, sweetie, think of the money you could make."

She shook her head. "No, I have money. I don't want to live in the city. I'm not you. If Callen wants to go back, he can do it without me. I'm staying right here."

"You know, sometimes you are so impossible. So, what did Callen tell you? Is he going back with the guys?" She just shook her head and walked away. "Come on, Lys, don't be mad." She just kept walking, then getting in her car, she drove away.

"Unbelievable. Well, if he wants to go, then let him." She was talking to herself. Before she realized it, she was parked in her parking spot at her apartment. "Screw this shit." She started her car and headed to the doctor's office.

Walking in, she smiled. "Would it be possible to see the doctor? I don't have an appointment."

The receptionist smiled at her. "We just had a cancellation, so have a seat and she'll call you when she's ready."

Lyssa stood there looking at her. "Seriously?"

She nodded. "It's a slow day. Not a lot of sick people."

Lyssa went and sat down, and a few minutes later, the doctor called her in. "Is everything all right, dear? You look a bit flustered. Upset."

"Oh, I am very upset, but that's not why I'm here. This is kind of embarrassing, but I had sex last night, and it was without protection, and I was wondering if there was any way you could tell me if I am pregnant?"

"Lyssa, you weren't raped, were you?"

"Oh, God no. I just want to get on birth control. I'm sort of in love with him, but I'm not sure how he feels exactly. I just don't want to get pregnant, because well, he's the kind of guy who would do the right thing. Even if it's not what he really wants."

The doctor sat there looking at her. "Lyssa, what is going on?"

She shook her head. "Nothing really. Is there some way to tell this soon?"

"Well, when was your last period?"

"A few weeks, maybe three. I'm actually due to get it this coming week."

"Then the chances are slim that you're pregnant, but I can do a blood test just to make sure. But, Lyssa, sperm can stay viable inside your body for up to five days."

"Is there any way to get it out?"

The doctor sat there looking at her. "No, there is not."

"What am I going to do?"

"Well, if you are due to get your period, then abstain until then and we can get you on birth control."

"Can I get one of those implants? My friend has one."

"Yes. Lyssa, if you need to talk about anything, I'm right here."

"Thank you, but really I'm fine. So, should I make an appointment for some time this week?"

"That would be fine. I'll see you then. And don't worry so much. The chances are slim."

She nodded. "Thank you." Getting up, she left, made her appointment, and headed home.

When she walked in, she went right to her datebook to make sure she was right. Counting the days, it had been twenty-seven days. Taking a deep breath, she went in and took a shower, and then gathered her clothes to do some laundry.

Her phone rang, and she ran to get it. "Hello,"

"Why did you leave?"

"Ken, I just need some time to myself. Please, just let me be. I've got a great deal to think about."

"You're thinking about Chicago?"

Taking a deep breath, she told her, "No, Ken, Chicago is not an option. It's not even part of the equation. If that's what Callen wants, then that's what he wants."

"What do you want, Lys?"

"To be left alone. Please, Ken, just leave me alone." She hung up the phone. Taking it off the hook, she stuffed the receiver into the laundry basket, then went into her room and climbed into bed.

She didn't want to be pregnant, so she prayed she wasn't, not if this game was still in play. *Why are they trying so hard to get me to Chicago? Was Callen really honest about how he felt?* God, she was so naïve. Not one thing was holding her down on this planet. Nothing made sense to her. *Why had I done something so stupid? Why did I sleep with him?* Her mind whirling in a million different directions, she closed her eyes and willed it away.

CHAPTER TEN

As Callen drove away from the ranch, he felt different, almost like he shouldn't be leaving her. Shaking his head, he continued to his house. Once he got into town, he called Tom.

"Hey, you guys up?"

Tom laughed. "Yeah, where are you?"

"Pulling in my driveway. I'm going to jump in the shower."

"We'll be over in a few minutes then. I think we need to talk."

"Give me ten and I'll be ready. Hey, bring me some food."

"You got it."

He hung up and went inside. It took him a few minutes to shower and throw some clothes in a bag. As he walked out of the bedroom, the guys were at his door.

"So, how'd it go last night?" Stu asked.

"Slade, what was all that about?"

"Listen, we want you to come back. We miss you. We know Lyssa is your choice, so we thought we would ask her if she would be interested. Kennedy seemed to think she would come."

"Kennedy doesn't know a thing. She is a self-serving person, only thinking of herself. I don't know how many times the girl has propositioned me, and she had no clue who I was."

"Yeah, maybe not, but she knows who you are now, and between you and me, I'd be careful," Mitchell said.

Callen looked at him. "What the hell does that mean? She's Lyssa's best friend."

"That may be so, but she has a hard-on for you."

"What the hell does that mean? I thought she was going after you."

Mitchell laughed. "Yeah, me too, until she came up with this plan. She knows damn well Lyssa wants no part of the city. So, she thought she would plant a bug in her head. Apparently, Lyssa isn't as confident as you think she is. Big insecurities."

Callen stood there looking at him. "Kennedy told you this?" They all nodded. "This is her idea, to get me back to Chicago?" Mitchell nodded. "She wants me?"

"It isn't anything new for you. Come on, Callen, you know how women respond to you. She's another…"

Callen put his hand up. "Don't."

"Sorry, but Kennedy wants you."

Callen laughed. "I'm in love with Lyssa. I'm not going back to Chicago. This is my life now. Here. If I wanted to come back, I would have years ago."

"Don't you miss it? I mean, I get the laid-back lifestyle here, but do you really like all this dust and slow-paced life?" Tom asked.

Callen busted out laughing. "I'm doing honest work, and I really do enjoy the quiet."

"Come on, Callen, look at this little house you live in. It's like you're dirt poor. You're a fucking billionaire, and you are living like a ranch hand," Slade said.

"You guys just don't get it, do you? All those people we hurt by destroying companies just to line our pockets. I never thought about it until *she* destroyed me. I've lost my bloodlust for it all. I'm the only one who knows what *she* did to me when *she* left. As the years have gone by, and I have lived it over and over again, I realized something. Karma is a bitch with fucking claws. What *she* did to me is exactly what I did to all those people, to all those companies. This, what happened here, this was the other side of what we did. Innocent people, doing innocent jobs, were left with nothing. I don't have it in me to go back. It's not who I am anymore."

They all just sat there looking at him, then at each other. It was Tom who spoke up. "For what it's worth, I'm sorry I wasn't a better friend. I never really looked at it like that. But you're right. We were in it for the glory, for the rush of the kill."

Callen nodded. "Yep, and I'm just not that guy anymore. Listen, what I have with Lyssa is so real it scares the shit out of me. She is so vulnerable when it comes to matters of the heart. She is like a terrified kitten, and God help me, she is so fucking beautiful it hurts. Guys, I am in love, and I am not leaving here. I want to marry this girl and have lots of fat babies with her. This is my life now. Please understand that and accept it. This is probably the reason I didn't call. I knew you wouldn't understand it. How could you? I lived my whole life in the city, moving from one company to the next, like a fucking piranha, eating up everything I wanted. I'm not that man anymore."

Mitchell laughed. "You want to marry her? Jesus, Callen, from what I understand from Kennedy, you just met her."

"Mitchell, what the hell is your problem with Lyssa? What is your problem with me? Why are you working so hard?"

"You aren't the Callen I know. He was merciless, cunning, and fun. This country life has made you boring as hell and soft."

Callen laughed. "Thanks, and you're right. I'm not him anymore, and trust me when I tell you I don't ever want to be him again. When that woman looked into my eyes and saw me, saw the arrogant asshole I was, it scared the shit out of me. So much so that I ran away from her, and in the process, I hurt her. I physically hurt her. That cut on her eye, I did that. She had bruises all over her face. When she jacked me, I was stunned. She called me out on my shit, and she's been doing it every day since. I hadn't learned a fucking lesson by what *she* did to me, not until that day. Not until I was so arrogant and so pissed off, even eight years later, that I physically hurt a woman. A woman who is about a hundred pounds lighter than me.

"I felt like shit. I was so disgusted with myself that I was embarrassed. She didn't do a fucking thing but exist and smile at me. That is not the kind of man I want to be, but that's the kind of man I was, that I have been my whole life. Untouchable. Well, guys, I don't know how to tell you this, but she touched me. She woke me up, and let me tell you, it's a whole other side of life when you finally open your fucking eyes to see yourself for who you really are."

"You're right, I don't understand. You're a fucking billionaire. You can have any woman on the planet. Why this one? Because she's a virgin?"

Callen busted out laughing. "The money means nothing to me. I've done two things in eight years with that money. I bought my truck and this house. I don't give a shit about that money. I'm glad I have it because I finally got to do something good with it. Lyssa doesn't give a shit about it."

Mitchell laughed. "Sure she doesn't."

"You know, Mitchell, you are coming real close to getting your ass beat. She has her own money. So much that she never has to work another day in her life. Life is not about money. This conversation is useless. I don't need to justify myself to you guys. I don't need to explain my life to anyone. I'm not going back to Chicago, not now, not next week, not ever. That Callen McCabe died a long time ago. This Callen McCabe is going to love, get married, and have lots of fat babies. Now, let's get Charles' truck back to him. You guys need to get to the airport. I really appreciate all that you have done for me."

They hugged it out and headed to the ranch. When Callen pulled up, he was surprised to see that Lyssa's car wasn't there. It wasn't down at her place either. They piled out of the trucks and headed up to the porch, where Charles was sitting with Kennedy.

Callen couldn't help but notice the way she looked at him, watched him. "Good morning, gentlemen," Kennedy said.

"Charles, I'm going to run these guys to the airport and then I'll be back to tear down the backyard," Callen said.

"Don't worry about that. Seems my daughter and her best friend had a falling out this morning."

Callen looked at Kennedy.

"What?" she said. "She needed to hear what I had to say."

"And what exactly did you have to say?" Callen was pissed.

"I told her she was an idiot for not going to Chicago with you. That the two of you could make so much money."

Callen tilted his head, looking at her. "I don't know what your problem is, but let me clarify a few things for you. First of all, I am not going back to Chicago, not now, not next week, not next year. Second, I am in love with Lyssa. I've asked her to marry me, and she said yes. Third, I am going to marry her and live here and have lots and lots of fat babies. I am going to work here on this ranch and live down the road in that house," he pointed to Lyssa's house, "with the woman I love for the rest of my life. Stop interfering in her life. She doesn't want to live in the big city, and even if she does, I don't." He looked at Charles. "Where is she?"

He shook his head then looked at Kennedy.

Callen looked at her. "Where is she?"

"Her apartment."

"Charles, I need to go." He turned to the guys. "You ready? I need to go."

Kennedy spoke. "I'll take them." She sounded defeated.

She didn't have to say it twice; he was off the porch and in his truck. The drive seemed to take forever. He pulled in next to her car and took a deep breath. He had a feeling she was going to be destroyed. Climbing the stairs, he made his way to her door. It took a good ten minutes for her to answer, and when he looked at her, his heart broke.

"Why are you here?"

"Well, I can't call you because I don't have your number. Can we talk?"

She pulled the door open to let him in. She moved to the couch and sat down, pulling her knees up to her chest. Callen took off his boots and sat on the coffee table in front of her.

Her beautiful blue eyes, those eyes he'd found himself in, were red and puffy. He wanted to hold her, to tell her that he loved her, that everything was going to be all right. But he also knew he needed to let her talk. His heart froze in his chest when he saw the unshed tears forming in her big blue eyes.

"Am I really what you want?" she whispered as the first tear overflowed. He watched it slowly tumble down her cheek.

"Yes," he whispered, not knowing what else to say.

"What about Chicago?"

"It's not my home." He watched as another tear fell and traveled down her cheek. With all that he was, he wanted to reach up and wipe it away. But, somehow, he knew it would be wrong. She was feeling vulnerable, and he didn't want her to feel manipulated.

"I'm not sure this is the best choice for us, to do this. I think you miss what you used to do. I feel that if I continue this with you, eventually, you will try to convince me to go there. It's not what I want."

Callen closed his eyes and took a deep breath. "It's not what I want. It's not who I am. Lyssa, I was on the other side of what I used to do this past week. When I did what I did before, I never once thought of how the people who owned those companies felt, how those workers who worked in them felt when I tore them to pieces. For me, it was about the kill, about the money I made. It was about becoming a terrifying force, an egotistical, untouchable piece of shit."

He opened his eyes to look at her, to hopefully touch her soul, because he was sure he was going to die if she ended what they had.

"I spent the last eight years acting, feeling, and doing what I did in the corporate world to women. When I hurt you, it snapped me out of the haze I had allowed myself to live in. The guilt, the disgust, the shame that I felt for doing that to you still eats me alive. You didn't do a fucking thing but see me. I know you felt it, too. It was like, the connection to this life that I severed a long time ago was reconnected and shorted out my brain. Woke me up, woke my heart up. Something I closed off a very long time ago."

Her tears fell as her eyes slowly closed. He couldn't stand it anymore. His hands moved to her face, his thumbs wiping them away.

"I think the connection I felt to you scared the shit out of me," he whispered. "I've never felt this before. I never knew how to love so completely."

She reached up and moved his hands off her face, and he felt like he was going to scream. This feeling of fear was something he'd never known.

"Callen, I am so confused, so scared of what we've done. I never wanted anything more than I wanted that with you. I know why I never did that before, and it's because of the way I feel now. I am torn to shreds. My best friend wants you. She is doing everything she can to give me reasons to push you away, so she can move in on you. I don't know how to deal with that. The fact that there is Chicago hanging in the background. The possibility that I might already be pregnant. These are things, along with many other factors, that I need to figure out. I know Kennedy; she always gets what she wants, and right now, she wants you."

"What about what I want?"

"I can't think about that right now. I have to think about me and how I am going to handle this, deal with this gut-wrenching pain that has me so shredded. I just need some time. Can I have some time?"

"You can have anything you want."

"It's you I want. I know it's you I need. And I have never desired anyone except for you," she whispered. "I also have no idea how to deal with that. I'm terrified, Callen. I am beyond in love with you, and I'm terrified that you aren't with me."

He smiled. "I know you find it hard to trust, but I also know you can see right into my soul." He moved closer to her. "Look at me, beautiful. Look." Her eyes looked deep into his, and he prayed she saw it. "I love you. I feel you. I need you. I desire only you. I want only you." He paused, lowering his voice. "I love only you." She nodded. He leaned in and kissed her on the forehead. "I'll be waiting for you, beautiful. I'm not going anywhere."

"Thank you."

Callen got up and made his way to the door. She watched him put his boots on. He picked up her phone and dialed his number. "Now, you can call me if you need me. I love you."

She smiled a small smile, and he walked out the door. Lyssa laid down on the couch and cried herself to sleep.

Callen got to his truck and finally let his emotions take over, letting out tears he'd be holding back all through their conversation. When he finished, he went home and crawled into bed. He wanted to be with her, but he also needed to not suffocate her. Love is an emotion he wasn't familiar with, and he knew she wasn't either. Pulling his phone out of his pocket, he saved her number. Laying it on the pillow next to his head, he just went to sleep.

Kennedy had taken the guys to the airport. "'I'll work on Callen," she said to them.

Slade shook his head. "We already had a talk with him. He isn't coming back, and that's fine. We all have other jobs, other businesses. He's happy here. He's happy with Lyssa."

"She is my best friend, but there is no way she can give a man like Callen McCabe what he needs in this life. Give me some time to work on this. I think I can get him back there in about a week."

Mitchell turned and looked at her. "Why would you hurt your friend like that? Why don't you just leave the two of them alone? He is in love with her. They are getting married."

She laughed. "I am doing her a favor. Callen isn't the kind of man who is ready to settle down with a mousy woman. Do you have any idea of his reputation in this town, hell, in this county? He is with a different woman every other night. I'm experienced. Lyssa is a virgin. Who do you think could show him a better time? I'll work on him."

Stu chimed in, "Kennedy, no offense because you are a very beautiful woman, but I know my friend. He wants this life. If he didn't he would have come back to Chicago a long time ago."

She smiled at him. "Why don't you leave Callen McCabe to me? Nice plane."

Tom laughed as he headed to it. "It's Callen's."

Kennedy stood there with her mouth hanging open. "It was nice meeting you, Kennedy. have a good life," Mitchell said as he headed to the plane.

She stood watching them board the plane. "Fuck me," she whispered. "Even Hugh didn't own his own plane. This should be easy." Climbing in her dad's truck, she headed to Callen's house.

Pulling up, she could see his truck wasn't in the driveway, so he must have gone to Lyssa's. Smiling, she was pretty sure she gave cause for her to stop what was happening between them. She headed home to shower and change clothes. She was going to seduce Callen and keep him for herself. Lyssa wouldn't know what to do with all that money or a man who looked like him. As she drove back to the ranch, she couldn't help but think about his fucking perfect body. She smiled. "I bet he's got a huge cock. Lyssa said it was big, huge, but she doesn't know any better. Oh, I am going to have some fun."

She made it back to the ranch in no time. It took her a good forty-five minutes to get ready, then she took her car back to Callen's place. When she pulled up, his truck was in the driveway. Hopefully, he was alone.

She stood at his door for a few minutes and then knocked. She had a plan in case Lyssa was here. When the door opened, she knew she wasn't. He looked like shit.

"Kennedy, what the hell are you doing here?"

"Well, I came by to see how you are. I got the guys to the airport and thought I would stop by. So, is Lyssa here?"

He just stood there looking at her. "For some reason, I think you know she's not. What are you up to? I don't want you. She was right about you."

"What the hell does that mean?"

"There is no reason for you to be here, dressed like that and with perfect makeup. Do I look like an idiot?" He found a bit of pleasure in watching her face as she worked her way through his insult. "Listen, Kennedy, I'm in love with your best friend. Why are you here?"

"Because my best friend isn't the right woman for you. You need a woman who can stand beside you, who can give you what you need."

He chuckled. "And what do you think I need, exactly?"

Her hand moved to his chest, her fingers spread apart. Callen looked down, his eyes catching her very well-endowed chest. Her hand moved up to his neck, and his eyes landed on hers. "I can give you the best time of your life," she whispered, stepping closer to him.

"I've already had the best time of my life. Last night and this morning."

She stopped, looking at him. "It wasn't the best time, because it wasn't with me."

Callen grabbed her hand, throwing it off him. "You really are a piece of work. She knows what you are doing. She told me this morning, but I didn't want to believe you were this kind of woman."

"I can be anything you want me to be."

"I want you to be the best friend of the woman I love. Not this conniving bitch who is trying to seduce her future husband."

Kennedy laughed. "You won't marry her. She will never make you happy."

"And why is that?" Lyssa said from behind her.

Kennedy froze. Turning to face her, she said, "Lyssa, you're an emotional mess. A man like Callen needs a strong woman."

"A woman like you?"

"Yes, like me."

"A superficial woman who believes it's all right to sell herself for things?"

"I know my worth," she said.

Callen stood there listening to the two of them with a smile on his face.

"Kennedy, I'll tell you what. I'm going to leave. You stay here with Callen and do what you do best. Whore yourself out. I don't have a problem with it."

Callen said, "I do."

Lyssa tilted her head, looking at him, "You know where I'll be."

He smiled. "I do."

She turned and walked away. Kennedy turned to look at Callen. "See, Callen? Trust me."

Shaking his head, he reached for his boots, "Kennedy, it isn't going to happen. That woman that just drove away is going to be my wife. You and I are not going to happen. She is the one I want. She is the one I am going to marry. She is the one I want to be the mother of my children."

"But, I do everything."

"That's the difference between you and her. You do everything, while she is everything. Now, if you don't mind." He walked over, grabbing his bag, then nudged her out of the house, closing and locking the door behind him. He climbed into the truck, leaving her standing there watching him. She was parked behind him, so he just drove through the grass.

He headed to the farmhouse. Pulling up, he saw her car, and his heart started beating in his chest again.

Lyssa was standing in the backyard looking out on the field when he walked up. He didn't touch her, just leaned on the fence next to her. "I didn't want to leave you today. I wanted to stay and help you through all of this."

"See, you can't help me. But your consistent actions and your words are keeping me grounded. Callen, we can't have sex again. I don't want to have a baby yet. I don't think it would be a good idea. I'm not saying I don't want to have a baby, I just don't want one yet. I've never felt this way about someone, and I want to make sure we are going to stand the test of time. If I get pregnant, you will stay with me because it's the right thing to do. I don't want you that way. I want you to want only me for the rest of our lives. You told me that you would show me every day how much you love me."

"I did, and I will."

"Well, I'm due to get my period in a few days, and if I don't get it, well, that's another story. But if I do, I already went to see the doctor today. I have an appointment next week to get an implant put in my arm. When we are ready to move down that road and start having lots of babies, I can have it removed. But, until then, we can't do that again."

"I'm fine with that."

"I stopped at the store on my way here to get some food. I was going to get some condoms, you know, in case we can't control ourselves, but you're the only man I've seen, so I didn't know what to get. Who knew there were so many sizes?"

He chuckled. "It will be the only one you ever see."

"I'm sorry for Kennedy. She sees your bank account. She set me up, and she set you up."

"I know, and I'm sorry she hurt you."

"She didn't. I did it myself. I let my heart love you, and then my mind got in the way. I know you don't want that life anymore. I just thought it was the logical thing for you to do."

"To be honest with you, the only logical thing I've done in the past eight years was work on the ranch. Listen," he turned to face her, "I accept everything you are offering me here. No making love until you are ready."

She smiled. "Oh, I'm ready."

"Good to know. Now, can I kiss you please?"

She turned and walked into his arms. Slowly and sweetly, he kissed her. "You said something about groceries?"

Laughing, she nodded. "In the car."

"Well, come on, let's get them in the house and just be us. We have today, and then tomorrow, I need to give Charles his ranch back."

They headed for her car. "He gave me the house as payment for helping him."

"Are you going to move out here?"

She opened the trunk then walked to the back door and pulled out her suitcases. "I think I am. I'm going to open my own law office in town."

Callen grabbed what groceries he could. "That's great."

They made a few trips back and forth to the car, carrying everything she could fit in her car. They laughed and talked the whole time. Kennedy had driven by and stopped on the road to watch them, but neither of them acknowledged her. They were just busy having a good time and being together.

Callen put everything away in the kitchen, while Lyssa unpacked her things. When he finished, he carried what she needed upstairs, and then they unpacked a few boxes downstairs.

"Did you want to go back to your apartment with the truck?"

"Well, I was thinking maybe we could go to your house and get your things?"

He stopped and looked at her. "Lyssa?"

"I mean, you'll probably be here every night anyway. So, I just thought, maybe... Never mind, I shouldn't have assumed you would want to stay here with me."

Shaking his head, he moved toward her. "I would love nothing more. Are you sure?"

"Yes, I'm sure. I like sleeping with you."

"Okay then, let's go. I don't have much. It didn't matter to me what was there. The only thing that I would want would be my bed. It's a great deal bigger than yours."

She laughed. "Yes, it is. Okay, well then, we should move the one in my room. Will it even fit in my room?"

"It should, or we can just put it in the master. That room has a bathroom now."

"Really? I guess I didn't look. All right, then let's go move that bed out of there."

He chuckled. "Let's go."

Together, they moved the bed out and into one of the other bedrooms. Then they headed to Callen's to get his things and his bed. Getting his giant bed upstairs proved to be complicated. It took far longer than they anticipated, but they finally did it, collapsing on it, exhausted.

"We are going to need sheets and pillows and blankets."

"Yeah, I only have what's here. Tonight, we can sleep in the other room, and tomorrow after I give the ranch back to Charles, we can go shopping. He owes me a few days off. I mean, I haven't taken a vacation for eight years, and I work seven days a week."

She turned her head to look at him. "Really?"

Laughing, he said, "Really."

"I'm hungry. You want something to eat?"

"Mmm, yes."

She squealed as he grabbed her up in his arms, kissing her. They rolled around on the bed, laughing and kissing, then headed down-stairs to cook. When they finished, they found themselves lying on the couch wrapped around each other.

"This is nice," he said softly.

"Yes, it is. I'm so tired."

"You want to go to bed?"

"No, I'm too comfortable to move."

"I know what you mean."

They fell asleep holding one another.

CHAPTER ELEVEN

Callen woke needing to use the bathroom. He managed to maneuver around her and got up. After using the bathroom, he went back into the living room to climb back on the couch. He stood looking at her. She was so small. Smiling, he gently picked her up and carried her up to bed. He laid her down and moved the hair off her face, and her eyes opened slowly.

"Callen." She smiled.

"I'm right here, beautiful." Pulling off his shirt and jeans, he got into bed with her.

Rolling into his chest, she paused. "You took your clothes off."

"I did," he said, kissing her head. "Go back to sleep."

"Mmm." She rolled over, taking off her jeans, then sat up to take off her shirt and bra. Laying back down, she rolled back into his chest. "This is better. You're so warm."

Chuckling, he wrapped himself around her. "You are so beautiful."

"Thank you." She tilted her head up to kiss his neck. "So are you."

When she pushed her knee up between his thighs to rest on his balls, his heart exploded. Closing his eyes, they fell back asleep. The sun rose and filled the room with sunlight. Lyssa woke before Callen, her smile automatic. She knew this was where she belonged. She knew this man was hers. Her lips landed on his chest, just shy of his nipple.

Slowly moving her hand around his body, her fingers finding his nipple, she teased it. Callen laid there letting her touch him. As she fingered his nipple, he felt himself get harder and harder. It was when her head moved and her lips wrapped around it that his whole body woke up.

"Mmm, what are you doing to me?"

When she pushed on his chest, he laid on his back, her hair surrounding her head like a golden halo, his hands on her thighs. He couldn't help but look at her. Everything about her was perfect. His eyes traveled down her body as she sat up. Her nipples puckered, poking through her hair.

"God," he moaned as he scanned her body down to her lace panties. His hands slid up her thighs, his thumbs brushing along her core. He closed his eyes when he felt how wet she was. Her swollen bud was very prominent as his thumb brushed over it, and he felt her tremble. "Remember that day you asked me what naughty things I wanted to do to you?"

His fingers slipped into the side of her panties as she smiled and nodded. Wrapping them around the fragile lace, he tore the sides away, flipping her over on the bed.

Lyssa squealed and busted out laughing as he pulled the lace from her body and threw it on the floor. His eyes landed on her core as she lay on the bed with her legs spread open before him. "Look at you." He smiled as his thumb brushed lightly over her swollen bud. "So beautiful."

Her back arched. "Callen," she moaned.

She was his obsession, his great love. His head moved down. He needed to taste her, to feel her perfection on his tongue. His tongue moved slowly, his lips wrapping around her bud.

"Ahh, Callen," she cried out. Her whole body trembled, and he could feel her pulse. Sliding his tongue through her, he slipped inside of her to get every drop of her release. When he was sure he got every drop, he moved up her quivering body, taking his time, making sure he devoured each of her nipples then moved to her mouth. Laying down next to her, his hand slid down her side, pulling her thigh over his to open her up. He deeply kissed her, letting his fingers slip slowly inside of her. Pulling back, she moaned out, "Ahh," licking her lips and locking eyes with him as his thumb brushed along her sensitive bud.

Callen watched as her eyes rolled back into her head and closed. Her mouth formed that sweet 'O'. Even against his finger, she was tight. "That's it, baby." He could feel her tightening again. He slipped a second finger inside, his thumb pressing a bit harder on her. He felt her arch her back and press into him. His mouth covered hers, and she exploded into a deep orgasm. He felt her clutch his fingers and then cover them with her release.

Her hands in his hair, pulling it, only made him harder. Her fingernails pressed into his skull. She was coming hard. Callen felt her teeth grab his lip and bite down. His smile grew against her lips. He could feel her slowing down, her body starting to relax. Opening her eyes, he could see her desire. He could feel her love.

"I love you," he whispered to her.

They lay in each other's arms, touching, kissing, and falling deeper in love. "Callen, I want to touch you. Can I touch you?"

"Beautiful, I belong to you. Yes, you can touch me."

"Yeah?"

"Oh, hell yeah."

Smiling her sweet shy smile that he loved so much, she began her exploration of his body. "Will you roll over?" She moved out of his way as he turned on his stomach.

Callen moaned as she laid her naked body on his back. "Feel me," she whispered in his ear, nipping it.

Pushing up, she trailed her nipples down his back, followed by her tongue, coming to his boxers. She gently pulled them off, tossing them on the floor. Her hands moved on their own. She had no idea what to do, so she just let herself go. His legs were covered in dark hair that tickled her fingertips. His ass was defined and sculpted.

"Callen, you are so beautiful," she said as her fingers dug into the flesh on his ass. Trailing her fingers along his crack, she could feel his body twitch. Spending more than a few minutes touching and feeling his ass, leaning forward, she bit into the skin, causing him to moan. Liking his response, she let herself go. When she had her fill, she put her hands on his hips, wanting him to turn over. Callen slowly rolled over so not to hurt her. Lyssa sat on her knees between his spread legs, looking at him.

His balls fascinated her, and after looking at him for permission, her fingers moved to touch them. She watched as his eyes closed and his head fell back on the bed. Callen thought he was losing his mind as she squeezed his balls. Her feather-light touches along his cock caused him to twitch. It was when she picked it up in her hands that his eyes opened to feel the warmth of her mouth as she pulled his head in.

He couldn't move. He didn't want to move as she methodically worked him into her mouth further and further until he felt the back of her throat. "Aww, beautiful," he groaned as she pushed down on him. He felt himself slip past the tight ring in her throat. "Ahh." She gagged a little pulling him out. He couldn't open his eyes, because if he looked at her, he would lose it. "Lyssa."

She opened her mouth and tried again, her eyes watering as she pushed him down her throat. She nearly touched her nose on his hair. Slow with her pull back, she picked her head up to look at him. His stomach was tight, every muscle defined. Her smile was huge as his eyes slowly opened. Licking her lips, she leaned in and pushed her head all the way down, touching her nose to his hair and wrapping her lips around the base of his cock. She felt him as he released, calling out her name. His hands moved to her head, his body lifting off the bed as she slowly pulled back. His release filled her mouth, and her tongue wrapped around his head as she sucked it.

Callen's hands wrapped in her hair, pulling it as his mind was blown by the phenomenal sensations quaking through his body. When his last pulse left him, his hands released her hair as she sat up licking her lips. Looking at his limp body lying on the bed, the way his mouth was slightly open, Lyssa crawled up his body. She laid on top of him, his hands slowly wrapping around her. Callen closed his eyes.

"I love you," she whispered as they fell asleep.

Callen didn't sleep long. Opening his eyes, his nose filled with her beautiful, flowery, musky scent. He tightened his arms around her, gently rolling over to see her big blue eyes looking at him. Smiling, he shook his head and kissed her with slow, long, deep thrusts of his tongue. His mind was on nothing but the woman in his arms, this woman who he would move the moon for.

As he pulled back, she smiled at him. "Hi."

He laughed. "Hi. Lyssa, that was incredible."

"Did I do it right? I mean, I guess I did since you came in my mouth."

"Yes, I did. And, oh my God, did you ever do it right. So much so, beautiful."

Her fingers moved to his mouth. "You make me feel things I've never known with these lips, with this mouth. I wanted to give you the same. I love you, Callen."

"I love you, beautiful. We should get up. I'm sure Charles is wondering what happened to us."

She laughed. "I'm sure he knows."

Laughing, Callen untangled himself from her. "I'm sure he does, too."

Lyssa got up and headed to the shower. When they were finished, they headed to the ranch. Lyssa noticed that Kennedy's car was gone. Callen looked at her with a small smile. She wasn't sure how she felt about what her best friend did, but she decided it didn't matter. He was with her, and she believed that he loved her.

Charles and Emily were on the porch when they walked up.

"Good morning, you two. I see you worked everything out," Charles said with a smile on his face.

Lyssa smiled. "Yes, we did. I suppose we are still getting to know one another."

"You ready to have your ranch back?" Callen asked.

"I'm not in any hurry. You two go on do what you need to do. We can take care of this later." Charles laughed. "It's not like I don't know where you'll be."

Emily stood up and hugged Lyssa. "He is a good man."

"I know. I just need to make my brain understand that."

Emily laughed. "It will catch up. Kennedy asked me to give this to you when she left." She handed Lyssa an envelope. "She went back to the city this morning."

Lyssa took the envelope and put it in her back pocket. Not sure she wanted to read anything Kennedy had to say to her right now. "Well, if we aren't taking care of the ranch today, we should get going." Lyssa hugged Charles and then Emily.

As they got ready to leave, Charles said to Callen, "You take all the time you need, son. You've been here eight years with not one day off. Tiny and the boys can handle it. If I need you, I know you'll be down the road."

"It should only be a few days."

"Nonsense, you take the time. I know what Kennedy tried to do. You seal your fate with that woman. Don't let her go."

Callen chuckled. "Oh, I have no intention of ever letting her go. I'll see you in a few days."

They climbed into the truck, and Callen dropped her off at her car. He had to make a stop so Lyssa went ahead of him. When he got there, Lyssa's car wasn't there so he just waited. A few minutes later, she pulled up with a huge smile on her face. He got out and headed to her car.

"I stopped and got some boxes," she said as she got out of the car. "I thought we should go shopping first to pick up some sheets for your bed."

Wrapping his arms around her, he said, "Our bed. Come on, I'll drive."

They headed to the little mall in town. They picked out sheets, blankets, some towels, and other stuff. As they were walking toward the exit, Callen spotted a lingerie store. He steered Lyssa toward it. "I owe you a pair of panties," he whispered to her, watching her blush.

"Oh, it's fine," she whispered back.

He chuckled. "Come on, let me get you a new pair." He pulled her toward the door.

"No, really, it's fine." She was totally embarrassed.

"Come on, there is nothing to be worried about."

She stopped. "Callen, please. I can't do this with you."

He smiled, running his finger down her jaw. "Fine, you wait here and I'll go in. Tell me what size you wear."

Taking a deep breath, she said softly, "Size zero."

"Now, see, that wasn't hard. What size bra do you wear, in case I see something I like?" Looking at the store window, he leaned in. "Although, I think I might like a great deal in there."

She smacked him on the chest. "A thirty-two C. You really don't have to do this."

Kissing her on the forehead, he set the bags on the floor. "Yes, I do. You wait here."

She watched him stroll through the door. She found herself leaning against the wall peeking into the store, watching him talk to one of the sales girls. The girl was flushed in the face. He was so good looking. Lyssa watched as he bought multiple bras and panty sets. He held up a few things for her to see, and she nodded her approval. She giggled a few times, was shocked a few times. But all in all, the man had incredible taste.

Twenty minutes after he walked in, he walked out with two bags. "You didn't have to do that," she said as he picked up the bags.

"Yes, I did. I can't wait to see you in them." Her face was redder than red with embarrassment. "Don't be embarrassed, you'll look beautiful in them. Come on, I need to stop at the drug store to pick up some essentials."

They walked hand in hand to the truck. Callen put everything in the back seat, and they headed off to the drug store. Lyssa picked up a few things she needed, while Callen was off getting what he needed, but then she found herself in front of the huge variety of condoms. She wanted to make love to him again, but she didn't have a clue what kind to buy.

Callen stood and watched her as she looked over the selection. She kept shaking her head and putting each box back. Her face was flushed with her blush. He walked up behind her, whispering, "What are you doing, beautiful?"

She leaned into him, turning her head to face him. "I want you, and well… God, Callen, I don't know what I'm doing."

Chuckling, he kissed her neck as he reached around her, grabbing the brand he used. "These ones, beautiful," he whispered.

Closing her eyes, she said, "I'm dying here, can we go now?"

Laughing, he wrapped his arm around her and turned her away from the display. They checked out and went back to her place.

"Hey, there is nothing to be embarrassed about."

"Says the man who knows just what he wants."

He laughed. "I do, and it's you." His hand came up to her face. "I'm honored that you want me. There is nothing to be embarrassed about. Now, let's get busy because I plan on using that entire box when we get home."

Her face turned bright red. "The whole box?" she whispered.

"Oh yeah." He kissed her forehead, grabbing a box. "So, tell me what to do."

She just stood there looking at him. "Books," she said. "Pack the books."

It didn't take long to fill the boxes she had. Callen ran up to the store and grabbed a bunch more, along with some food. They sat laughing and eating, then filled the boxes he bought. When they were finished, they carried them down to the truck and to her car, filling both.

"I think I need more boxes. I didn't realize I had so much stuff."

"How about we empty these and then come back tomorrow to get the rest. What about all this furniture? We could take it to my house, maybe rent it out as a furnished rental."

"That's a really good idea, but I don't want to move furniture. I'll call a moving company when we are done. Let them move it. Hey, what about work?"

Callen wiggled his eyebrows at her. "Charles gave me some time off."

"Well, that was nice of him."

"It was, so, you ready?"

She nodded, and they headed out. By the time they had everything unloaded, they were both exhausted and collapsed on the sofa. Callen wrapped her in his arms. "That was fun." He snuggled into her.

Giggling, she said, "So not fun. I swear, if I stay here long, I'm going to fall asleep."

"What's wrong with that?"

"I'm hungry and dirty. We still have to wash the new sheets and make the bed."

"No, we don't. Why don't you go take a shower, and I'll make us something to eat? Then I'll take a shower and we can just go to bed."

"Mmm, that sounds like a good idea."

Kissing her, they got up. He headed to the kitchen, while Lyssa took the bags of lingerie he had bought her upstairs. Callen watched with a smile on his face. He hadn't felt like this in all of his life. He was happy, his heart full of love for this woman. Making his way to the kitchen, he started dinner.

Lyssa took her bags upstairs and unpacked them. Her face flushed at some of the things he had purchased for her. But there was one thing she didn't see him buy—a beautiful cream-colored negligée made of the softest satin. It had a matching robe. She stood there touching the fabric with a smile on her face, totally unaware that Callen was standing in the doorway watching her.

"Do you like it?" His voice was soft.

She nodded. "It's so beautiful."

"I thought you were taking a shower." He moved into the room, wrapping his arms around her. He loved the way she leaned into him.

"I am. I thought you were cooking dinner."

"I am." He kissed her neck. "It's in the oven."

"Then take a shower with me." Turning her head, he kissed her.

"You sure? I might not be able to control myself."

She giggled. "What if I don't want you to? What if I want you to take me right here."

He shook his head. "We have an agreement. Not until you're sure, one way or another."

She walked out of his arms and headed to the bathroom, leaving the bathroom door open. Callen stood there watching her get undressed. It was when she pulled her lip into her mouth that he was moving. His clothes seemed to just fall away from his body. Stepping into the shower, his breath caught in his chest. She was standing with her back under the shower head, her hands in her hair, her nipples hard and sticking out, beckoning him. He stood in front of her, looking at her. She was perfectly proportioned, her tiny hips, her spectacular waist, her perfect tits. And God, her perfect core. His hand slid down her stomach to her fluff, his other hand wrapping around her neck pulling her mouth to his, just as he slipped two fingers inside her.

Callen pressed his thumb on her bud and proceeded to give her a fantastic orgasm. His mouth never left hers, swallowing her cries and her mews. She soaked his fingers. Sliding them out, he brought them to her mouth, slipping them in so she could taste herself. Feeling her tongue wrap around them made him even fucking harder if that was at all possible. As he pulled them out, his mouth covered hers, and he could taste her on her tongue.

Lyssa was so blown away by his beautiful assault on her that she was unable to move. When he finally let go of her, she leaned against the shower wall, pulling her lip between her teeth. Her eyes traveled down his body to his cock. "Touch yourself." Her voice was barely a whisper.

Callen smiled, his hand slowly wrapping around his cock. "Like this?"

She nodded, her eyes glued to him. She watched as he slowly pumped his cock. "What does it feel like?"

"It feels good, baby." He groaned, "Mmm, this isn't going to last long."

Her hand moved to cover his, and he stopped. "Don't stop, I want to watch."

With her hand on his, he continued to move it up and down. "Lyssa."

Her eyes moved to his. "Come for me, Callen." Moving her eyes back down, she watched as his stomach pulled tight. His legs went stiff, and a low hum rumbled from his chest.

"Oh, God." His voice was deep.

When he pulsed, she could feel his cock twitch as he released. His cum landed on her stomach as it shot from him. "Oh my God," she whispered.

When the last drop poured out of him, he released his hand, grabbing her face, and his mouth covered hers. The kiss was deep and intense. Pulling back, she smiled at him. "I've never done that before in front of someone."

"No?"

He shook his head. "No."

"I thought it was incredible. Will you do it again for me sometime?"

She watched his face blush. "I will do anything you want." Leaning in, he kissed her again.

They showered and got out. Callen grabbed a pair of jeans, deciding to go commando, while Lyssa debated on the silk nightgown or just a t-shirt. Not knowing what was for dinner, she opted for one of Callen's t-shirts that went nearly to her knees.

When she came bouncing down the stairs, she was stopped short when she realized Callen was sitting at the kitchen table with a stunned look on his face, looking into the kitchen. Then she heard him. "You fucking people destroyed everything. Do have any idea how much money you and that little bitch cost me?"

Callen's eyes didn't shift when he felt her. He stayed looking right at Knox. "Listen, I have money. How much do you want?"

Knox laughed. "I'm sure, you're a fucking ranch hand. How much money could you possibly have? I know that bitch has money. I saw her bank book."

Lyssa stepped back. She made her way to the front door, quietly opening it, and backed out onto the porch. Without thinking, she took off running through the field. She hit the porch of the ranch, flinging open the door, yelling, "Charles!" There was no answer. She started moving through the house yelling his name. Running into their bedroom, she saw Emily's feet. "No!" she screamed. Moving to the side of the bed, she saw the blood. "Oh my God, no, no, no." She grabbed the phone off the base and punched in the Sherriff's number.

"Sherriff's office."

"Oh my God, this is Lyssa Dawn. I'm out at the Greenvale ranch. Emily has been hurt. I don't know where Charles is, and there is a man in my house holding a gun on my boyfriend. Please hurry. Send an ambulance. God, please hurry!"

She heard talking, and then the voice came back on the phone. "Lyssa, this is Alex Middleton. We are on our way. Is Emily breathing?"

"I have no idea. There is blood everywhere. Please." She started to cry, "Please hurry. Knox Fairfield is at my house with a gun, and he has my boyfriend. I can't find Charles. Please, Alex, hurry."

"The Sherriff is less than five minutes away."

"Tell him to go to my house. My boyfriend is there. Hurry. Knox is going to kill him." That's when she heard the gunshot. "Oh my God. NO!" she screamed, dropping the phone.

She forced her body to move. Her lungs hurt from running so fast. She made it onto the porch as Knox was walking out the door. She slammed into him, knocking them both to the floor just inside the door. Knox slammed his head on the tile floor. Lyssa scurried off of him. Seeing the gun, she grabbed it and ran toward the dining room.

Callen was lying on the floor with blood all around him. "No, no, no, no," she cried as she made her way to him. She pushed him over. He was bleeding from the upper righthand side of his chest. "No, Callen." She touched his face. "Oh, God, baby, please." Her tears were coming hard now. She managed to get his head in her lap, her fingers shaking as she felt his neck for a pulse. "NO!" she screamed when she couldn't feel anything.

The Sherriff came running in the door. Stopping short of Knox, he bent down to feel for a pulse, then looked up to see Lyssa holding Callen's head and the blood pouring from his chest. Rushing over to her, he asked, "Is he alive?"

Lyssa couldn't move. She couldn't talk. The Sherriff put his fingers to Callen's throat then spoke into his radio. "Alex, I've got one causality and one gunshot victim at the Dawn Farm. I haven't been over to the Greenvale ranch yet. Get me some medical out here. Get the fucking chopper in the air."

"On it, the ambulance is five minutes out."

The Sherriff looked at Lyssa. "He's alive. The ambulance will be here in five minutes. I need to get out to Charles'. Are you going to be all right?"

She just looked at him, picking up her hand with the gun in it. She nodded.

The Sherriff took the gun. "Mr. Fairfield is dead. You'll be all right. Are you hurt?" She shook her head. Then she heard the ambulance siren. "They will take care of him." She nodded.

She watched as he got up and ran out the door, passing the paramedics along the way. Three people walked in the house, one stopping by Knox and the other two rushing over to her. One of them helped her up while the other worked on Callen. She didn't move from her spot while they started an I.V., bandaged his chest, and took his vitals. Then two of them left and went to get the gurney.

Lyssa knelt next to Callen, her shaky hand reaching for his face. Her fingers gently touched his eyes then his mouth. "Callen, come on, baby. Open your eyes." Her voice was soft, fighting the tears. "Please."

The medics came in with a gurney, and one of them said, "The helicopter is landing in the field. Let's get him out there." He looked at Lyssa. "You can come with."

She nodded and watched as they picked him up and put him on the gurney. Then they were all moving out the door and into the field, and then into the helicopter. The next few hours were a blur for her. She was given some scrubs to put on, and she found herself sitting in a chair in a waiting room. Not knowing how long she was there, a doctor put his hand on her leg.

"Are you waiting for information on Callen McCabe?"

Lyssa looked up at him. "Yes." She was so afraid of what he was going to say to her.

"He's out of surgery. He's going to be all right. They have him up in the I.C.U., so you can go up now if you want."

The tears fell from her eyes. "Thank you."

He helped her stand. "I'll take you up. The Sherriff called. He wants to come and talk to you."

She just nodded as he led her to the elevators. When she walked into his room, he was hooked up to some machines, which caused her to stop moving. "The bullet nicked his lung. That's why he is on the machine. We have him in a drug-induced coma so he doesn't struggle to breathe. It's only for twenty-four hours, then we are going to wake him up and take the machine off. You can stay here if you want."

"Thank you," she said through her tears.

He walked her over to the chair next to his bed and sat her down. "Miss Dawn," he said. She looked up at him. "Are you all right?"

She nodded, wiping her tears. He smiled at her and left the room. She just sat there looking at him, looking at the bandage on his chest, his beautiful chest. Scooting the chair closer to his bed, she reached for his hand, holding it.

Lyssa had no idea how much time had passed. She must have been sleeping when she felt a hand on her shoulder. Opening her eyes, she saw the Sherriff and Alex Middleton. She and Kennedy went to school with him.

"Lyssa," the Sherriff knelt next to her, "can you tell me what happened?"

She sat there looking at him, then proceeded to tell him what she knew. "How are Emily and Charles?"

The look on the Sherriff's face told her what she had already known. "I'm sorry, Emily didn't make it, and I'm afraid Charles had a stroke and isn't expected to make it through the night."

The scream that came out of her mouth was shattering. Alex moved around the Sherriff and wrapped her in his arms. "I'm so sorry, Lyssa," he whispered to her. She sobbed and hit him and screamed again. He didn't waver in his hold. The gut-wrenching pain that seared through her was nothing she had ever known before.

The Sherriff left the room, leaving Alex and Lyssa alone. She cried for a long time while this man she hadn't seen in years held her. They were all in the same grade, all through school. She started to calm down. Pulling back, she looked at Alex. "I'm sorry," she whispered.

He let her go. "It's fine. Can I get you something to eat or drink?"

She shook her head. "Where is Knox?"

"He's dead," was all he said. "I'll leave you alone. I'll be back with something for you to eat."

She just nodded, turning her head to Callen, listening to the damn machine breathing for him. For hours she sat staring at him. Alex had come with food, but she didn't see or hear him. She just stared at Callen, and her finger didn't stop moving on his hand the entire time. She forced her eyes to stay open.

The doctor came in. "Lyssa?" She turned her head. "We are going to start to wean him off the medicine now. Then we will remove the tube."

She nodded, letting go of his hand for the first time in twenty-four hours. She moved to the other side of the room while they worked on him. "There are some people in the waiting room if you want to go out there." She shook her head, her eyes never leaving him.

It took twenty minutes for them to finish, and she was right back in her chair holding his hand. Her finger moved methodically across his hand. Her eyes watched his, waiting to see them move, waiting for them to open.

The doctor came back in. "Lyssa, I just wanted to let you know that Charles has passed."

Her eyes filling up with tears, she nodded to him. "Thank you."

"Kennedy is in the waiting room. She asked if you would come out to see her."

Lyssa snapped her eyes up at the doctor, her heart racing. She stood up and leaned in, kissing Callen on the lips. "I'll be right back, my love." Then she looked at the doctor. "How long until he wakes up?"

"It shouldn't be long, maybe an hour."

She put his hand on his stomach and walked out of the room, headed to the waiting room. When she walked in, Kennedy was in the arms of Mitchell, her eyes red and her face puffy. They all stood up when she walked in. She still had blood on her hands and arms and in her hair.

"Lyssa," Stu said.

"How did you know?" she asked him.

"It's all over the news."

Her eyes moved to Kennedy. "This is all your fault. I don't know what the fuck you are doing here, but you need to leave. There is nothing here for you. Our friendship is over. You are responsible for your parents' deaths and for what is happening to Callen. You are a fucking waste of time and space. I don't ever want to see you again."

She turned and went to walk out of the room when she ran right into a woman. "Excuse me," she snapped at Lyssa.

Lyssa stood there. She could hear the guys. "No fucking way," they whispered.

"Jessica, what are you doing here?" Tom asked.

The woman was stunning, although dressed a bit too fancy for a place like this. She was sneering at Lyssa. "I heard about what happened to Cal. Of course, I would come. He is fighting for his life. How do I get in to see him?"

Lyssa just stood there looking at her. *This is her.* "Excuse me?" she said to the woman.

"I'm here to see Cal McCabe. He's been missing for eight years, and then I hear he's been shot and is fighting for his life." She looked at the guys. "You said you didn't know where he was. Why would you lie to me? I made a huge mistake all those years ago, and now, I may not get the chance to make it right." She looked at Lyssa. "Who are you?"

Lyssa smiled. "I'm his wife." She turned and walked out of the room and headed back to Callen.

CHAPTER TWELVE

The room went silent as Jessica watched Lyssa walk down the hall. She turned to look at Stu. "He's married? Why would he marry someone else? I've been looking for him for eight years. I can't believe you all knew where he was."

Stu stood up. "Jessica, we didn't know where he was until last week." Turning, he looked at Kennedy. "When did they get married?"

She shook her head. "After what I did to them, I'm pretty sure she is never going to talk to me again. I'm still trying to figure out what the hell happened. Has anyone talked to the Sherriff?"

Just as she said it, the Sherriff and Alex walked in. "Kennedy, I can't tell you how sorry I am, about your parents."

"What the hell happened? No one is telling us a damn thing, and Lyssa isn't talking."

"From what we can gather, Knox Fairfield got out of jail and ended up at the ranch. He shot your mother, trying to force your father to tell him where Lyssa and Callen were. Your father had a stroke when Knox shot your mother. When Knox was fleeing, he saw the cars at the farmhouse. We got a call from Lyssa from your folk's place, saying that Emily was hurt and she couldn't find Charles, and that Knox was at the farmhouse with a gun on Callen."

Alex spoke. "I was on the phone with her when she heard a gunshot and started screaming. She dropped the phone."

"I was about three minutes away. She ran all the way across that field. When she ran in the door, she ran into Knox. They hit the floor pretty hard, and he cracked his skull open, died instantly. When I walked in the door, Lyssa had Callen in her arms. He had a gunshot to the chest. We got him here in the helicopter, and your dad came in the second one. He didn't make it through the night. They just took Callen off life support."

Everyone gasped. "He was in a drug-induced coma. The bullet tore through the upper part of his right lung. He should be waking up anytime. Listen, Lyssa hasn't slept, and I know she hasn't eaten a thing. She has been sitting in there holding his hand since he came out of surgery. Kennedy, she is your best friend. You have to get her to eat."

Stu stood up. "Can you get me in that room? I'll get her to eat."

The Sherriff nodded. "Come on."

He looked at Mitchell. "Why don't you take Kennedy home. It's obvious that she isn't going to be able to help Lyssa." Looking at Kennedy, he said, "We told you not to do what you did. She needs you, and you betrayed her." Kennedy dropped her head as the tears fell from her eyes. Walking past Jessica, he said to her, "You are not welcome here. You destroyed him when you left. He is happy now. He has a happy life here with Lyssa. Just go." He followed the Sherriff out.

Jessica stood there looking at them. "He still loves me. I'm not going anywhere until I see him."

"Yeah, well, I'd be careful, Jess. Lyssa isn't some country bumpkin. She is a force to be reckoned with," Mitchell said as he helped Kennedy up.

"She's a mousy little thing. I'm not worried. You don't love someone like we loved each other and get over it. I'll be back."

They all stood there watching her walk down the hall. "What a bitch," Kennedy said.

Tom laughed. "You haven't seen anything yet."

～

Stu went down to the cafeteria and grabbed some finger foods, some coffee, a few bottles of water, and some juice. The Sherriff helped him carry everything to the I.C.U., and the doctor was coming out of the room as they made it to the door. He smiled and nodded to them.

As they walked in the door, Stu felt himself get sick. Lying in the bed, hooked to machines, was his friend. A man he not only admired but loved. He took a step back to catch his breath.

Lyssa sat there looking at Callen. "Please, baby, wake up," she said softly. Her fingers trembled as she touched his lips. Her tears came when his tongue came out to lick his lips.

"Callen," she whispered as her body stood up.

She watched as his eyes fluttered open. He struggled to focus. "Lyssa?"

"I'm here." She squeezed his hand. "I'm right here." She watched as a tear fell from his eye. "Shh, I'm here."

His hand closed around hers. "I'm so sorry."

"You have nothing to be sorry for. I'm the one who is sorry. I'm so sorry I left you there alone."

He turned his head to look at her. "No, beautiful, you did the right thing. He was going to kill you. I couldn't let him hurt you. Not again."

She was crying. "So you let him shoot you?"

"I fought with him. The gun went off. What happened?"

"We can talk about it later. You're going to be fine."

"I love you," he whispered, pulling her hand to his mouth to kiss it.

She bent down, touching her lips to his. "I love you."

Stu and the Sherriff walked in. Lyssa looked up. "He's awake."

Stu nodded to her, putting everything he bought for her on the table, then walked over to his bed. "Hey," he said to him.

"What are you doing here?" He looked at Lyssa. "Did you call them?" She shook her head.

"You made the world news. Tom saw it, and we jumped on the plane," Stu said

"What do you mean? No one knows who I am."

"Well, someone did. But it's not here nor there. I am so glad you are all right. Listen, I just came in to bring this lady some food. She won't eat. She's been sitting here since they brought you out of surgery."

He looked at Lyssa. "You have to eat. How long?"

"Just a day or two. I don't know. I'm fine."

"Lyssa, please eat. I'm not going anywhere."

"I will, I promise."

"Listen, I'm going to go and let the guys know you're awake. I only got in here because of the Sherriff. We'll head out and come back when they put you in a regular room."

Callen looked at him. "Thanks for coming."

"Always," Stu said. He looked at Lyssa. "You don't worry about anything, all right? We'll get your place cleaned up and bring you some clean clothes." She smiled at him. He looked at the food. "Eat, please."

With that, he turned and walked out the door.

"You sleep, I'm not going anywhere."

He smiled as his eyes closed. She did what he wanted her to do and ate. In fact, she ate everything Stu had brought.

She sat in the chair by his bed, talking to him when he was awake, and holding his hand when he was sleeping. Stu brought her back a bag of clothes, and he sat with Callen while she took a shower.

He stayed in the I.C.U. for two more days. They moved him to a regular room, and that's when Lyssa told him about Emily and Charles. They both cried.

"The service is on Saturday," she told him.

"We are both going to be there," he told her.

"Callen, you can't leave the hospital yet."

"It's three days from now. I'll be fine. I want to go home. If I learned anything from this, it's that life is too short. I love you, and I want to marry you."

She smiled. "Well, you might not want that after I tell you this."

He chuckled. "It doesn't matter what you say to me. I am going to marry you."

"Jessica is here or was here. I don't know if she is still here."

Callen sat there looking at her. A strange feeling came over her, a feeling of fear. She could see it in his eyes: confusion, fear. "What?" She nodded.

"She said she's been looking for you for eight years. I guess she has asked the guys repeatedly where you were."

"Where is she?" His words were short and hard.

Lyssa let go of his hand and stood up. "She's been in the waiting room every day, waiting with Kennedy, Mitchell, Stu, and Tom."

He watched her body change as she moved to the door. "Where are you going?"

She just looked at him as she fought her tears. Not saying a word, she walked out of his room. It was the first time she had left him. She could hear him calling her name as she made her way down the hall to the elevators. He was going to leave her; she could feel it. He didn't want her. He wanted *her.* Pushing the button, she stood still, not moving, not breathing.

The doors opened, and Stu walked out. "Hey," he said, putting his hand on her arm. "Lyssa, what happened?"

She shook her head and got in the elevator and pushed the button, not picking her head up as the doors closed. She walked out of the hospital and just stood there. She had no money, no purse, nothing, so she started walking. She found a police station and asked them if she could use their phone, then dialed the number. "Sherriff's office."

"Could I please speak to Alex?"

"May I ask who's calling?"

"Lyssa Dawn," she said softly.

"One moment."

A few minutes later, he answered the phone, "Alex Middleton."

"Alex, it's Lyssa. I was wondering if you could come and get me and give me a ride home. I don't have any money or a car."

"Lyssa, what happened? Why aren't you at the hospital?"

"Please, Alex," was all she said as the tears fell from her eyes.

"I'm leaving right now. Where are you?"

"Hold on." She looked at the officer. "Could you please tell him where I am?" She handed him the phone and went to sit down.

An hour later, the door opened, and Alex walked in, kneeling in front of her. "Hey, what happened?"

She shook her head. "Can you please take me back to the farmhouse?"

There wasn't a word said the entire drive back. When Alex pulled up behind Callen's truck, she looked at him. "Thank you," she said and got out of the car.

The lights were on in the house, but she didn't understand why. When she got to the door, she tried the handle and it turned. She didn't look at anything, just went upstairs and packed a suitcase. She needed to get the hell away from here. Grabbing her purse and her keys, she made her way down the stairs and back out the door.

CHAPTER THIRTEEN

When Stu walked into Callen's room, he had tears on his face and was trying to get up. He rushed over to him. "What the hell are you doing?" He helped him back into bed.

"I have to find her."

"Who?"

"Lyssa, she just left."

"I know, I saw her at the elevator. What the hell happened?"

Callen laid back down, looking at Stu. "I don't know. I think she mistook my reaction to Jessica. What the fuck is she doing here?"

Stu just stood there looking at him. "She told you?"

Callen looked at him. "Why wouldn't she tell me? Jessica being here means nothing to me."

"Yeah, well, we all know how in love with her you were. She claims to have been looking for you since you left."

"Yeah, that's what Lyssa said. Listen, you need to find her. I need to find her. She thinks I don't want to be with her, that I want Jessica back."

"Do you?" Stu said.

Callen sat there. "I love Lyssa."

"But you love Jessica, too."

He shook his head. "No, I don't. Lyssa is who I want. Lyssa is who I love."

Stu sat down. "We have clearance to come and see you now. I'm sure she'll be here sometime today."

"Who, Lyssa?"

"No, Jessica. She's been here every day. Lyssa told her she was your wife."

Callen chuckled. "She is going to be, just as soon as I put the ring on her finger that I bought."

"No shit? I'm happy for you. But you are going to have to end this with Jess."

"There is no ending anything. It ended eight years ago when she walked out."

"I'm sorry to say this, but you're not very convincing right now."

Callen looked at him. "What the hell does that mean?"

"We've known each other for what, nearly fifteen years? You may believe in your mind that Jessica means nothing to you, but your eyes and your reaction say otherwise."

There was a knock on the door, and both Callen and Stu looked at the door as it pushed open. There she was, Jessica.

"I'll be back," Stu said, squeezing Callen's leg.

He sat there looking at her. She hadn't aged a bit since the last time he saw her. Smiling, she walked into the room.

"Hi, I came as soon as I heard."

Callen felt his heart lurch when she spoke. He didn't want this. He didn't want to feel like this. "Why are you here?"

She smiled and walked over to his bed. "Cal, I've been looking for you. I wanted to say how sorry I was for leaving like that. I was just afraid. You were so serious about us. I wasn't ready for you."

He laughed. "And what you are now?"

"I was after I had time to think. You're pretty intense with your feelings."

Callen sat there thinking about that. He was serious. Is that what was so scary for Lyssa? "You did a number on me, Jessica. I got your message loud and clear when you emptied our bank account."

"I have every penny I took. Cal, I'm sorry. I'm here to get you back. I want us. I've wanted us for the past eight years."

"You tore my heart out, Jessica. I can't forgive that."

"Can you try? Can we try? I mean, you can't possibly love that mousy thing, not like you love me."

His heart swelled at the mention of Lyssa. "You don't know me anymore."

"I may not know you, but I know your heart. It belongs to me. It's always belonged to me. You can't deny that. You can't possibly be happy here. You're a financial god. You don't belong on a ranch in the middle of nowhere."

"Listen, I have a good life, a minimalistic happy life. You don't own my heart anymore. It doesn't beat for you anymore."

"Then who does it beat for? Certainly not that mousy thing."

"Her name is Lyssa, and yes, it does. She is going to be my wife. She is going to be the mother of my children. You have no idea who she is."

"She got you shot. She nearly got you killed. From what I understand, she's the reason those other two people are dead. At least, that's what that woman in the waiting room said."

"Who said that?"

"The blonde all over Mitchell."

"Kennedy? Kennedy's here?"

"I suppose that's her name."

Callen laid there not saying a word, his mind whirling in a million directions. He knew he didn't love this woman. He loved Lyssa. His heart and soul belonged to her.

He looked at Jessica; she was stunning, perfect in every way. But she didn't hold a candle to Lyssa. Lyssa was everything Jessica wasn't.

"You need to leave," he said.

"Cal, I'm not leaving without you. I love you."

He laughed. "You don't know the meaning of the word. If you did, you would have never left. I'm not going anywhere with you. I am going to marry Lyssa, and we are going to have a happy life. A good life, an honest life. Not one based on the size of my bank account. I don't want you. I could never be with you again."

"How can you say that? I told you I didn't spend the money. I'll give it all back. Cal, you're the love of my life."

"Just get out of here," he said as he closed his eyes. "I want nothing to do with you."

"I know you love me," she whispered, touching his hand. He pulled it away. "I know you do. I'll leave for now, but I'm coming back. I want you back, and I am going to make you realize that you still love me."

"I don't, and you are wasting your time. Just leave. Take your money and get the hell out of my life."

He listened as her footsteps carried her out of the room. When he opened his eyes, she was gone. He needed to find Lyssa, to tell her how he felt. He needed to make sure she understood how much he loves her. Throwing the covers back, he attempted to sit up. The pain was horrific, but he managed to get up. When his feet hit the floor, Mitchell came walking in.

"What the hell are you doing?" He rushed over to help him.

"I'm going to find Lyssa. Can you help me?"

"You aren't going anywhere. You've been shot and had major surgery. Callen, you're just going to hurt yourself more. I'll go find her. Hell, we all will. Just get back in the bed before you kill yourself."

"No!" he shouted. "She's out there thinking I want Jessica. Thinking I don't love her. I need to find her."

Mitchell stood in front of him. "Don't make me knock your ass out. Get back in the damn bed. I will find her. I promise."

Finally nodding, Callen let him help him. With tears in his eyes, he said, "You need to find her."

"I will, buddy. I promise. You get some rest. I'll be back."

Callen nodded and closed his eyes. Mitchell left and went to the waiting room. "Come on, guys, we have something to do." He looked at Kennedy. "I'll be back."

"I want to come. What are you doing?"

"Finding Lyssa."

"What? She's not in with Callen?"

Stu stood up, and Mitchell told her, "No."

They all left, leaving Kennedy at the hospital. Outside, Mitchell said, "All right, we have one car, but we need at least two. Let's head back to the ranch and get Callen's truck. We need to find her and get her back here before he kills himself trying to do this himself."

They all agreed. Stu drove, and he didn't take notice of the speed limit signs. They made it back to the farmhouse before Lyssa. Going in, they waited for her. No one knew she had come in until they heard her car start. Mitchell was the first one out the door with Tom and Stu following him.

He threw himself in front of her car. "No, Lyssa, stop!"

Stu opened her door. Reaching in, he turned off the ignition. "You can't do this."

"Just leave me alone." She was crying.

"No, beautiful, you can't do this to him. He is trying to come after you. We promised him we would find you and bring you back."

She shook her head. "He doesn't want me."

"Yes, he does," Tom said from the back seat.

"Listen, I was in that room with him. I had to threaten to knock him out if he didn't get back in the bed. Lyssa, he loves you." Mitchell smiled. "He loves you. Not her."

Lyssa just sat there, tears running down her face. "You didn't see him. You didn't feel what I did when I told him she was there."

"He was angry, that's what you saw and felt. Nothing more. He threw her out, told her he was going to marry you. That he loved you."

"He did?" she whispered.

"He did. Now, come on, let us take you back. He can't get out of bed and drive, and he will if we don't come back with you. Lyssa, he might have thought he loved her once, but he didn't know what love was until he met you. We've known him a long time, and he isn't the same man as he was. You changed him. The love you two share has changed him. He doesn't want her," Stu pleaded with her.

"Fine, I'll go back." Taking her purse, she got in the truck while Mitchell shut the farmhouse up.

The ride back was long and very quiet. No one said a word. When they parked at the hospital, everyone got out but Lyssa. "Stu, can I talk to you please?" He nodded and got back in the truck. She sat there and watched Mitchell and Tom walk into the hospital. "Why would she come here?"

"Because she wants him back. She said she's been looking for him for eight years."

"Has she?"

"She's talked to all of us over the years about his whereabouts, but none of us knew where he was."

"You were his friend when they were together. Did he love her like that, enough to consider going back?"

"He loved her deeply. Everything he did, he did for her, because of her. When she walked out, he died that day."

"He's your friend, but please don't lie to me. Do you think he wants her back?"

"I think a part of him is intrigued that she's here."

"That's not what I asked you."

"I don't know, I can't answer that question. I will say this, though. He threw her out and then proceeded to get out of bed to come and find you. Lyssa, Callen is the type of man who loves with all that he is, with his whole heart. He wouldn't tell you he loved you unless he did."

"But he loves her still. I know what I saw. I know what I felt."

"Then you should be having this conversation with him. Lyssa, I can only tell you about the man I knew eight years ago. I don't know this man like I did that one. He has changed, and it's you who has woken him up."

"I suppose you're right. Thank you, Stu."

"Anytime. Now, come on, before Mitchell has to knock him out."

She smiled and got out of the truck. Together they walked into the hospital. "Oh, Kennedy is here. She really wants to talk to you."

"Yeah, I really have nothing to say to her."

"All right then."

Stu headed to the waiting room, and Lyssa continued to Callen's room. She paused outside the door when she heard *her* voice.

"Callen, I told you, I will give the money back. Please, don't do this. We would be together if you hadn't run away."

"Jessica, you are not hearing me. I don't love you. I don't think I ever did. I think, with you, it was the idea of being in love."

"And you're in love with that mousy thing?"

"Her name is Lyssa, and yes, I am. I told you I am going to marry her."

"No, Callen, you can't. You are the love of my life. I am the love of yours. We spent five years together."

"And you drained my bank account and walked out on me. Jessica, I was there for five months after, selling everything. Not once did you come back. Why are you doing this? I don't want you."

"I know you do," she said softly. "You're just mad at me, and that's all right. I know what I did hurt you."

Lyssa stood outside the door, leaning against the wall and listening. She knew she should go in there, but this was his test. This was his past.

"Jessica, you are not hearing me. I spent the last eight years getting over you."

"See, it took you eight years, so that just tells me that you still love me. She is just a substitute for me, for what we had. You know what we had was as real as it gets. I was scared, Callen, so very scared. When I realized what I had done, I came back. Ask the guys, they know."

"No, Jessica, no. I can't. I won't do it again. I could never trust you."

And there it was. He still loved her. Lyssa felt her eyes fill with tears. A nurse saw her standing there, shaking, with tears running down her cheeks. "Miss, are you all right?" she asked, standing in the doorway.

Lyssa just looked at her. She heard Callen call her name. "Lyssa? Oh, God, Lyssa."

"Cal, what the hell are you doing? You can't get out of bed. Jesus, help me please," she called out to the nurse.

Lyssa watched the nurse as she ran into Callen's room, and then she walked away, listening to Callen call out her name. Stu saw her walk past the waiting room and got up to follow her. He caught up with her at the elevator. "Hey, what happened?"

She shook her head. "Could you please take me to my car? I can't do this right now. I need to sleep. I need to think."

"Come on," he said as the elevator doors opened. They both walked in. Picking her head up, she saw Kennedy looking at her with tears in her eyes. She turned her head; she didn't want to see her.

Stu helped her into the truck and started driving. When they got back to the house, she got out and thanked him. He nodded and just sat there watching her. She didn't get in the car. She walked to the backyard and stood by the fence.

She wasn't sure what she should do, how she should feel. Her heart loved him, but her mind had convinced her that she was a fool to think he could love her the way she wanted to be loved. *Is this what love is?* The tears came, and she couldn't stop them. Her knees started to fail her, and she felt her body lower to the ground. Then the scream came. Again and again, she screamed.

Stu watched her go down and got out of the truck. He had never seen a woman in this much distress. When she screamed, he was moving. He didn't know what to do, so he just knelt on the ground next to her. When the third scream came, he pulled her into his arms and sat on the ground. Lyssa wrapped her arms around him and cried into his chest.

Stu had never seen a woman this destroyed before. *What the fuck happened?* Time had no meaning while he hung onto her. He felt her pull back and move off his lap to sit on the ground.

"Lyssa," he said softly. "What happened?"

She looked at him. "I told you he only thought he loved me. It's just guilt. I don't know if it's guilt for what he did to me, or guilt because he can't have what his heart really desires."

Stu pulled his eyebrows together in confusion. "What do you mean, what his heart really desires?"

"He told her he couldn't forgive her. That he waited for months before he left there, that it has taken him eight years to get over her hurting him. He loves her. He will always love her. He will never love me the way he loves her."

"No, that's not true."

She just stared off into the field. "I heard him say it. If I'm not around, he can find his way back to her. She is who he wants. He's wanted her for eight years. I was just another way for him to forget her for a while."

Stu just sat there looking at her. "I don't believe that."

She turned her head to look at him. "It's the truth. Thank you for bringing me back here. I'm going to go. You guys need to take care of him. After the funeral, I'm just going to go. Thank you for everything."

Stu sat there and watched her get up and walk to her car. He couldn't move; he was in shock at what an asshole his friend was. Shaking his head, he got up and ran after her, jumping in front of her car. "No!" he shouted. "No! I won't let you do this. Fight for him."

"Just get out of my way," she yelled back.

"No! Turn off the car. Turn off the car, Lyssa, and let me take you back. Fight for him. He loves you."

She slammed the car in park and got out. "You don't know a fucking thing, Stu."

"Bullshit. I'm calling bullshit on you." He grabbed her arms. "Fight for him. Do you love him?"

"Yes!" she shouted.

"Then goddammit, fight for him. Don't let that bitch do this to you, to him. He loves you. Let me take you back."

"He doesn't want me. He is still in love with her."

He shook his head. "No, Lyssa, he's in love with you. Don't you see the way he looks at you? He loves you. He never looked at her like that. Never. Please, let me take you back. Don't do this to him, to you."

She took a deep breath. "Stu, he has to do this. He has to make the decision. I can't do it for him."

"Then do it for you. Get your ass in that truck and go tell him. Go tell him how you feel. By running away, you'll never know for sure if he loves you like I know he does."

After a few quiet moments, she nodded. Stu walked her to the truck and helped her in it. They didn't say anything while they drove. When he pulled in the parking lot, Stu opened the door but Lyssa just sat there.

"What's wrong?" he asked.

"She's in there. I can feel it."

"Then I'll get her out of there. Come on. I'm on your side."

Nodding, she opened the door and climbed out. Together they walked in the hospital. Together they walked to his room. Stu pushed the door open, and they walked in together. Jessica was sitting in the chair.

"Get the fuck out of this room," Stu said to her.

"I'm not leaving him." She looked right at Lyssa. "He doesn't love you. He loves me."

Stu grabbed her by the arm and pulled her out of the chair and out the door. Lyssa looked at Callen, then turned and followed Stu down the hall. She watched him push Jessica into a room and shut the door. She stood outside and listened.

"He doesn't want you. Why are you here? Did you run out of money? What is your fucking deal, Jessica?"

"I love him, and he fucking loves me."

"No, no, he doesn't. He is in love with Lyssa. You don't know that man in there. You know nothing about who he is now. For eight fucking years, he has been working on a ranch out here and loving his life. You don't know him. You are a self-centered, egotistical, materialistic bitch. Just like Kennedy, you take what you want, and you don't give a shit who you destroy while you are doing it. It wasn't Lyssa's fault he got shot. It was fucking hers." He nodded toward Kennedy. "She is exactly the same as you are. Only she destroyed her best friend and had a hand in the murder of her own fucking mother, and all she does is sit here and blame Lyssa for helping her parents. You don't know a fucking thing about either of them."

"I don't really care who she is or what she thinks she feels for him. He is in love with me. I love him. Why should I care about that mousy thing?"

Stu shook his head. "You fucking little bitch. We all know about the countless men you've fucked over the last eight years. So, don't stand here and pretend you love him. Get the hell out of this hospital and don't ever come back. Callen is going to marry Lyssa, and there isn't a fucking thing you can do about it. Just go, because you are not getting back into that room."

"You can't stop me."

Lyssa pulled the door opened and walked into the room. "No, but I can."

Kennedy stood up, and Stu smiled.

Jessica glared at her. "You have no rights. You aren't married to him."

Lyssa stepped forward, causing Jessica to step back. She saw the fear in her eyes. "Why would you want him? Are you planning on moving here? Because he isn't going anywhere. I know he's not. You know how I know? Because he loves me, not you. You are just like Kennedy. The only thing you want is his money, his name, what he can give you."

"And you don't?"

Lyssa laughed. "See, the difference between me and you is I don't need his money, nor do I want it. He isn't going back to Chicago."

"I wouldn't be so sure of that," Jessica snapped.

Lyssa stepped forward again, causing Jessica to step back. Leaning in, she said with a smile on her face, "Trust me when I tell you this. I am so sure he isn't going anywhere. He fought for me. He fought hard for me, and I am going to do the same for him. If I see you anywhere near him, or me, or this hospital, I will call my friend at the F.B.I. and I will let him know that you stole five million dollars from Callen. I believe that's a felony charge, which means at least twenty years in a federal prison. You want to fuck with me, then let's go. I'm fighting for him, for what's mine. His heart belongs to me. So, take your skanky ass out of this hospital and go back to your whoring ways in Chicago."

Turning her head, she looked at Kennedy. "Why are you even here? I told you, there is nothing left. Because of your self-centered, egotistical ass, your parents are gone. You have nothing. You are nothing. I can't believe I fixed everything for you your whole life. Just get the fuck out of here. After Saturday, you don't ever have to think of me again."

She looked at Stu. "Please get these two bitches out of here. I'm going to see Callen."

"You can't stop me."

"Watch me," he said, picking up the phone by the door. "Yes, can I get security to the eighth floor waiting room please?"

"They can't stop me," she smarted.

Stu didn't say a word. He could hear Kennedy sniffling behind him, but he didn't give a shit about either of them, not after what he just went through with Lyssa. There was a knock on the door. Stu opened it. "Could you please remove these two women from the hospital? Our friend was shot, and they are both a threat to his recovery."

The security guards took both Jessica and Kennedy by the arm and started out of the room. "Is it possible to make sure neither of them can get back in?"

"We will take care of it. If they happen to get back in here, you just call us, and we will get the police involved."

"Thank you."

Stu stood there watching them being dragged down the hall to the elevator. "What the hell has gotten into you?" Tom said.

He spun around. "You don't even want to know. I'll be in Callen's room. Their house has blood all over it. Go out there and clean it up for them. Or just do what you want. I don't really care. Neither of those bitches is getting anywhere near him. I'm going to his room to wait for him to wake up. It's time I'm the friend I should have been eight years ago. He was right. We've turned into egotistical assholes. That's not the man I want to be."

Stu walked out and headed to Callen's room. Lyssa was standing by the bed holding his hand. "The nurse said he would be out for about eight hours. I'm going to the hotel down the street. I need some sleep. I don't feel good. Will you stay with him and let him know that I was here and that I'll be back? I promise I'll be back. I don't have any money. I left my purse in my car."

Stu smiled at her, handing her all the cash he had in his pocket. Then he opened his wallet and took out his bank card. "Go, I'm not leaving here until you get back. The code is six, one, eight, two. In case you need anything."

Lyssa leaned in and kissed Callen softly on the lips. "I love you," she whispered. Looking at Stu, she smiled. "Thank you."

"He would have done the same for me. Go, get some rest and eat."

She smiled and left. As she walked out of the hospital, she saw Mitchell and Tom talking to Kennedy and Jessica. Shaking her head, she got in a cab and went to the hotel.

CHAPTER FOURTEEN

Stu sat in the chair with his eyes closed. He must have dozed off because when Callen touched his arm, he jumped.

"Where is she?" he asked.

Stu sat there looking at him. "You fucked up."

Callen closed his eyes, feeling tears coming. *How in the world did this get so messed up?* "Stu, I love her."

"Who?"

Callen opened his eyes. "What the hell does that mean?"

"Well, I think you need to tell me that. You gutted her. I've never experienced pain like that in my life."

"Fuck," he said. "Where is she?"

"I don't know. The question here is not where she is, but what the fuck are you doing?" Callen looked at him. "Listen, man, Jessica fucking destroyed you. So much so that you sold every fucking thing you owned and disappeared. Yeah, she has been coming around looking for you. But none of us believed it was because she wanted to be with you. Over the years, we have all seen her with countless men. That woman doesn't love you, and if she does, well, you don't want that kind of life."

"I don't want any kind of life with her. Why won't anyone believe that?"

Stu chuckled. "Because your convictions are less than believable. Even I can see it, feel it. Can you even imagine how Lyssa feels? You're the one who told us how special she was. So, imagine how she feels. I was there with her when she cracked, and let me tell you, she cracked. That woman loves you deeply. So much so that she is willing to walk away so you can learn to love Jessica again. She knows, you fucker. She knows that you still have feelings for *her*. You can deny it all you want, but Lyssa knows."

"So, I have unresolved feelings for a woman who I thought was the love of my life. But she wasn't. I love Lyssa."

"See, I don't understand you. You are the smartest man I know. How can that fucking ego of yours be so stupid? She took five million dollars from you and left. She never loved you. That was all in your fucking head. I don't know if she drugged your ass or what, but she never loved you. Not like Lyssa. That woman is the embodiment of how a person should love. Cal, tell me you didn't sleep with her. Tell me you didn't take her virginity with residual feelings for Jessica."

Callen didn't say a word. *Did I do that? Was my heart not completely with her? Was it just the idea of having a virgin? No, she is incredible.* "No, I have no feelings for Jessica, and if I did, they were gone the minute I met Lyssa. She is who I love. Knowing her has made me realize that I never loved Jessica. Not the way someone should love another person. Lyssa is that woman. The way her smile lights my fucking soul. The way her laugh makes me feel like I am in heaven. The way she looks at me, looks right into my soul. She has to know I love her."

"Oh, she knows."

"Then what is going on?"

"She also knows that you still have feelings for Jessica. You can't love two women like that. A woman like Lyssa is a rare find in this life. You have been given a gift."

"Stu, where is she?"

"Cal, I swear to God, if you hurt her."

"Stu…"

"She's at a hotel down the street. She told me to tell you she would be back after she got some sleep. She tore into Jessica in the waiting room. Kennedy too."

Callen smiled. "I'm so fucking tired. Can you do me a favor?"

"Sure," he said.

"When she gets back here, can you go out to the farmhouse, and in the closet of the master bedroom in the far back corner, can you get the box that's there and bring it to me?"

"Of course, what's in it?"

Callen smiled. "The ring I bought her."

Stu smiled. "I'll do it. You get some rest and let yourself heal."

"Good, thank you. Thank you for looking after her. Man, I am so fucked up. I can't lose her. For weeks, she has been the only thing in my heart in a long time. Everything about her is everything I can't breathe without."

Lyssa slept only because her body was so exhausted. When she woke, her heart was still hurting. She loved him, there was no denying it. But she was strong. She wasn't this wimpy woman. She had her break-down, but now, it was time to put on her big girl panties and face the facts. There was a woman out there who wanted the man she loved. The question was, would she fight for him or would she walk away?

But every lesson she learned from the men in Kennedy's life taught her to just walk away. You can't make someone love you. Did he love her, or was she so far gone that she was just believing what he wanted her to believe? She couldn't even tell. She had nothing to base it on.

She got up and took a shower. She was getting dressed when she realized that it was Wednesday. "Shit." Dialing the phone, she said, "Hi, this is Lyssa Dawn. Did I miss my appointment?"

"It's in fifteen minutes. Did you need me to re-schedule?"

"No, I can make it. Thanks."

She dressed in lightning speed and rushed out of the hotel. Hailing a cab, she rushed into the doctor's office with one minute to spare.

Laughing, the receptionist nodded to her and then they headed back to the examination room. "She'll be right in." Lyssa nodded and sat down.

When the doctor came in, she smiled. "So, I take it no period?"

"No, so what do we do?"

"Well, let's get some blood and we can go from there. I'll send the nurse back in. It shouldn't take long."

Lyssa sat there freaking out. She wanted babies, lots of babies, but she couldn't tell him. He would stay just because of the baby. The nurse came in and took her blood then left. She found herself getting a bit excited. She had enough money to have a baby alone. Lots of women did it. She could sell the little farmhouse and have more money. Her mind whirled.

The doctor came in and sat down, looking at her. "Lyssa, I'm not sure how you are going to take this news, but, sweetheart, you're going to have a baby."

She sat there looking at the doctor. "But you said it was highly unlikely."

"It is. Now, there are plenty of options. You can terminate, or there's adoption."

"No, none of those are options. I'm having it. I want it."

"Okay, well, I'm going to give you a prescription for prenatal vitamins. And I want you eating lots of folic acid-rich foods. I want you to come back in three months. If not, then to a doctor in three months."

Lyssa just nodded. She didn't really hear what she was saying because she was still in shock. She was having a baby. "Are you sure?" she asked the doctor. "I mean, there is no way to make a mistake now, is there?"

The doctor smiled, handing her the paper. "No, I'm sorry, no mistake. You are having a baby. Lyssa, are you all right?"

"Yes, I'm just shocked. I had sex three times in my life with one man, and I'm pregnant." She laughed. "What luck. Thank you." She stood up and left the office.

She needed to walk so she did, stopping off at the drug store to fill her prescription. Then she went to the diner to get something to eat.

She was in a daze, wandering around. Eventually, she ended up at the hotel, sitting in a chair in the lobby. *Is this really what I want to do? Do I want his child even if I can't have him?* She knew she wanted babies, just never expected to do it alone.

Getting up, she went to her room and laid on the bed, resting her hands on her stomach. "Hey, little thing in there," she said. "I'm your mommy. I'm sorry things are crazy now, but hopefully, it will get better. I'm not sure if your daddy is going to be around when it's time for you to come out. He might be in love with someone else, and I'm sorry about that. But I think we will be all right. I'm hoping that he is in love with us. Well, he doesn't know about you yet. I just found out about you. I can't tell him you are in there, because he will choose us, and I will never know if it's me he really loves. Not sure if I am ever going to tell him you are in there. No, that's not true. One day, I will tell him, one day, when he figures out who has his heart. Me or that evil bitch from Chicago."

She rolled over and closed her eyes. Sleep was what she needed. So much had happened in such little time. Tomorrow, she had to go say goodbye to Charles and Emily and to face Kennedy. She wasn't sure she wanted to do that.

Callen slept for nearly two days, and Stu sat vigil in his room. There had been no sign of Jessica or Kennedy. Mitchell and Tom had stopped by to let Stu know that they got the farmhouse cleaned up and there was no sign of Lyssa.

They let him know where the funeral was and what time. They had brought Callen's suit and the ring. Stu sat looking at the ring. It wasn't something horribly big, but then again, Lyssa wasn't that kind of girl.

As Callen started to stir, Stu closed the box, setting it on the table next to the bed.

"How do you feel?" Stu asked him.

"Like I've been shot. Did she come back?"

"Who?"

"Lyssa, who else?"

Stu smiled. "No, I haven't heard a word from her. I talked to the doctor. He said you can go to the funeral and the wake, but you have to promise to come back here when it's over."

"I don't care. As long as I can pay my respects and get my girl, I don't have a problem with that."

"I'll have a nurse come and help you get dressed. I'll get changed in the bathroom down the hall." Stu stood up, handing Callen the ring box.

He smiled and watched Stu move out of the room. It took a great deal to get him dressed and ready to go. When Stu came back, Callen was in a wheelchair in his suit. "You ready?"

"Yep, let's go."

They were early to the wake. Callen paid his respects, and they made their way to the back of the church. Little by little, the church filled with people. He could have sworn the whole county was there. He had seen a few of the women he had fucked, but none of them approached him. He waited through the whole service for her, but he didn't see her. His heart raced, thinking she didn't stay for the funeral.

Everyone followed the hearse out to the ranch, to the family burial plot way up on the hill. There were more than a hundred people there. Callen saw Kennedy and Mitchell, along with Tiny and the guys from the ranch. But not Lyssa. He started freaking out as the people were leaving. He could feel the tears building in his eyes. "She didn't come," he said softly. But then some people moved out of the way and there she was. His heart stopped when he saw her. She looked destroyed, standing next to a tree on the far side of the graves.

Getting out of the chair proved to be very difficult, but Stu helped him. He managed to walk on his own toward her. She didn't see him through her tears. In her hand, she held two roses, waiting for the people to leave, then she moved slowly toward the graves. She still hadn't noticed him.

He watched as she bent down, laying a rose on Emily's grave, her mouth moving. He couldn't make out what she was saying. Then she turned toward Charles' grave, her back to him. She didn't notice him when she stood up.

He was a few feet from her when she turned around. Her eyes were down as she walked. She felt him before she saw him, and stopped in her tracks, lifting her head, her breath hitching in her chest.

Taking a few more steps toward her, he watched her shake her head. "Why are you here?"

"Lyssa, I don't want her. Please, beautiful, believe me. I love you."

Her tears fell. "I saw it. I heard you. You still love her," she whispered. "Things are different now."

"Stu said you would come back. Why haven't you come back?"

"I've been thinking and sleeping. I needed to get my head straight. Why are you here? You should be back in the hospital."

"I had to be here. I needed to say goodbye to them. I needed to see you."

She smiled her shy smile. "I was coming back today. Come on, you need to get back. You don't look so good."

He chuckled, his hand reaching up to touch her face. Her instinct was to move away. His hand dropped. "Please, beautiful. Let me love you."

She smiled. "You own my whole heart, but I heard you. I heard what you said to her. Callen, you still have feelings for her."

"No, I don't. I love you."

"I know you do, and I love you. But it's different now. She is here and fighting for you."

He smiled. "So are you."

He watched her blush. "Because I love you."

"I'm so sorry this is happening. I just want to love you, to have the life we want. I want to marry you, have a life with you, and have lots of fat babies with you." His voice was soft.

Stu, Mitchell, and Tom stood there with Kennedy watching.

Lyssa stood there looking at him. "You're just afraid to go back. I can feel her pulling you away. I can't, Callen. I can't." She turned to walk away.

"No!" he shouted. "No!"

She stopped, wanting to believe him. She needed him now more than ever. Her hand moved to her stomach, and Callen saw the instinctual movement. His heart stopped. "Lyssa," he whispered as he moved toward her. "Don't run. Please, baby, don't leave." He was right behind her. "Let me love you." He wrapped his arm around her. His tears fell when she leaned into him. Bending his head down to her ear, his eyes glanced at her hand on her stomach. "I love you, beautiful. Marry me."

Her eyes closed. She loved him. She wanted a life with him. He was here with her. He came for her. "I love you so much," she whispered. "I want so much with you. You own my heart. Please don't hurt me. Fight for me."

"It will never happen. Let me love you, beautiful. Live this life with me. Be my wife, my partner."

Kennedy whispered, "Come on, Lyssa. Say yes."

Stu looked at her. So did Mitchell.

"Beautiful, turn around." She turned slowly, her tears falling slowly on her cheeks. Callen's hand tilted her head up. "Marry me? I can't live without you. I need you. I can't breathe."

She smiled her shy smile at him and nodded her head. He bent the best he could to kiss her. "I love you," she said on his lips.

"I belong to you and only you. Forever."

She wrapped her arms around his waist, laying her head on his chest to listen to his heart. It was slamming in his chest. No one moved. No one said a word. They just stood like statues waiting to see what happened.

Callen and Lyssa didn't let go of each other. "I am so sorry for everything that happened," he said.

"I'm sorry for all of it. If it wasn't for me…"

"You did the right thing. You helped Charles and Emily. You helped me. We have to believe that this was meant to be, that it all happened so we would meet. I'm not going anywhere. I love you. I'm not letting you go. I need you to fight for me, just like I am fighting for you. I am not going to lose you over her. She isn't who I want. You are, only you, beautiful. Only you."

She lifted her head, and Callen's hand came up and wrapped around her neck. "I love you," he whispered on her lips as he kissed her. When they pulled apart, she smiled her shy smile at him. "I love you."

He chuckled. "I think I need to get back to the hospital. I'm not sure I feel very good."

She felt his body slump onto her. Out of nowhere, Stu was next to him. "Come on, buddy," he said, helping him stand. Mitchell came up with a wheelchair, and they sat him in it. "Lyssa, can you take him back in your car? I'll follow you."

She nodded. When they got back to the hospital, and Callen got back in bed, the nurse gave him some pain medicine. As he was falling asleep, he said to her, "Please don't leave."

Smiling her shy smile for him, she leaned in and whispered in his ear, "I love you. Go to sleep. I'll be here when you wake up. I'm not going anywhere."

His smile stayed on his face as he crashed. Lyssa got comfortable in the chair next to his bed. Holding his hand, she closed her eyes with her hand on her stomach and said to herself, *Well, little one, I guess your daddy loves us. We are going to have a wonderful life.*

CHAPTER FIFTEEN

Ten days after the funeral, Callen was released from the hospital. "Take it easy. No working for at least three weeks," the doctor told him.

"Oh, he isn't going to be doing anything but lying on the couch," Lyssa said.

The doctor laughed. "He can do just about anything that's not strenuous."

"Thanks, Doc, for saving me." Callen smiled at him.

Stu stayed the entire time. He was standing behind the wheelchair waiting for him to get in. "Let's go, your chariot awaits."

Callen chuckled. Walking over, he sat down in the chair and smiled at Lyssa. "You ready, beautiful?"

"Oh, you know I am."

When they got to the doors, the press was all over the place. "Shit," Callen said. "This is ridiculous."

"Yeah, well, it's not every day that someone with your reputation disappears and then reappears with a bullet in them." Stu looked at Lyssa. "You ready for this?"

"No, but let's just go. I'm tired of being here." She looked at Callen. "You ready?"

He reached up and took her hand. "So fucking ready. Just promise me you aren't going to listen to what they say."

She laughed. "I'm more worried about one of them hurting you."

Callen laughed. "I'm sure they won't be expecting the ass kicking they'll get if they do. Let's go home, beautiful."

The three of them walked out the doors. The crowd erupted, flashes going off, people shouting questions at him.

"Callen, is it true you and Jessica are back together?" He hung on to Lyssa's hand.

"Callen, is it true you're going back to Chicago?" Lyssa smiled.

"Callen, is it true your girlfriend's lover shot you?" Stu busted out laughing. He knew Callen was her only lover.

"Callen, is it true that you're here because you're broke?"

They finally made it to the car. Callen stood up and climbed into the front seat, and Lyssa shut his door and made her way around to the driver's side. Stu headed to the truck, ready to run interference in case the press followed them.

Lyssa started the car with a huge smile on her face. They were going home. She needed to tell Callen about the baby, but she didn't want to do it with a bunch of people around. So, she kept her secret to herself. She was only a few weeks along, so she had a bit of time left.

"You happy?" he said softly to her.

"I am," she said and smiled.

When they pulled up to the farmhouse, there was a car in the driveway that she recognized. "Who's that?" Callen asked.

"My boss, well, my old boss. I wonder what he's doing here." She opened the door just as Stu pulled up alongside her. Walking around to Callen's side, she helped him out and they headed toward the house.

Mr. Slate walked from the back. "Lyssa," he called out.

"Mr. Slate." She moved toward him. "What are you doing here? How did you find me?"

He smiled. "First, let me just say how sorry I am for everything that happened to the two of you." He nodded to Callen. "Mr. Greenvale sent me an envelope. Inside was a letter for you, to be opened upon his death, and I have a revised copy of his will. I couldn't find you, but in his letter to me, he told me you were living here now."

"I've been at the hospital with Callen. Mr. Slate, I don't understand."

Callen smiled. "Why don't we go inside? I could use something to drink."

They moved into the house and sat around the dining room table. Lyssa watched as he pulled a huge envelope out of his briefcase. Pulling a letter from it, he handed it to Lyssa. She sat there looking at it, then at Callen.

"Hey," he said gently, reaching for her hand. "You don't have to read it now."

She nodded. "You said something about a revised will?"

Mr. Slate nodded. "I have it here."

"Well, shouldn't Kennedy be here? I mean, I'm sure her parents would want her here." She watched Mr. Slate, but something wasn't right. "Mr. Slate, what's going on?"

"Lyssa, you should read the letter before you read the will."

She looked at Callen. Taking his hand, she stood up, and he followed her as she walked out onto the back porch, leaving Stu and Mr. Slate in the house.

"I'm scared," she whispered.

"I'm right here. Do you want me to read it?"

She shook her head and opened the letter.

Lyssa,

I know you are wondering why we have written you a letter. Emily is sitting here confident that we are doing the right thing. Even though you are not our daughter, we have always thought of you as ours. I know that your life growing up wasn't a good one. We know that your daddy hit your momma, and we know that he hit you as well. You did a great job of making up excuses for the bruises, but we knew better.

There aren't words to express to you how grateful we are for everything that you have done over the years to protect Kennedy. We can't figure out where we went wrong in raising her. She was such a wonderful child, but she grew up to be a horrible person. I don't believe that Hugh made her do what she did. She always hated this place, and I think, in the end, she hated both of us.

When Callen crashed his truck into our fence post and we brought him into our home, he became, to me, the son I never had. Sure, I had all the ranch hands, but he was different. He is a genuine human being. Honestly, I thought maybe Kennedy would show an interest and come back home, but he didn't have enough for her. She was always looking for something bigger. In the end, she will land on her feet as she always does.

Emily and I want, more so now, for you and Callen to have our ranch. We are happy in knowing that you both will love it as we have. He is a good man, Lyssa, and he loves you like you deserve to be loved. So, we are leaving the ranch to Callen and everything else to you.

Please don't say no and refuse. We want you to have it. Have a happy life like we've had here. Raise your babies here and give them the deep love the two of you share. It's rare to find that kind of love. We were lucky to have found it.

We love you both as if you were the children we wanted.

You live a happy life here and think of us often while you do.

Love,

Charles and Emily

Tears were streaming down her face. Callen held her while she cried. She gave him the letter to read, and she held him while he cried. "I can't believe they did this," he whispered.

"Callen, Kennedy got nothing. Shouldn't we give her something?"

"Let's not make any decisions right now. Come on, let's go back inside and read the will. Maybe they left her something."

Together they went in, and Mr. Slate read the will. Kennedy was given nothing. Callen got the ranch, and Lyssa got all the money. Mr. Slate and Stu left after the reading. They just sat there at the table, not saying a word, for the longest time.

Looking at him, she said, "I'm going to go to bed."

He nodded and watched her get up and go upstairs. Callen got up and walked out to the backyard and stood leaning on the fence looking out over the ranch. It was all his now. He couldn't help but think back on his life and how he got here. Reaching into his pocket, he pulled out the ring he bought for Lyssa and smiled. He was going to marry her, and they were going to live here and be happy.

Turning, he looked up to the window. The woman he loves was up there. She needed him. So, he went back in, locked the house up, and made his way to the bedroom. She was lying on the bed in her panties, with her back to the door. He took his clothes off and climbed in behind her, wrapping her in his arms and pulling her to his chest.

"I missed this. I missed you," he whispered. "I love you, beautiful."

Slowly, she rolled over into his cocoon. "I love you."

Wrapped up in one another, they slept and slept. Being in the hospital with people coming and going all day and night, it was hard to get any good sleep; plus, they couldn't sleep in each other's arms at the hospital. Lyssa woke first, getting out of bed to use the bathroom.

When she walked out, Callen was looking at her. "You are so fucking beautiful," he whispered to her, loving the blush that covered her body. He reached his hand out for her, and she walked toward him, climbed on the bed, and snuggled into his side.

"Why don't we get something to eat?" she whispered. What she wanted to do was make love with him, but he still had a bandage on his chest, and he was still weak.

"What if I want to starve to death holding you."

She giggled. "Not going to happen. I need you. You can't die on me now."

"Fine." He pouted, and she kissed him. "I'll get up."

Lyssa rolled over, grabbing a sun dress out of the closet. "I'll go make us some breakfast." Callen sat on the bed smiling at her. She smiled back at him. "What's going on in your head?" She walked up to him, running her fingers through his hair.

"Nothing, I just feel like the luckiest bastard on the planet." His arms wrapped around her.

"I'm the lucky one, Callen."

Tilting his head up, he took in her sweet smile. "We will never agree on this."

Laughing, she bent and kissed him before moving out of the room. Callen bent down, picking up his pants, and pulled the ring out of his pocket. He grabbed a pair of pajama bottoms and headed downstairs with the ring on his pinky finger. He was going to ask her to marry him. When he walked into the kitchen, she was at the stove, so he got down on his knee and waited for her to turn around.

When she did, she froze. "What's wrong?"

He smiled. "Lyssa Dawn, I would be so honored if you would consider spending the rest of your life with me. Will you marry me, beautiful?"

She could feel her eyes fill with tears. "Yes," she whispered. "Oh, God, Callen, yes." She knelt in front of him.

Slipping the ring off his finger, he put it on hers. "I love you," he said against her lips as he kissed her. "I want you. I've missed you."

"But the doctor said not to do anything strenuous," she whispered as his hands moved her dress up. She lifted her hands above her head.

"Making love to the woman who is going to be my wife is not something I would consider as strenuous." Laying her back on the floor, he kissed her while maneuvering out of his pajama bottoms. He made love to her, and she made love to him. After, she laid on his chest as he held her, the both of them content and looking forward to a life together.

"We didn't use a condom," he said softly.

"It doesn't matter."

"You said you didn't want to get pregnant yet."

"It doesn't matter anymore," she said, lifting her head. "Callen, I'm already pregnant." She looked deep into his eyes, wanting to see the truth of how he felt. His smile grew slowly across his lips, and she saw what she hoped she would see.

His eyes filled with tears. "Really?" His voice was softer and filled with nothing but love.

Nodding her head, she told him, "Really. I found out a few days after you were shot. I didn't know how to tell you. I didn't want you to stay because of it. I wanted you to want me, to want us."

"Aww, beautiful, there should have never been a doubt in your mind or in your heart. I am so in love with you."

She leaned in and kissed him. "I love you so much, Callen. So much."

EPILOGUE

18 MONTHS LATER

Callen and Lyssa were married a month later in a small ceremony on the ranch. Stu had decided that he was going to stay, so he bought Callen's house from him and took a job on the ranch. They had begun restoring the old ranch house together while Tiny and the guys took care of the ranch.

"Callen, come on! We are going to be late," Lyssa yelled up the stairs. "What are you two doing up there?"

"We're coming. I had to make sure his bow tie was just right," he said as he appeared at the top of the stairs.

"He's only nine months old. A straight bow tie isn't going to matter by the time we get to the church."

Callen walked down the stairs holding their nine-month-old son, Charlie, named after Charles. "Relax, he can't get married without me. I'm the best man." He kissed her, pulling her to his chest. "Don't my girls look beautiful?" he whispered on her lips.

Laughing, Lyssa said, "Thank you, but this little girl isn't happy with being late." Her hand moved to her baby bump. She kissed Charlie on the forehead as he reached for her hair. "Come on, will you put him in his car seat? I need to pee."

Callen laughed. "Well, hurry up. We don't want to be late." He smacked her on the ass as she moved past him. "Come on, little man, let's get this show on the road." Yelling toward the half bath, he asked, "Baby, did you pack the diaper bag?"

"It's already in the truck."

Callen walked out the door. He was putting Charlie in his car seat when he heard a car coming down the road. He made sure the little boy was all strapped in then closed the door as the car pulled up.

Stu got out. "What are you doing here? You're getting married in like an hour."

He shook his head. "I'm not sure I can do this."

Callen smiled at him. "What are you talking about? Sherry loves you."

"Yeah, that's just it. I'm not so sure it's me she loves."

"Okay, I'm a bit lost here. What is going on?"

"Well, a few days ago, we were talking, and she made a comment about getting out of this tiny house."

"I used to live there. It is a small house."

"So is this one." He nodded to their house just as Lyssa walked out the door.

"Stu, what are you doing here? I was just telling Callen that we were going to be late." She walked up and hugged him.

"Stu is having second thoughts."

"Don't be silly. Sherry loves you."

Stu shook his head. "I'm not so sure that's true." He looked at Cal. "How did you know Lyssa wasn't after your money?"

Callen laughed. "Well, the fact that she beat the shit out of me a few times was my first clue."

"So, you admit it? Finally!" Lyssa laughed. "What happened?" she asked Stu.

He leaned against the car and watched as Lyssa opened the truck to get the baby out. "We were talking a few days ago about painting the house, putting in some trees and bushes, and she said, 'Why waste the money? Aren't we moving into a bigger house after we get married?'"

Lyssa turned and looked at him. "Are you serious? She's been working in my office since before you two started dating. She has never led me to believe that she wanted anything more than you."

"Lys, I can't do this. I don't feel that she loves me like you love Callen. Although, I know you two are like the exception to the rule of being in love." They both smiled at one another, and Callen wrapped his arm around her, kissing Charlie on the head.

"Stu, how do you feel about her when you're not together?" Callen asked. "I mean, love is different for everyone. It's not defined by any set of rules or examples. When I met Lyssa, the minute I looked into her eyes, I knew she was going to own me. So much so that it freaked me out."

"I don't think I feel that way with Sherry. I mean, don't get me wrong, I think she is beautiful, and smart, and a total sweetheart. But I don't know if it's who she really is, if it's me she wants and not my bank account. Do you know we have never had a fight?"

Lyssa busted out laughing. "I'm sorry, seriously? You two have been together for nearly a year and you've never had a fight?" Stu shook his head. "Callen and I have one at least once a month."

Callen chuckled. "I fight with her because making up is so much fun."

Lyssa laughed, slapping him in the chest. "Stu, if you don't think you love her, then don't go through with this. Please don't hurt yourself. Yes, Sherry is sort of my friend, but you are family. If she hurts you, I'm going to be pissed."

"I think part of the reason I came here was because I needed to know if you've felt anything different about her."

"She's never really talked to me about you. She just thanked me for introducing her to you. But that's about it. Please don't do this if you aren't sure. Because in this state, it's a fifty-fifty state. If you get divorced, she gets half of what you own."

"I know, and I also know you don't give a shit about money, but she could walk away with a couple hundred million."

"Stu, man, what is this really about?"

Stu looked at Lyssa. "Can I talk to him alone?"

She smiled. "Not a problem, I think this man here needs something to eat anyway. Don't leave without talking to me first."

Callen kissed her on the forehead. "Thank you," he said softly. They stood there and watched Lyssa walk into the house.

"I know this shouldn't be in my mind, but I can't get what Jess did to you out of it. I'm not sure if I'm really in love with this girl. I mean, yeah, we have good sex, but our conversations feel sometimes like they are choreographed, like she says what she thinks I want to hear."

"Well, if you're worried about the money thing, have you given her access to it?"

He shook his head. "No, I haven't. Did you with Lyssa?"

"Lyssa has her own money. We have a household fund that I keep padded for her, but she's never indicated she wanted or needed more. You two have lived together for a while now. Who takes care of the bills?"

"I do for the most part. What about you?"

"No, Lyssa does it. I don't know what to tell you. Why don't you call her and have her come out here? We can get Tiny's girl to come out and sit with Charlie, since he's going to want to take a nap soon, and we can go over to the ranch house and you can talk to her. See if Lyssa can gauge her. If she blows up, I don't want her to scare the baby."

"Do you think she would do that?"

Callen laughed. "It's not like she can turn it on or off. It is what it is. But the woman knows when someone is lying."

Just then, Lyssa walked out of the house with Charlie on her hip. "Callen can you take him?"

"Come on, little man." He reached for the baby.

"Lyssa, will you do something for me?" Stu asked.

"I would do anything for you. Yes, go call her. I already called Sarah. Tiny is bringing her over."

Stu stood there looking at her while Callen laughed. "I told you." He pulled Lyssa into his embrace as Stu walked away to call Sherry. "I love you, woman."

"You better, I'm knocked up again."

"Mmm, and what a beautiful pregnant woman you are. I plan on keeping you that way. Barefoot and pregnant in my kitchen."

She laughed. "You think?"

His mouth covered hers. "I know," he whispered on her lips. "If you weren't already my wife, I would ask you to marry me."

Lyssa laughed, putting her hand on his face. "I want to fuck you, husband," she whispered.

"Damn, Lys." He kissed her deeply, lifting her in one arm while the baby patted his face. Laughing, he set her down, pulling back, and looked at the baby. "What's the matter, buddy?"

Charlie smiled at him and laid his head on his shoulder. Lyssa ran her fingers though his hair. "You tired, little guy? Daddy, why don't you take this bow tie off him and these clothes and put him down for a nap?"

"Come on, buddy." With a kiss on her head, he took Charlie into the house as Stu walked up.

"She's upset and crying because I'm not at the church."

"I would be as well. Is she coming?"

"Yeah," he said, turning his head as Tiny came down the road. "Lys, I don't think I can do this."

She rubbed his back. "Then don't. You are doing the right thing by telling her. I mean, you could have just left."

He smiled. "To be honest with you, I couldn't understand why Cal wanted to stay here. I mean, we had such a fantastic life in Chicago, but once I was here for a while, I understood. I'm not leaving here. I want what you two have, to be with someone who wants just me, who wants a life with me."

"I wasn't sure he was going to stay with me. I was terrified to tell him I was pregnant with Charlie, because I didn't want him to stay because of that. But, it turns out, he is just as in love with me as I am with him. Stu, I'm your friend. If Sherry isn't it for you, then she isn't it. Callen and I knew it from that first day. Is that how you felt with Sherry?"

"No. I mean, she is smoking hot, and she says and does all the right things, but I don't think that's how I feel. I didn't tell her I loved her until four months in, and I think I only said it because she said it to me first."

"We're you two having sex when she said it?"

Chuckling, he nodded. "It was right after, yeah."

"If you want my advice, take sex off the table. Make sure next time."

"Is that what you two did?"

She busted out laughing. "Stu," she whispered. "I was a virgin, remember. I didn't want to have sex with anyone."

"Then why did you with Callen?"

"Because my whole body loved him, wanted him, needed him, desired him."

"As did mine," Cal said as he wrapped his arms around her stomach, cradling her baby bump and kissing her neck.

Tiny's truck pulled up, and Sarah got out of the truck. "I thought you were going to a wedding?" she said to Lyssa.

"We were, but something came up." Looking at Tiny, she said, "Thanks, I'll have Callen bring her home when this is over, or to the wedding."

Tiny nodded to her and pulled out of the drive. Lyssa headed into the house with Callen. They stood talking for a few minutes, and then Sarah went in and they all headed over to the ranch house.

Twenty minutes later, Sherry pulled up in the car, she was wearing jeans, had her makeup done to the hilt, and her hair looked beautiful. Stu stood on the porch looking at her. He wasn't sure he felt what he should feel toward this woman. Her makeup was impeccable, but yet she was crying on the phone.

As she walked up the stairs, she looked at Stu. "Why would you do this? It's our wedding day."

Lyssa walked out the door carrying a tray full of lemonade. "Hi, Sherry." She smiled, and Sherry nodded as Lyssa set the tray down. She picked up a glass and went to sit on the stairs.

"Come and sit with me," Stu said, putting his hand out to her. She took it and they went to sit in the rockers. "I'm not sure we should do this today," he said sweetly.

"I gathered that when you called me and asked me to meet you here. Stu, what's going on?"

"I'm not sure, it just doesn't feel like it should. I don't feel like I should. Cal and Lyssa knew the second they met. Me? I wasn't sure."

"Why did you ask me to marry you?" She had a bit of a bite in her voice. Lyssa turned, leaning her back against the post so she could look at her.

"I think because you wanted me to. You had mention it a few times."

"So, you didn't ask me because you wanted to marry me?"

He chuckled. "If I didn't want to marry you, I wouldn't have asked you."

"Then why are we here sitting on the porch at the ranch?"

"What do you expect out of this life with me?"

She sat there looking at him. "I don't understand."

"I want children, lots of them. What about you?"

"How many is lots?"

Lyssa could see she was very uncomfortable.

"I don't know. Four, five, maybe six."

"I don't want that many. I really don't want any, but I'm willing to have two maybe. I just don't want to destroy my body having babies."

And there it was. Stu knew, as well as Lyssa, that she was in this for the money.

"Would you be willing to try some different things in the bedroom?"

Lyssa nearly spit her lemonade all over the place when Sherry's face contorted. Her voice very soft, she told him, "I'm not into kink. No, Stu, that stuff is not for me."

Stu sat there looking at her. "Sherry, I can't marry you. I don't think or feel like you love me. Not like the way we should."

"Why, because I won't do kink with you or have a heard of babies for you? I mean, really, how are we supposed to have that many children in such a tiny house. You have all that money, and you live like a poor ranch hand."

Stu busted out laughing, shaking his head. "I knew it. The only reason you are willing to do this is because I have money. Sherry, I'm sorry, but I am more than my money. I can't do this. I'm sorry, but we are over. Keep the ring. I'll pay your parents for the wedding, but you and I are through." Lyssa watched as he got up and walked to his truck and then drove away.

Turning her head, she looked at Sherry, who just sat there looking at the ring on her finger. She looked at Lyssa. "I can't believe how humiliated I'm going to be. There are a hundred people at that church."

"Can I say something?" Sherry nodded. "Even if he went through with this, you were just going to marry him for his money. Why would you do that?"

"Because I want to get out of this fucking town, and with all the money he has, we could have left here."

"He doesn't want to leave here. It's the same with Callen; he just wants to have a nice quiet life with a woman he loves who loves him in return."

"No offense, Lyssa, but that's pretty funny coming from you. You're married to a billionaire."

"Yes, I am, but it's not my money. It's his. I didn't marry him because he's rich, Sherry. I married him because he set my heart on fire. That should be the only reason you marry someone. Not for their money. I'm sorry that you feel this way, and I'm also sorry that I don't want you to work for me anymore. Stu is my friend, and you hurt him. You took advantage of him, and well, I don't want someone like that around me. Please, just leave. You can come by on Monday and empty your desk." Lyssa stood up and walked back into the ranch house where Callen was standing just inside the door.

His arms wrapped around her, and he kissed her forehead. "Come on, beautiful, let's go home."

"I am home. You are my home. I love you," she whispered.

His hands moved to her face, and he kissed her deeply. "I love you, wife."

They walked out as Sherry was pulling away. "I'll take you home then take Sarah home. I'm going to stop by Stu's. I'll probably be late."

"That's fine, he needs you."

Callen laughed. "He has the guys. I just want to make sure he's all right."

He opened the door for her and helped her climb up into the truck. When they got back to the farm house, Callen left to take Sarah home and then he headed to Stu's. By the time he got home, the lights were off and the house was dark. Smiling, he went in to find dinner in the oven for him. He sat and ate it then put the dish in the dishwasher and headed upstairs. Charlie was wrapped in her arms, and they were lying in the middle of the bed. His smile was huge as he reached for the baby. "Come on, buddy," he said, gently cradling the baby in his arms. He put the baby in bed and went back to their room. Dropping his clothes, he crawled into bed, and Lyssa rolled into his arms.

"Mmm, did you eat?" she whispered as she snuggled into his neck.

"I did. Thank you, beautiful."

"Callen," she mewed.

He knew this voice, knew what she wanted. "Yes, baby," he whispered, his cock getting hard. Her hand moved up his chest, setting his skin on fire. Rolling her over, his mouth covered hers, and somehow, he managed to get her pajamas off. His hand rested on her belly. "God, beautiful, I love you."

More Books by Cin Medley

Broken
One Hundred Acres
Six Months
Beautiful Liar
Justice
Within The Ashes